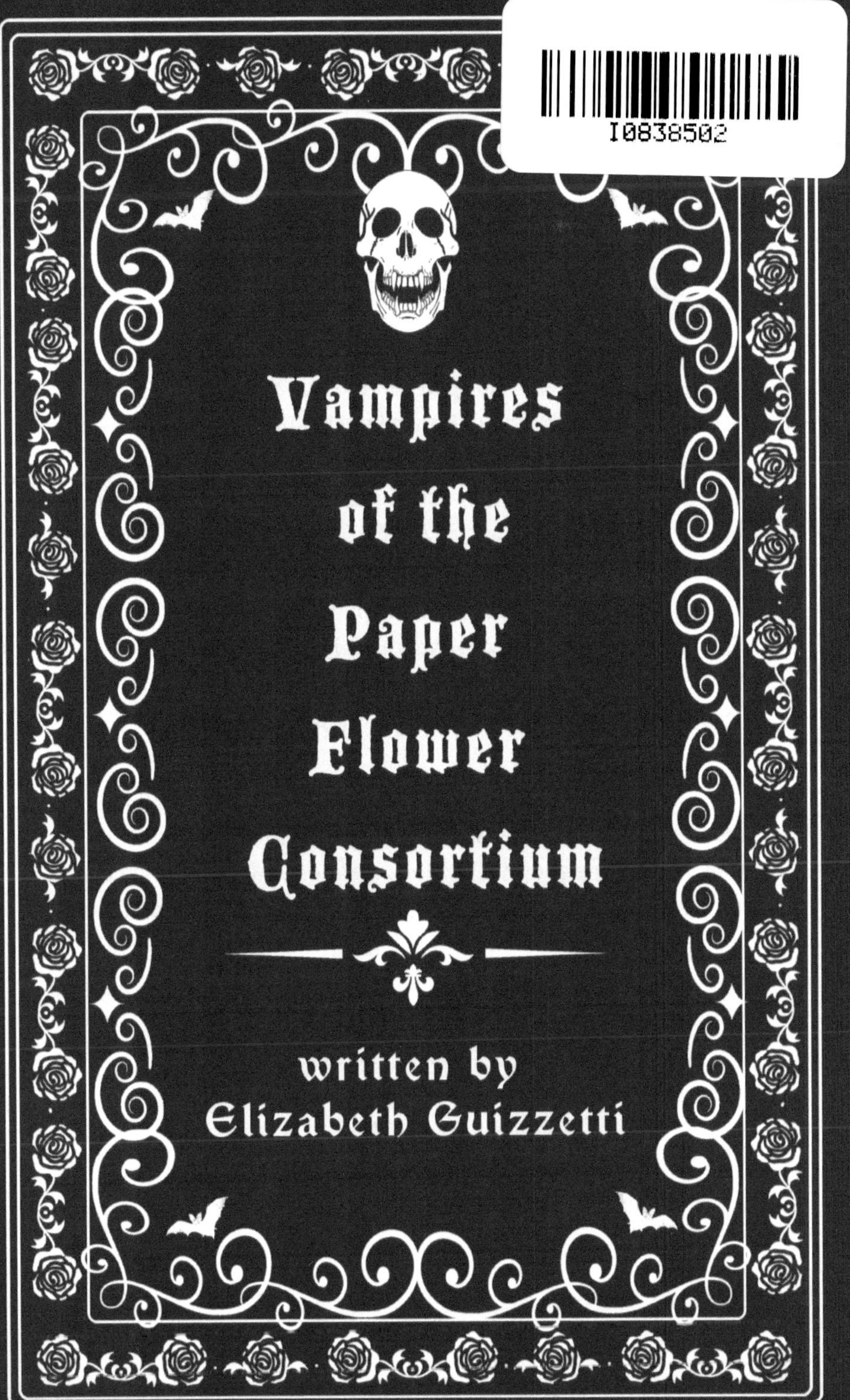

Vampires
of the
Paper
Flower
Consortium

written by
Elizabeth Guizzetti

This book is dedicated to
Evan Witt,
a great friend and listener.

Preface

Beloved Initiates,

Like so many of my artistic endeavors, I jumped into doing a podcast headfirst and did not plan as well as I should have. This anthology holds the first twenty regular episodes in season 1. (It does not hold the "Holiday Specials" as those stories are from Accident Among Vampires or What Would Dracula Do?)The illustrations were either created as episode art or as prints or cards to sell at conventions.

I began this podcast during the Covid-19 Pandemic, so don't be surprised when I mention it. It helped me connect with fans of my work and my author buddies, but it was already in my mind, as was this anthology. I performed as Loretta Fabron Onfoy, so the stories in the anthology are also from her point of view. That being said, these are not direct transcripts of the show. When I edited the stories for the book, I primarily used Chicago Style with some vampiric touches as I did to keep it consistent with the other novels.

Therefore, if you are reading along while listening, expect minor alterations. One of the most significant differences is the importance of identifiers in the spoken stories, which were not dramatized with voice actors. When I was correcting my podcast, I often added, X said. Sometimes, you might find a line cut from the podcast, which is still in the original story. Listeners may also notice some affectations such as "Indeed" or "As you may know," when I played Loretta, but not in the story at all.

I always planned to write from one of the three vampire women who founded the coven. At the time, Loretta was not a significant character in the published books, so I could make up her personality as I went along. Besides, as a historian and librarian, Loretta had access to all the stories which were hinted at in the books but didn't fit. For example, way back in 2018, I wrote a scene in Honor Among Vampires, which was cut for pacing and simply hinted at elsewhere in the book. However, now it is the fourth story in this book. A few stories were taken from the novels, but told by Loretta's perspective as the story fit.

I learned how to do a podcast as I went along. I bought a few packs of sound foam and started recording with a Yeti Blue, which I already had. I edited the podcast with Garageband for the first episodes. Then I moved to Logic X. Though most "lessons" are just me as Loretta, I want to shout out to the voice-actors who played roles in the radio plays or regular episodes. All the work was done remotely due to the pandemic, so I am thrilled with how everything turned out. I primarily hired my author buddies or friends from the convention circuit with podcasts or a solid microphone.

Evan Witt wrote the fantastic intro and outro music and played Derrik Miller in the radio plays. However, most importantly, he lent an ear as we went on our regular walks as I blathered on and on about vampires. Somehow, we are still friends! Stevie Rae Causey brought Norma Mae Rollins to undeath. Gretchen SB played Pascaline. Jennifer Brozek played Agata, Mrs. Washington, and Initiate Ellen. Ronnie Mason played Jeffry Conway and Augustus. Adam Watson played Marcus and Oskar, ND Fessenden played Sydella, a mom singing to her infant and Ona.

Finally, my super supportive husband, Dennis Roberts, did several one-line roles when I needed a deeper voice. Plus, due to the pandemic, he was working remotely when I recorded most of the episodes in our 640-square-foot apartment. He was a metaphorical rockstar in quietness. Plus, he double-checked the fonts I used in the anthology for readability.

Whether you are a fan of the show or you are finding out about the Vampires of the Paper Flower Consortium for the first time, I hope you enjoy this anthology!

Elizabeth

As recorded by Loretta Fabron Onfoy,
former Lady of the Kingdom of France,
Current Historian and Librarian
of the Paper Flower Consortium

Born 1670, Reborn 1692

INTRODUCTION

Initiates,

Languages change so much through the centuries, as do the methods of recording one's thoughts and history. I fear the change that is coming to English.

Our initiation manual was written in 1917 and published in 1921. So many words have changed in the past century. In truth, keeping our history has always been a full-time occupation.

Old journals crumble with time; paper makes way to digital. There are and have always been change. The French I spoke as a girl is gone. My English is not so old, as I learned it in the 1940s from our fledglings. And yet, sometimes I know I sound like someone's great grandmother trying to stay hip. So before English gives way to Emojis or whatever our next dominant language will be, I have made an effort to record journal entries in order to show the next generation of vampires what it is to be a vampire in this modern world for fear we fall back into our old ways. The old ways will mean Final Death.

So let us begin with the subject of transformation. People seek vampirism for fundamentally individual reasons. Some came for eternal love, others for vengeance or a certain lifestyle, and some to see what the future holds.

While Gothic fiction, films, and myths suggest vampires choose to steal the soul of their victims and force them into eternity, most vampires consent to vampirism. It is our greatest shame when a vampire is created without their blessing, but I will not lie and say that it doesn't sometimes happen.

The initiation education law was enacted in 1921, but by then, most legitimate covens only allowed transformation with an individual's agreement and instruction explaining the reality of our existence. Not just because immortality destroys one's former life, but it also dissolves any chance for an easy or culturally "good" death

Before the initiation laws, the most common reason for failure was the creator took too much blood and the initiate exsanguinated before blood could be restored.

The law brought in other guidelines: initiates must be twenty-five years of age and weigh at least 110 pounds in the United States or 50 Kilos internationally. It is also suggested there is no more than twenty pounds difference between creator and creation, which protects the initiate.

Rebirths are now coven-wide affairs. Several vampires are present to ensure the initiate does not lose consciousness until death takes them. These guidelines slashed fledgling mortality rates. All that being said, the transformation is still dangerous. Movies create the illusion that any human can be transformed into a vampire. That is simply not true. All creatures lose offspring, and vampires are no exception. Many come to the coven believing eternal life is absolute, but the initiate must defeat death.

This is why we inform all potential newcomers that some transformations fail. The biggest fear for any vampire progenitor is failure to thrive. We have no idea why it happens. Some believe God, and I am not claiming any single God, but whichever God the vampire believes in, sanctions our undead existence. Some believe in an intrinsic defiance against the natural order. And some believe in simple luck. The truth is no one knows. There are those who shouldn't have survived the rite, and they endure while others perish. Most discussion around failure to thrive is filled with the fallacy that the vampire gently disappears into the night.

But I mean to set the record straight. It is a horrifying experience for the creation, the creator, and their bloodline.

FAILURE TO THRIVE, 1903

The Paper Flower Consortium experienced this agony in 1903 when my husband lost his Firstborn, Walter Davidson, after his transformation.

Walter's conversion started off well. He had come to us under his own free will after finding us in the telephone directory. A former soldier, like my husband Charles, Walter sought an existence of peace. He looked at both of our first-generation male vampires but chose Charles as his mentor due to the similarities in their history and dispositions. He was quite a jolly fellow. We all liked him.

Charles was ecstatic. He was so excited to experience the connection between vampire and Firstborn. Charles had been a vampire for two hundred and eleven years. I had my Firstborn ten years prior. Now that the coven was settled in the Seattle area and we were financially stable, Charles was thrilled to be chosen.

Walter was twenty-nine and sound in mind and body on the night of his rebirth. He had spent two years in instruction and swore he looked forward to eternity. He did not tremble as he relaxed on the gurney, covered with a thin mat and quilt for his comfort.

As a Christian, he read a prayer to our shared God.

Charles opened Walter's radial artery with his fangs and drank in his blood until Walter grew pale. Agata, a learned healer and the eldest of our number, listened to Walter's pulse slow.

As his consciousness began to fade, Charles stabbed himself in the chest and gave Walter his lifeforce. It seemed Walter drank deeply. Flush with vampire blood, he lay back on the table in order to die.

Charles stabbed him in the carotid artery.

Walter didn't have time to scream, but his eyes showed the agony of death. That was to be expected. Even the quickest death pains the direct bloodline. Jakub and Agata felt Walter pull existence away from them, seeking their gifts and their blessing. Jakub's second son, Derrik, and Agata's daughters, myself and Pascaline were immune from this pain, so we were there to assist.

Agata signaled to us that Walter's heart began to

beat again.

Walter awoke as a vampire a few minutes later. He screamed as most new vampires do.

"Are you hungry?" Agata asked.

"Ravenous," Walter said.

Pascaline, Derrik, and I gave the fledging our blood until his complexion mimicked life.

Once he was able to sit up, the coven's two other young vampires, my son, Xiao, and Pascaline's daughter, Alice, brought him the flesh of animals, wine, and boiled sweets. We sang songs and prayed till the sun rose.

The transformation seemed a success.

We happily went to our coffins. However, the next night, Walter was not seen either at work or the public parlor.

Charles, gifted with Clairvoyance, knew his son was in his apartment. We went to check in on him.

We found Walter's enthralled human sitting half-dressed in the hallway.

"He kicked me out," she said. She swore she was not injured. She had not even been touched.

"Go on to our apartment. Our thralls will ensure you eat breakfast and give you a robe until we can work this out," I told her.

We gently knocked on Walter's door.

He did not answer.

We knocked again. Still no answer.

Charles turned the knob. It was unlocked. "Walt, it's Loretta and I. Are you decent?"

Walter, dressed to his waistcoat, sat at an east-facing window. He did not speak as we entered the room.

A cup of cooled blood sat on the table beside an unfolded newspaper. His thrall's breakfast was uneaten. I made a mental note to ensure my thralls took care of his until this was all sorted.

"Walt?" Charles asked.

No answer.

Charles pressed his hand upon Walter's shoulder. "My son, what are you looking at?"

"The vastness of eternity," he said in a slow, cryptic voice. "It will never end."

"What won't end?" Charles asked.

"Wars. There's another war," Walter replied.

I caught a whiff of musty death on his breath. Something inside him was rotting.

"But we will live in peace," I said.

Walter sighed deeply. "Does that make me a coward? Not fighting anymore."

Charles glanced over at me; his eyes filled with apprehension.

"Walter, you are not a coward, nor is Charles or Jakub. You have all seen battles. Many battles."

"But they don't ever stop..." Walter said,

If I am honest, I knew Walter was lost, but we still attempted to save him. Charles was still weak from the transformation, but I had blood to spare.

"Do you need another infusion, Walt?" I asked.

"No, lady, thank you."

"I can bring a thrall to you?" I asked.

"No, lady, thank you," Walter repeated and looked

out the window.

I asked: "Does your gift trouble you?"

He said, "No." But I could see the lie in his cold and empty eyes.

I bled into a bottle and set it upon the windowsill with a cup. "For when you get hungry, my husband's son."

I bent down and kissed him. The rot smelled stronger as my lips pressed against his cheek.

Walter made no move to take it. He sat and stared at the window, which only cast the reflection of his clothing. The bottle of blood coagulated on the windowsill.

An hour before dawn, Charles closed the shutters. We retired to our coffin. My sweet husband tossed and turned that day. Though I was worried, I held my beloved close and told him not to worry.

The next night, Walter was still unresponsive. The smell of decay was pungent in the same clothing he had worn the night before. His eyes were no longer just empty, but they had lost their luster. They were milky.

We phoned Agata and asked her to check on him.

Though Walter was indifferent to her exam, his temperature was normal; his pulse was slow and steady as it should be. His reflexes seemed typical. Not knowing what to do, Agata consulted the ancient vampires who ran Strawberry Fields, the coven over in Bellevue. They did not have good news.

Jakub cut open his wrist and pressed it to the other man's face. Walter did not move to take it. He just sat there.

Charles begged: "You're my son. My Firstborn. Don't you know how much I love you?"

In a slow, hollow voice, Walter replied, "Outside is a city full of sentiments and anguish, yet it all feels so distant in the vastness of eternity."

"Please drink! Just a sip," Charles cried. Bloody tears crested his eyes and cascaded down his face.

"Even your sorrow is hazy, and you stand beside me," Walter said in a monotone voice.

We did not know those words would be his last.

By the third night, the smell of corruption and putrefaction filled the apartment. The wraith, which had been Walter, just stared out the window.

I tried to embrace him and coax him to take just a sip of blood, but his flesh squished under my hand as if our dear Walter had become a bag of watery, moldering offal.

His once-strong muscles had disintegrated until he was folds and flaps of loose skin hanging on bone. As a lady of the court, my training kicked in, and I forced myself not to vomit or show my discomfort.

Charles raged. "It is my lady's blood. Drink it. How dare you not drink it?"

Walter did not answer.

On the fourth night, Charles opened his wrist again and begged him to drink.

The wraith ignored the blood on my husband's wrist and cheeks. He stared out the window into the night until Charles closed the shutters before dawn.

We returned to our coffin to a day of not sleeping in worry.

I tried to sing Charles a sweet song to comfort him when suddenly my husband shrieked and pushed me away.

"Run, Loretta! Run," he shouted and tried to slap inexistent flames from his body. I moved out of the way of his thrashing limbs and rolled onto the floor before I realized his nerve endings must be on fire.

Bloody sweat stained his pajamas and coated his hair and beard.

I ordered the thralls to fill our bathtub with cold water. We struggled to get my much-larger husband into it as he shrieked. When he was coherent, Charles claimed that I should run from him and the hideous day. At one point, he tried to order me to leave him. He didn't want me to see him so weakened and didn't want me to remember him so burnt.

I did not leave my husband's side as the connection between him, and his Firstborn was torn asunder. It took hours. Pascaline brought me ice for Charles and went to assist Jakub and Agata, who also suffered.

Charles hugged the ice. He rubbed it on himself until his skin blued, blistered, and cracked. Yet, he still felt the heat as Walter burned.

I tried to dominate his mind, but Charles kept repeating: "I see my son, his rotting flesh is burning off of him, his rotting flesh is burning!"

Not knowing what else to do, I finally cried: "Then sleep!"

Charles collapsed from agony and exhaustion.

I wiped my beloved's brow with cool water and washed the blood away. Too soon, he awoke again. Charles was strangely quiet and distant. He stared at the ceiling, but his expression was cold, hollow, and haunted as Walter's expression had been.

I shook him and cried, "Don't you dare leave me, Charles Onfoy!"

He blinked and looked at me as if he had realized I was there. "I think....I think Walter is mostly gone. Perhaps his brain has been destroyed. There is no pain, just wretchedness. But it still hurts."

"What should I do?" I asked him.

Charles put out his hand, so I helped him out of the tub and into a fresh sleeping-shirt.

We sat on the sofa and I ran my fingers through his hair until Walter's soul was freed from his body. Charles wept for a long time until finally, he fell asleep, this time naturally.

After the sun moved across the building, and it was safe to do so, I collected the ash into a glass container that now sits in a silver urn on top of our china cabinet. Surrounded by silver, Walter will be safe forever.

The rug and all of Walter's clothing and most of the upholstered pieces were later burned. The janitor needed several applications of lemon juice and wood oil to get the smell of decomposition out of the apartment's floors. As Walter's enthralled human was heterosexual and did not wish to leave the coven, she went to stay with Jakub.

My beloved never forgot his Firstborn. He blamed himself for decades. He didn't trust that his blood wasn't somehow wrong. In his pain, he sought answers, though there were none. He read hundreds of books.

He wrote to many of our ancient ancestors for advice.

One actually replied, "We all have had fledglings who failed to thrive."

As if that was supposed to bring Charles any comfort.

The only consolation Charles ever found is in his immortal memories of the two years which he and Walter had before the transformation and the belief his Firstborn's soul has gone on to heaven.

It was fifty years before my beloved tried to create another vampire. Thankfully, the transformation of Charles's Secondborn, Jeffry Conway was successful.

A WORD FROM OUR SPONSOR

Photos Ever More

Are you an initiate concerned that a creature of darkness is unable to reflect light and therefore unable to be caught on film and digital photography? Photos Ever More records your photograph for posterity, future documentation, and identification. We even can future-proof your social media with a hundred glamorous selfie-style photographs, which we can Photoshop into your future vacation, dog park, or dining pics! Affordable packages based on your needs. Visit us on our website to schedule an appointment tonight! *Before you stop reflecting light forever, think Photos Ever More!*

INITIATE QUESTIONS

WHAT IS AGATA'S BLOODLINE MORTALITY RATE?

Now, I will start off by admitting that Agata's bloodline mortality rate is skewed badly. You see, Derrik's Firstborn, William, experimented on over 100 humans in 1951. He wanted to create an undead army. Only one of his experiments survived—and by all rights, she shouldn't have. However, these were not coven-sanctioned initiations. So if you remove William's experiments, we have approximately a three percent Fledging Mortality Rate from the Bloodline of Agata.

WHO CAN BE INFECTED WITH THE VAMPIRE VIRUS?

Please understand that the ability to transform and the ability to legally transform are two different things. Before the 1921 Initiation Laws forbade such things: many vampires attempted to create vampires from beloved working animals or pets. However, Early Exsanguination and Failure to Thrive have even higher percentages among animals. In my existence, I have only seen one: a beautiful warhorse who existed for over two millennia.

Reptiles do not seem to be infected, or if they can be, they die quickly. This is perhaps because they need the warmth of the sun to function. This is unclear to us. Insects and birds also don't seem to survive the transformation. Or if they do, they die the first time they take flight. Though people relate bats to vampires, the truth is, that bats probably would not survive the transformation as most as tiny creatures.

Occasionally we have heard of hybrids between werewolves and vampires. However, prevailing science shows that to be a rare phenomenon. In practice, werewolves die if infected by vampires, and vampires also die when infected by werewolves. Merfolk seem to be immune from the virus. The Fey are more immortal than we, so there is no reason for them to wish to be vampires.

Legally, what that means is, only humans can be altered into vampires. However, as I said before, they must be 110 pounds, 25 years of age, educated in a trade, and have a complete medical workup before they are altered. This includes checking for other transformational viruses, such as those that might turn them into werewolves or zombies.

One more thing, when dealing with witches—which of course are humans--the transformation is more dangerous than most. Latent abilities become quite active, and training becomes obligatory. Derrik and all of his offspring have been witches. Their powers of the mind, though useful, are also quite dangerous to the coven. At one point, we had to decide if we should cauterize that branch of the bloodline, but that is a story for another time.

Good Day, Beloved Initiates, and Sleep the Sleep of the Dead.

Introduction

Beloved Initiates,

In the last lesson, I mentioned enthralled humans or thralls. Many listeners had questions or comments. It is amazing how judgmental people are! Personally, I blame Dracula and all other villainous vampires from films and books who break promises or kill their enthralled humans or other helpers.

A real vampire doesn't behave in that manner.

Vampires require blood, and human blood is preferable, but that does not mean we must be jerks. Admittedly, we can live for a while on animal blood, but we slowly weaken over time. Some of us have gone mad when our diet consists of nothing, but the flesh of animals.

However, vampires cannot survive in any number if we choose to hunt our neighbors. As seen in several films, this would get all our covens burned to the ground. So most of us keep enthralled humans.

There is another reason why people are judgmental of these relationships due to what I will refer to as Romantic

Paranormal Fiction. While some relationships between the human and vampire are romantic, some are just genuine trusted friends, some are just business, and some, how shall I put it, the human worships the vampire as a god or goddess.

Some relationships change over time. Just as relationships are varied, the reasons people come to the coven are varied and individualistic. Honestly, many humans enjoy the quiet, slow-paced vampire lifestyle but do not want the eternal commitment.

Do not let the title fool you. Enthralled humans, or thralls, are not under anyone's spell. Any human in good health can enter the program. And it goes without saying thralls are never touched by vampires without their permission.

Admittedly there is some ageism and classism by the humans. Older vampires, over a few centuries, who have not lost their foreign accent and dress out of time, are in quite high demand. Younger vampires, especially if they were born in America, are less coveted. However, the coven system ensures everyone's needs are met.

Now I hear looking for a thrall is a bit like dating, but ladies in 17th century France did not date, so I don't really know if that is applicable.

While some enthralled humans come to the coven for a summer or even a gap year, most, once tied to a vampire, end up spending their lives, and only death takes them from us. You see, vampires don't care about the outer shell. We couldn't care less when our enthralled grows old, wrinkled, or fat. We only care that they are healthy enough to donate blood—and if, and when, they cease to be after a lifetime of service, vampires tend for their aging thralls most diligently. Some vampires even take in their thrall's aging family members because we want them to be happy.

There are many benefits of being a thrall, such as housing at the coven for discounted or even free rent. They have Full Heath Benefits, including an Urgent Care Clinic, twice-yearly dental cleanings, a yearly eye exam, and a $500 stipend for glasses or contacts. There are also family discounts at all our Vampire-run retail establishments and services. We offer free personal tax assistance, Discounted Business Quarterly Tax Assistance, Attorney on Retainer, and of course, there is always the ever-popular Off-Site Cleaning Service.

Unlike the three years, one must study to become a vampire, to enter into the enthralled program, humans answer a questionnaire and give a statement, and sign a boilerplate enthralled human contract. Being a thrall isn't permanent until the thrall wishes.

The following statement was written by Sophia Shumaker, who came to the Paper Flower Consortium's Saturday night Fellowship back in April 2016. She is a college graduate and works for an internet marketing company in downtown Seattle. I am recording this statement with her permission.

SOPHIA'S STATEMENT, 2016

I wanted vampires to exist for so long, ever since I read Twilight when I was a teenage girl. I was Team

Edward—though now I understand how creepy that was—I didn't know when I was a teenager. Don't worry; I don't think vampirism is like that. The truth is to really know that there is something supernatural in the world is important to me.

The strange thing is, I'm not sure I want to be a vampire myself. Shouldn't I want to live forever?

I can't imagine filling immortality. Especially now I have met actual vampires. Perhaps I do want to be a vampire. I don't know. This is why I am signing up to be an enthralled human.

It all started last Friday. Not yesterday, I mean a week ago. All this will sound strange to you. Here I am writing about a happy hour of all things.

I hadn't seen most of my friends since we graduated from college two years ago. I had to schedule some flextime and come in early so I could leave work at 3:30 PM. Since I was going to be out for the night, my boyfriend, Matt, planned to meet with some of his own friends. The neighbor had been able to take Matt's dog out for a quick pee. All in all, I just kept thinking, adulting takes so much work.

The bar was empty when we arrived, and we found a table easily.

Politics and the coming election dominated the discussion; we were all Seattle-liberal enough that there were no shouting or bad feelings. Or if there was, it had been buried quickly and plied with alcohol.

Still, I think everyone was more comfortable when we moved on to the next topic of conversation. My friends all talked about their lives as if they were waiting for something. I didn't really feel that way, but I wanted to fit in with the crowd so I mentioned I couldn't wait for Matt to propose. We had spoke of marriage, but he hadn't proposed yet.

In the back of my mind, I felt this little twinge because I wondered if I wanted to get married so bad why I didn't I just propose to Matt.

It was when the group mentioned wanting to attend and experience an art installation on Free Thursday that I suddenly felt something was wrong. You see, they complained about the First Thursday crowds but were not willing to pay the normal entry fee to the gallery to attend a different evening. They babbled about how ideas and art ought to have more government funding. How our friend, so-and-so, would be an artist too, but it was too expensive even to get started. They complained about how they were all drowning in student debt. We were all too poor to pay to go to an art exhibit. I couldn't help but notice one less drink on everyone's tab and we could all go tonight. We were drinking $12 cosmos!

So leaving out the first thought, I asked, "Hey! Maybe we could all go tonight?"

One of my so-called friends spoke of the toddler-free freedom that she was experiencing at that moment. Her voice dripped with mockery as she expected to see a screaming child at a Friday night art show that served wine. The rest of my friends agreed with her.

The music grew louder as the bar shifted away from happy hour and into the night-time crowd when my friends' sweat-covered rosy faces blurred. I realized I didn't like them.

I switched to water, but I yearned for fresher air.

I cashed out my tab, said goodbye. I hugged my friends and promised not to wait another two years to see them again. I was lying. I would never call them again. Now don't get me wrong, I wish none of them ill-will. I hope they will all live happy, successful lives. I just hope they live somewhere that I am not.

However, as the cold outside air hit my face, I feared The Seattle Freeze. Locals know how it is.

Ignoring the pestering voice in my brain, I wished I had brought a heavier coat,

Like all Seattleites, I had learned the smell of coming rain in the wind which blew off the Sound, and of course, I didn't have an umbrella as I trudged up the hill towards the lightrail station and bus stop. The streets didn't seem as busy as they felt like they should be on a Friday night. But like I said, it was cold.

I thought I heard a moan as I crossed an alley. I glanced over and saw what looked like a drunk girl stumbling in the dark. She wore no coat, only a thin tee and jeans.

I called out: "Hey, are you okay?"

The girl's posture changed. She stood too quickly. Her blonde hair streaked with blue fell about her shoulders. I had the distinct impression the girl had only been playing drunk. Then I saw something— someone—lying on the ground beside Not-Drunk-Girl's feet.

Her shirtfront was covered in something dark. Was it mud, vomit, or some strange graphic playing with my blurred mind?

She said, "Hey."

I was drawn to her. Yet, feeling terror rise in my throat, I hurried up the hill. Panting, I made it to the lightrail station. Covered in sweat, I wanted to open my jacket, but then I knew I'd be too cold.

Now that there were people around, coming and going, I felt silly for my panic.

There were people in business attire heading to the trains and buses for the residential neighborhoods or suburbs. Young people in small groups wearing club clothes were ready for a night on the town. I was ready to go home.

I glanced over my shoulder. Not-Drunk-Girl nowhere to be seen. Relieved, I slipped inside. However, the too-blue LED light made everyone appear sickly. My stomach turned, and I regretted that third cosmo.

The train runs every twenty minutes, but I checked the lighted board anyway. And realized I had just missed the previous train. *Damn it. Now I have to wait twenty-minutes.*

A man vacated his spot on the metal bench, and I snagged it before it was swallowed up by someone else. Through my clothes, I felt the last shadow of the man's heat leech away into the cold metal.

I fiddled with my phone, doing nothing of importance. I tried to play a word game but could not get over the feeling that someone watched me. Someone unseen beyond the reach of the cameras. I caught a glimpse of Not-Drunk-Girl's blond hair streaked with blue.

I told myself: *It's probably someone else. Even if it was the same girl, logically, if she fell down in the street, she probably just wants to get home.* My mind refused placating logic.

Then Not-Drunk-Girl walked past. I pressed myself into the wall behind the bench.

Her flimsy shirt was too cold for the weather, but she did not tremble. Brownish red splotches stained her tee. It wasn't blood, I told myself. It was a graphic to some ghoulish band. *Something the kids know, but not me. Not anymore. Now that Life has become a series of repetitive actions: wake, shower, work, eat, television, make love when I was lucky, sleep.* I no longer had time for Seattle's independent music scene.

The Not-Drunk-Girl caught my eye. She smiled and gave a little halfhearted nod in the way common to Seattle when two strangers meet. I expected rows of fangs, but it was just a smile. *Was it just my imagination that her canines grew longer in front of my eyes?*

Then I realized the girl wasn't young. She wasn't old, just older than me. She looked like she might be in her late twenties or early thirties. I probably should have called her the Not-Drunk-Woman, but as she acted like a club kid, I'm going to keep using Not-Drunk-Girl.

Possibly just the alcohol, definitely terror warped reality all around me. Suddenly, I feared I might never see Matt's dog again.

Then I wondered why I was I not fearing I'd never seeing Matt again. *Why do I fear losing Matt's dog more than I fear losing Matt? What is wrong with me?*

I liked Matt. Do I love him? No. I feared I was going to die and leave Matt in a lurch on our lease.

I could no longer take my eyes off Not-Drunk-Girl, who pretended to stumble into a college-age man in a Huskies hoodie.

However, he did not react to the blood which covered Not-Drunk-Girl's chest.

Yes. I told myself. *It has to be a band. They both know it. And the girl is younger than she appears—let's just say she's led a hard life, and it shows.*

Not-Drunk-Girl and College-Kid started to flirt. He pulled out his phone, texted someone. The two left the station together.

Watching them leave, I thought of the phrase I had heard from so many other people, but I had never thought it or said it until now. Youth is wasted upon the young.

My train came, but I felt rooted to my spot. I needed to know what was going to happen to that College-Kid.

I sat there until the sky darkened even more, not that it mattered. The LED bulbs still glowed more blue. Outside, the buildings spilled light into the street. But I sat there. I sat there until it felt as if all the people around me had become shadows.

The Not-Drunk-Girl appeared again, wearing the Husky hoodie of the College-Kid. He was not with her. Her skin seemed more ruddy and she seemed more alive somehow. Her bright eyes scanned across the crowd.

Life is fragile. But I had to know.

She looked at me and smiled again. Her teeth stained. *Were they stained before? I don't think so...* My brain screamed, *Run, Stupid! Run!*

My instinct for self-preservation finally kicked in.

I stood and hurried to the platform. I scrambled onto the next train, not caring where it was going. I decided to propose marriage as soon as I got home. Matt and I already lived together. We had a dog. We both loved her. Some might say we were too young, but I am twenty-four, he is twenty-six. What are we waiting for? To pay off college debt? Save for our first home.

What am I waiting for?

I looked out the window and caught sight of the blue-streaked hair and Huskies hoodie chatting up another girl. I have to know. I scrambled off the train. I had to know if what I was seeing was real, but I had no idea how to find out without being a vampire's meal.

So I asked, "Siri, what to do when you see a vampire?"

Norma's Cleaning Service, a subdivision of the Paper Flower Consortium, popped up first. Siri asked if I wanted to call the number.

I called.

The phone connected.

"Norma's Cleaning Service." A young female voice said.

"Do you take care of vampires?" I asked.

"Yeah. But it depends on what you mean by take care of..." the young voice said.

"There's a vampire at the lightrail station. I think she might be killing people."

"And you are?"

"I am just sitting at the lightrail station. I think she

might have cast a spell on me or something," I said.

The voice asked a little more firmly, "And you are?"

"Sophia Shuemaker."

There was a pause. "You are a human?"

"Yeah. Siri brought you up," I said.

The voice sighed. "Okay, I see. No problem. We'll be there in a few minutes."

I watched as two vampires—or at least who I thought were two vampires—entered the light rail station.

One was a teenage White girl with black curls who scanned the crowd. Slightly uncanny innocence were plastered on her ivory cheeks. The Latino man beside her looked to be thirty. When you are alive, it is hard to describe the undead, but I suppose he was not as animated as the girl. She pointed and spoke. He just stood there and nodded.

I did not know what was going to happen as they crossed the crowd, but they just spoke to the Not-Drunk-Girl. I could not hear their conversation. Not-Drunk-Girl nodded, shrugged, glanced over at me and left.

I was still rooted to my spot when the vampire who I assumed was Norma's eyes alighted upon me.

I felt like she knew all my secrets. Of course, since I have since learned that she absorbed some of my secrets because she is a telepath.

"Thanks for letting us know," she said. "Public feeding is really frowned on nowadays."

She handed me a card: Paper Flower Consortium. "If you want to know, what I know you want to know, come to the chapel on Saturday nights. We have a church service and potluck. Don't worry. There'll be plenty of human food."

I put the card in my pocket.

It was strange.

When I got home, I still thought I might propose, but instead, as soon as I looked at Matt, we broke up.

He doesn't understand, and he's hurt. He thinks maybe I slipped, and this is my way of dealing with the guilt. But I know now there is something else for me, and I have to find it. So Matt and I are going to be roommates until our lease is up. Then I am going to move out, he will have to find a new roommate, I guess.

I really will miss the dog, but she was his first.

Tonight, I came to your fellowship. I came, and now I am here, and it is real. Moreover, zombies are real too. Tonight, when I spoke to Norma, she told me her friend is a zombie. (Insertion: Sophia refers to Carlos Fisher-Perez, Norma's friend and business associate. Statement continues.)

I appreciate everything the lady Pascaline and the lady Agata explained to me. So I am just letting everyone know I am heterosexual and would want to be pared to a man.

I understand that vampires are not monogamous with their human companions. I believe I can live with that. I also understand no children can come from this union. And if I want to get pregnant, I must tell the coven immediately, and all bloodletting will stop.

I grew up Christian, but I'm not anything anymore, and I am not sure if I want to go to your church service, but

I enjoyed your potluck very much. Norma was right; there is a lot of human food, and everyone is so welcoming here.

Over the next month, Sophia was introduced to several vampire men. She pared up with Scott Hansen, the Ninthborn of Charles. Scott does not have a vampire lover or any lover to the best of my knowledge, but he and Sophia seem to be quite content in each other's company. She moved into a small studio in the building after her former lease was up. Her career is one with the ability to telecommute, so switching to night hours did not affect her job.

I am happy to report though Sophia was once Team Edward, now she is on Team Scott.

PUBLIC SERVICE ANNOUNCEMENT

Before I get to the questions, I must announce: while vampires cannot be killed by most human viruses, our humans can.

I will just say all Paper Flower Consortium Businesses are closed as we are considered non-essential in the State of Washington, and all church services and social gatherings have been canceled for the foreseeable future. Please stay safe, stay at home, and when you venture out to the market or other essential business, practice safe social distancing.

INITIATE QUESTIONS

YOU TALKED ABOUT THE ADVANTAGES, BUT WHAT ARE THE DISADVANTAGES TO BEING AN ENTHRALLED HUMAN?

The biggest disadvantage is that all condos in our building—and most vampire covens work this way—can only be owned by vampires. This means thralls don't own property. If they choose to leave the coven, this can hurt them financially if they have not put the money they saved on rent into another investment. Of course, this also means they don't have a vote in how the condo is run and how we spend our HOA reserves.

IT SOUNDS LIKE THRALLS STILL HAVE JOBS?

Currently, most thralls have at least part-time jobs; many have careers they love. However, that is a decision between their sponsor vampire and themselves. The coven does not dictate this.

WHAT HAPPENS IF A VAMPIRE GETS TIRED OF A THRALL?

Vampires don't get tired of thralls. We need them. Thralls get tired of vampires. Most relationships dissolve because the thrall decides they want something else out of life. Thrall contracts are generous, and they have the absolute power to end the relationship.

Of course, there have been exceptions. It doesn't

happen often, but we have seen vampires ask their thrall to leave.

For example: We once kicked out a thrall who tried to rent out their free studio for $100 a night. Most condo buildings have rules against short-term rentals, and ours are no different. We also have a rule against allowing strangers into the building during vampire sleeping hours. They broke our trust, so we asked the offender to leave. They did.

Another reason a thrall might be asked to leave is domestic violence. In 2018, a thrall became very unhappy, but instead of leaving, she became abusive.

Domestic violence is an insidious thing, even in this modern era. The coven heard shouting on occasion, but the vampire never said anything. Until one night we witnessed her slap him, we did not realize how bad it had gotten.

But fear not, the vampire's coven sisters jumped in to help him.

The former thrall was given enough money for first and last month's rent plus a security deposit and told to leave. She was also given a key to a storage locker with six months paid, where she found all of her personal possessions and a vaguely threatening reminder that Norma will address all kinds of messes. Wisely, she went to a human-run extended leave hotel outside the city without argument.

Good day, Beloved Initiates, and Sleep the sleep of the dead.

INTRODUCTION

Dear Beloved Initiates,

Tonight's subject is horrid indeed: Vampire Hunters.

Though vampires are apex predators, as I said last week, in the modern era, most of us keep thralls, so we do not need to hunt.

Still, there are those who hate us and hunt us. These hunters believe, mistakenly, we are cold, evil creatures.

Of course, our body temperature is colder than that of a human. As with any population, some of us are evil. But one ought not to stereotype an entire species. Though vampires are difficult to destroy, we can be killed by sun, fire, among other methods. We used to keep these things a secret, but modern films and books have made our weaknesses public knowledge, so I am not disclosing anything people don't already know.

There are rumors of former thralls who become vampire hunters, but for the most part, we have never found that to be true. The thralls who leave most often think back to that time in their lives with a twinkle in their eyes. Most keep in touch—in this past through Christmas Cards, currently through Facebook and other social media.

From what we have seen, most hunters are rank amateurs. They like to think they are Van Helsing or Buffy saving the world from a vampire stretching our dead ashen limbs around some virginal youth and biting into their quivering flesh. But that is simply not the case. Most of the time, they are not heroes.

Hunters are just people who are angry and afraid about aspects of their lives that have nothing to do with vampires. They are often divorced, abandoned, or downtrodden in some way. You see, many feel they have nothing to live for, and hunting gives them a purpose. Those who go down the path of violence do not live long. —And those who seek vengeance find only coldness as their reward.

However, there is the professional vampire hunter, and these by far are more dangerous.

There is no intrinsic payment in hunting us, yet some people try to find grieving clients. These swindlers seek to fool a grieving human into believing that their undead family member came to us unwillingly. Since the Hunter can not return the vampire to the family alive, we have even heard of a charlatan who creates a phony séance using fake or real ghosts who cry that the vampire suffers in their eternal hell and who begs, "Give me final death!"

On June 6, 1889, Alice Munroe left our coven in a hired wagon for an afternoon appointment with her human father in the downtown business district. She had been transformed three nights before. Her father, who originally disowned her when she began dressing in womanly fashion, requested her attendance at his office. Yet, he had set the appointment when the sun was high. We didn't know what to expect.

Pascaline advised Alice to leave her humanity completely behind her, but Mr. Monroe's letter mentioned an allowance of some sort. She wanted to go.

Modern women, who have never needed an escort to ensure their safety, might not understand why Derrik accompanied Alice. Of course, he had the excuse of being her attorney, but in reality, Pascaline was worried. While a well-dressed woman crossing the lumber and redlight districts would most likely have been unmolested, there were not enough police in the fledgling city. And Pascaline never quite recovered from her and my perilous journey, though that happened centuries before.

Derrik was also there to ensure that during any heated discussions, Alice did not make a fatal mistake that might haunt her for eternity. Alice was only three nights old, and a young vampire needed blood. Like all concerned progenitors, Pascaline fed her offspring. She ensured her fledgling had a belly full of blood so no human might tempt her. You see, Alice is Pascaline's only offspring to survive the Rite.

But I should not get off track.

It is dangerous to go out during the day at the best of times. Still, Derrik and Alice's peril became tenfold because on that fateful day, at approximately 2:30 pm, a carpenter accidentally overturned a glue pot and began the most devastating fire in Seattle's history.

JOURNAL OF ALICE MONROE

June 6, 1889

I admit I am glad Derrik had been with me today. I fear I might have lost my way home without him. I have my creator's strength and speed, but we try not to show our vampire powers to humanity. I regret I am not a revolress. I never even held a gun. Of course, Derrik told me he never fired a gun either. Charles agreed to show me how to shoot once the city settles down from the day's tragedy.

So many times, our existence was endangered, but Derrik never lost his head. I wish I were as brave as he. If I am honest, I never saw what Pascaline saw in him until today. He isn't exactly hen-pecked, but he isn't commanding either. I suppose what he is with his quiet voice and gentle mannerisms is a bully trap. He certainly knew how to handle my father.

Derrik is so modest! The strangest thing of all is to hear him talk about the day's events; you would think I saved him.

We entered my father's office at exactly 2'o'clock for the appointment. My father's eyes moved over my dress and the feather in my hat as he stared at me with smoldering hate. He cleared his throat. His hands pressed flat against the inlaid leather of his pine desk. He cleared his throat again.

"Father?" I tried.

My father said, "Mr. Miller, I am not here to chew the rag with your client."

And Derrik spoke in his soft way: "You called this meeting, Sir. I am simply in attendance to act as Miss Monroe's advisor."

My father quivered in rage. Though he claimed he had nothing to say to me, he shouted: "This depravity is why I refused to let you come to the house. Your poor mother would die of shock if she saw you like this."

I told myself my father's hateful words didn't matter, but they did, of course. I shall never forget the revulsion in his tone.

"Is Alice's mother in poor health?" Derrik asked softly.

"How dare you speak of my wife?" He punched the desktop.

I flinched. Derrik did not. "Sit, if you please, Sir. We have business to discuss."

My father's pulse flew in his fury. I clenched my fists into my palms. I refused the bloodlust which was growing and allowed Derrik and my father to do business in my name. This is an aspect of womanhood that I do not like when I took off my outer disguise and accepted my femininity, but it is the way of humans. I told myself my father's hateful words didn't matter, but they did.

I wish my father knew me better. When I pretended to be my father's son, I was a useless ne'er-do-well. I spent my adolescence deadened with brothel alcohol in the establishments which served the carriage class. He did not care. He did not care that I was killing myself. I wanted to tell him as a vampire and a woman, I have begun to learn filing systems and business management so our coven can continue to grow.

My father was shouting again. "I won't be dictated to in my office—especially by two immoral reprobates."

"Very well. Mr. Monroe, if you won't do your duty by your daughter, then my wife will take care of her. Have a good afternoon."

We turned to leave.

My father put a pistol on his desk.

I wondered if I should speak. I didn't believe my father would shoot me, but I was terrified he might try. I couldn't find the right words, and even when I tried to open my mouth, my mouth was so dry, no words came out.

"Let's not make this difficult business more painful. You wrote to my client regarding a stipend," Derrik said.

"Against my wishes, my wife desires to ensure that creature has a small income. There are few jobs available to women in Seattle. Heaven forbid, this creature becomes a 'seamstress'." He made a gesture of air brackets at the word seamstress.

I felt like muck on the bottom of a shoe. I suddenly remember thinking I smelled smoke, but honestly, I have been so scared today I can't remember. I was still frightened my father would try to shoot us or call the police or even open a window and let in the terrible sun.

My father snapped, "I could call the police, Sir, for what your wife did to my son."

I think I winced then. I felt so small and insignificant.

This was an aspect of the decision that I didn't like when I made when I took off my outer disguise and accepted my femininity, but it was also the way of the world.

"You could," Derrik said in his soft-spoken way. "But that would hardly be to your benefit. Think of the scandal. It is, of course, a most distressing time for you, but we wrote this for your convenience."

He pulled out a paper with my obituary from his leather briefcase.

My father said: "A respectable daughter doesn't leave her family home unmarried."

"Then we will find Alice a husband," Derrik said.

"I would not have her marry that...."

Derrik did not allow him to say the profanity against our coven brother any more than he would allow a profanity to fall upon my person.

"Our coven brother is an American, Sir. But if Mr. Bao doesn't suit your family's limited view, there are plenty of other men. Georgetown and Seattle's population is still overwhelmingly male. Frankly, it matters little to the coven if the husband is even a vampire."

These words seemed to calm my father. He explained how my mother planned to deposit ten dollars a week of her own money into an account in my name— Alice Monroe—as she did for my sister—so we might have some of our own money to set aside for a trousseau. Of course, after I was married, my husband would care for me as was proper.

Father had opened the account for Mother but

otherwise wanted no part of it. After today, he would not look upon me again and told me if I had any decency, I would leave my mother and sister alone.

I wanted to say something about my father's hypocritical nature. He only pretended to be decent. He was part of the carriage crowd who visited brothels in his spare time, just as I had been. I said nothing. That life was over; a new existence had begun.

Derrik accepted the account information and set it in his briefcase. He asked how my family would like to be informed of my upcoming marriage.

Father told him to write to the office, not to the home. As we said our goodbyes, he reminded me that as long as I continued this debauchery, there would be no other monies coming in my direction. I was dead to him.

I almost laughed at that.

I looked at the aging bag of flesh which once was my father and understood that his world had already turned away into something new. He simply had no comprehension what being a vampire meant. Though I missed my mother, I wouldn't see her. I could never chance hearing that fragile heartbeat and destroying the life which gave me my first life.

As we exited my father's office, my father's errand boy past us, bumping us as if I were nothing. I told myself it didn't matter. He ran to a young man who stood on the raised walkway smoking a cigarette.

I noticed the hired cart which we rode to Seattle was gone.

Something was wrong. No. Everything was wrong.

People were moving too fast. Their heartbeats echoed inside me. It took all my will not to reach out and grab one of them and expand my fangs into their delicious flesh. The smell of smoke on the wind was strong, so strong it could not be just smoke from one of the mills.

Moreover, the sky had turned orangish and brown, but it was too early for sunset. My hand trembled under my parasol. The silk seemed too thin to protect me.

I looked around, hoping to spot for a cab for hire.

The young man walked towards us with a leonine authority a long machete scabbarded on his belt. His eyes were bright with rage and did not leave my face. His cowboy hat was too clean as was his shirt. His granite jaw was recently shaved, but his perfectly formed mustache betrayed, he was not a workman—even a freshly bathed one.

Derrik stepped closer to me and gently took my arm. "I don't like the way he stares. We dare not wait for the cab," he said.

We began to walk arm in arm southward, hoping to find some way home. I glanced behind me. The man was still there.

"Can you read his mind?" I asked Derrik

"I only know there is anger and hate within him." Derrik said, "Your father wouldn't have sent someone after us, would he?"

"Of course not!" But in truth, I wasn't sure.

I didn't want to believe my own father capable of that, but I knew that he could be a hard man. Very few men make their money in this world through benevolence. Still, ten dollars a week didn't seem like much to kill someone over.

"The allowance might only be a lure to get you away from those who would protect you," Derrik said.

We both glanced back that time. The man was still behind us.

Derrik's thin lip expression matched our pursuers. In a different set of circumstances, the mimicry might have been funny.

Derrik's brow furrowed. His facial muscles twitched, and the expression became full of bile as the other man's thoughts overtook him. A spray of bloody spittle came from his mouth, and he sounded like he couldn't catch a breath.

"The city's fear overwhelms me."

Suddenly, all around us, people started running. A shout turned into a thousand screams for water. A flash of orange fire leapt up the timber walls of a nearby building and onto the next. The timber building charred and blackened and sent up acrid smoke into the sky. The fire jumped again to the next building. And the next.

A fire truck clattered by. Horses were clopping over the brick and cobblestone. Bucket brigades were set up. Lumberjacks were drafted into the brigades.

Though he was in pain, Derrik pulled me along the dirt road, trying to find a way to escape.

We followed women with babes in arms, pulling screaming children beside us. The smell of their fear-laden bodies piqued my bloodlust. I wondered how many humans and animals were dying.

Nightmarish visions of flames danced in my head,

but what was in front of me was worse.

Rats, their fur ablaze, dashed past us screaming in ear-shattering panic. I choked on the ghastly smell of burning flesh as we crossed over several burning sewer pipes- hollowed-out scrap logs, filled with the city's feces. If I had not already died, I thought I might suffocate.

Popping and crackling flames danced from one building to another. Was it chasing us too?

Our pursuer did not seem to care about the burning buildings, panicked citizens, or ash-filled sky. He matched our pace and kept us in sight.

We passed the brothel I used to frequent. The women had formed their own bucket brigade and were trying to douse the fires, but there wasn't enough water. The building was lost. I had once known those women; it was they who never judged my needs. I wanted to help them, but the man was still behind us--his hand on the hilt of that terrible knife.

Derrik coughed beside me. "Alice, I finally caught a thought. The Old Man of the Forests killed his brother. Indeed, he is one of those misguided idiots who thinks he should remove monsters from the world."

An ember must have hit my parasol, because a small hole burned through the silk and then grew larger. I dropped it onto the dusty road. Moments later, it was trampled by a man leading cows away from the flames.

I glanced back; he was closer now, the man might overtake us. His hand was on his long knife. His eye were filled with hate.

Holding my arm tightly, Derrik moved down an

alleyway which cut into Washington Street. We crossed to First Avenue, which we could follow most of the way home --though it became a dirt road that hedged the mudflats once we left Seattle proper.

I glanced back again. For a moment, I lost sight of our purser. I felt a breath of relief run through me. All we needed to do was get around the fire, and we would be safe. We might even be able to hitch a ride with a farmer moving livestock if we got lucky.

Then the man was there again. "Bloodsuckers!" He shouted and drew his knife.

No longer worried about exposing our vampiric speed, Derrik and I darted past burning buildings, retreating people, and livestock. My eyes burned as we wandered through the thick smoke, dust, and smoldering ash. My muscles ached, but we did not stop until our progress was halted by an inferno that sparked and crackled and popped.

Derrik's pace was hurried, and though our strides are about the same, I struggled to keep up.

We lost him again and Derrik eyed me. "Forgive me the immodest question, but what do you have on under your dress?"

It wasn't like Derrik to be improper, but I didn't know how to answer.

"What?"

"The crinoline. Is it... Never-mind, just remove it. It is a cage. And take my jacket. Wool will offer more protection than your silk."

"But what about you?" I cried.

"The ash will protect me from the sun. Besides,

there is no way I could return to the coven without you. Pascaline would kill me."

I unpinned and untied my lower layers as he muttered, trying to figure out the safest path. "West to the harbor or east up the hill? All the people are running to the harbor."

I pulled off my crinoline. It made the outer skirt drag on the ground in an unattractive way. Fearing I would trip on it, I found the seam and ripped off the lower flounce so I could run unencumbered.

"People will be using the water, so east," I said.

Derrik nodded.

Now Derrik was sure, I wouldn't catch on fire, we hurried east, up the mill road, also called skid row. Normally this time of day, the logs were greased and skidded down the hill to the harbor. But the ground was wet from the morning's work, the road had been emptied as the lumber jacks had gone to smother the fire.

However empty or not, the road was a slurry of accursed mud, manure, and grease. Mud and donkey manure splattered up my skirts with every step. My heeled boot slipped and I fell to my knees. Derrik pulled me up by my forearm. Every step needed two to gain traction. I wished I wore more sensible boots, but Derrik wasn't doing much better.

He dropped his briefcase, and while he immediately picked it up, for the first time he looked like he might weep as he clutched the leather case to his chest, but then it might have just been ash in his eyes. My eyes ached and burned.

Heat radiated behind us. *Was the flames climbing*

the hill? I couldn't tell there was so much light. I cried out as a loose steel cable caught my skirt and sliced into my flesh. But filled as blood as I was, the ripped flesh quickly closed. I kicked some of the muck off my boots and took another step.

Finally we crested the hill and hurried into a forest of stumps. Twigs snapped with every footfall.

We ducked; unsure where the hunter was and if we were safe from the fire this high on the hill. I hoped we would be better shaded, but the thick stumps offered little protection. The lumber jacks had been quite efficient in this part of Seattle. We moved on.

Suddenly the wind shifted and the sun came through the ash. Beside me, Derrik grunted, and lifted his briefcase to shade us.

His flesh started to smoke as the sun pierced his cotton shirt. I used his jacket to press the flames on the back of his neck. The flesh blistered and popped and the fawn-colored wool became stained with blood.

We found a piece of woolen tarpaulin, and Derrik pulled me under his arm and used it to block the sun. We both cringed as another scream sounded from lower on the hill.

Then we saw the silhouette of the hunter in the distance. We raced across a grassy clearing towards some houses. Derrik tightened his grip on my wrist and drew me along. He pushed me to run even faster. Pain began in my heels, up my calves. My knees threatened to give out. I gasped, unable to breathe, through the thick ash-coated shoulder. Beside me, Derrik gasped. Bloody sweat coated his brow and stained the underarms of his shirt.

We took shelter on the east side of a house. The sun's terrible rays no longer upon us. Derrik wheezed, trying to hide his agony. I saw that his right hand had blistered, as did his right ear and the right side of his neck above his collar. Thankfully his hat and briefcase had offered some shade on his face. Flushed by the exertion, smeared with ash, Derrik's undead face looked mottled and completely dead.

I had no way to heal him--except my blood. I offered it.

"I can't take your blood," he said. The wheeze in his chest grew deep and horrid.

"Take it. We still have miles to go. I trust you." I removed my glove and put my hand towards him.

"But Pascaline..." he said. "I can't weaken you."

"Lady P. will understand."

Derrik wiped his face, smearing the ash with his uninjured hand, and muttered something under his breath.

"What did you say?" I asked.

"That Charles and Jakub would know how to protect you better," he said.

"Please, take just a sip, we have so long to go." I said. "And if you are to protect me, I need you strong."

Doubt made his blue eyes stormy. Still Derrik expanded his fangs, bit on the flesh of my palm, and took a short gulp.

I replaced my glove and watched as his blistered skin heal. He cried out and dabbed his face with his handkerchief.

We sat there, resting, for a few minutes more, praying for the ash to hide the sun and the fire to remain in the valley. I never wanted my coffin so badly. I wanted to sleep in the beautiful darkness. And I wanted Derrik to be well.

Then the hunter came around the house with a dangerous smile on his lips. The large machete left its sheath.

"Did my father send you?" I asked.

"Your father!" The man cackled. "Bloodsuckers don't have fathers! I will kill you. I hate bloodsuckers. How dare you think to walk in the day!"

Derrik put his hands, palms up. "Let us go, I have money."

The man swung his machete at me.

Ahead of his swing, Derrik pushed me into the wall, but the blade caught him on the shoulder. My coven brother yelled as blood poured out of the wound. His scream grew agonized as the flesh knitted back together. My God, if he hadn't taken my blood, he would have been badly injured. And I couldn't leave him any more than he could leave me. We both had to get back to Pascaline.

Then I saw it. The man's heartbeat panicked as Derrik's wound closed. This was the moment I might have to get the upper hand. His eyes were on Derrik, not me.

I leaped on the hunter's back and expanded my fangs.

"Don't bite him!" Derrik shrieked. "I don't know his species!"

I stopped. In my hesitation, the hunter threw me

off. He rose his knife again.

"My species! My species," the hunter bellowed.

The machete flashed sunlight into my eyes, and I scurried back into the shade of the building as I tried to escape the terrible reflection.

With a momentous growl, Derrik rushed the man. They barreled into the street. Derrik screamed as his back smoked through his clothing. He lifted the man off his feet and rammed him into a woodpile. Then the man was screaming.

I heard cracking—most likely wood. I don't think it was bone. Gore poured from the man's thigh.

Derrik's eyes were open wide. He slowly backed away from the woodpile; his whole body trembled. "How did I do that? I'm sorry. I'm sorry."

I yearned to drink that blood so badly, but Derrik was right. We did not know his species.

The man shouted guttural obscenities at us. He claimed I was in hell, and he would save me from damnation.

Derrik didn't move. I edged closer to the man and kicked his knife out of reach.

"Your father sent him. I am sorry."

"That doesn't matter now. We have to go!" I yanked Derrik's arm, forcing him to run.

Derrik jerked away from me. He opened his billfold and gave the man ten dollars. "Use it for a doctor. Next time, I will not be this forgiving."

I grabbed Derrik's hand again; he ran beside me. But tears dripped out of his eyes and down to his bloody ripped waistcoat and shirt.

Trying to calm him, I said: "He probably survived. But we have to go."

He gasped and hiccuped. I admit I did not understand my coven brother's feelings. He had protected us.

I shouted at Derrik. "We left him alive!"

Thankfully, my coven brother snapped out of his morbs. We dashed from house to house, glancing back every few minutes. The trees grew thicker as we moved southward. Fortunately, we were able to remain in the shade of the forest for the last two miles.

Then in the distance was our wooden barn, but it looked blackened. "Do you think….Are they all right?" I asked, my stomach in my throat.

"We would have felt it if something happened to Jakub or Pascaline, correct?" Derrik said. But his face was grim.

"Correct. You're correct," I said.

We drew closer and felt sweet relief as we could see the coven move across the blackened barn. In thick hooded robes, Pascaline, Xiao, and Jakub had climbed up to the roof and had put thick wet woolen blankets on the roof. Charles, Loretta, and Agata had collected some water from the bay and packed wet sand around the base of the barn creating a break in the vegetation.

Suddenly Agata called our names and ran toward us. Pascaline leapt down from the barn and dashed to us, overtaking Agata. My creator cried out something in French. Bloody tears streamed down my creator's eyes as she embraced both of us around the neck. She kissed my cheeks. And Derrik on the lips.

Then she started asking at the closed wound on Derrik's shoulder. They spoke a few words in French. She kissed him again and pressed his hand to her cheek.

I regretted not studying French, but I understood her expression well enough.

When Agata arrived, she eyed Derrik's wounds and opened her wrist. She ordered us to both take a sip of her blood. Unlike with me, he did not argue with Agata.

Nor did I. No one argues with Agata. There was hot agony all across my body as minor burns and scratches healed within seconds. I cried out, but in front of his beloved Pascaline, Derrik would only grimace.

Agata told us to open a jug of deer blood and drink our fill. Which we did. Then she told us to bathe in the slough and when we returned to bring up more buckets of water. And then told us we had quite a day. The barn was safe. We ought to try to sleep a little.

Derrik collapsed into his coffin. I cannot sleep. I am too afraid of the wind turning the fires this way.

No, that's only half of the truth: what is really on my mind is why in the world did my father send the hunter after us?

Pascaline was correct. I should have never gone into the city. *What is ten dollars a week compared to my existence? And what if Derrik had been killed or seriously injured?* I will never forgive myself if I caused Pascaline to lose someone so dear to her.

A few notes for our listeners. Though millions of rats and other pests died during the Great Fire only one human life is known to have been lost. Thankfully, no vampire existences were lost that day.

For listeners who are confused by Mr. Monroe's comment about "seamstresses": in the late 19th century, Seattle had a tax on "seamstresses". They did not want to tax the lumber jacks so instead they taxed the women who serviced the lumber jacks. The Old Man of the Forest which Derrik mentioned is a legendary vampire who wandered the deep forests of Washington State before it was Washington State. However, stories of the Old Man disappeared once Seattle was founded.

As for Alice, she did not marry right away. That stipend (Approximately $285 in 2020) allowed her freedom she wouldn't have had otherwise. She never saw her human family again though her mother sent Christmas letters and an announcement of her sister's nuptials. Only after her father's death in 1927, Alice attended the University of Washington and found occupation in the budding telecommunication's industry. She married in the 1990's to a lovely ancient vampire and moved to Strawberry Fields in Bellevue where she joined the tech industry. This worked well as the greater Seattle area had begun to grow and traffic has really gotten terrible.

We miss Alice of course, but we see her often enough that she is still known as Pascaline's Firstborn and it's better to reside where she doesn't have to commute over a bridge.

A WORD FROM OUR SPONSOR

Paper Flower Credit Union

Tonight's lesson is sponsored by Paper Flower Credit Union established 1918. For those vampires and ancient Gods who have enjoyed a recent torpor you may remember it as the Paper Flower Savings Fund, established in 1871. As a member owned, not for profit credit union, we are committed to our members prosperous financial well-being. We offer excellent interest for our savings accounts and CDs not seen for decades. We also offer flexible extended term mortgages with low annual APR for vampires of every budget. We take the long view!

INITIATE QUESTIONS

LADY LORETTA, DO YOU OFTEN PAY OFF VAMPIRE HUNTERS OR DO YOU HAVE TO KILL THEM?

Most of the time if we pay them off they go away. And presently, if they come back, we can always call Norma. She and her associates are quite good at cleaning up little messes.

Good day beloved initiates and sleep the sleep of the dead.

INTRODUCTION

Beloved Initiates,

I shall discuss the vampire powers, sometimes called talents. Before I start, I ought to clarify I shall not be speaking on the broad powers all vampires seem to have. I speak of how when vampires are reborn, one or two talents, often extrasensory, come to the forefront.

In our experience: the progenitor's most potent gifts seem to be passed on to the fledgling. However, that is not always the case. An intelligent coven learns what gifts all members are reborn with so they may be useful rather than a hindrance.

Though not a part of the Paper Flower Consortium, we can trace many of our gifts through our ancient ancestor, Gaius Lepidus Severus, a former general in the Roman empire. He created the vampire who attacked and ultimately infected Lady Agata with vampirism. Agata and Gaius's history, how shall I say it, is complicated, and speaking about that specific vampire would be in truly bad taste. So I shall not be speaking about either of them without permission from the existing undead parties.

The three major gifts Gaius gave us are Clairvoyance, Celerity, and Mesmerism. True Telepathy, also called mind-reading, is quite rare and entered the coven more recently through Derrik Miller.

As Agata is our oldest vampire, let us begin with her gift of Mesmerism. Mesmerism is the ability to direct minds. It can be used to control someone; however, it works best when the subject of Mesmerism wants to do what is asked. Some call it hypnotism or domination.

Her Ladyship Agata was born the daughter of a Count and married at age fifteen to Jakub, the younger son of a different Count. Beyond being a wife and mother, she was also a learned midwife and healer. However, since she was attacked and left to die, she had no true teacher. She did not know of her vampire talents until months after her transformation.

Agata, alongside Gaius's concubines, killed Agata's progenitor, so we do not know his primary gift. Agata shared only a few words with him. She did not know her powers or how to use them. She did, however, and still does, have an observant, scientific mind, and an aptitude for estate management.

Agata quickly realized she was stronger than she had been as a human woman and healed quickly as long as she had blood, but of course, she was weak in comparison to the other vampires she met in her first weeks as a vampire.

After her turning, Agata experimented on herself. She kept two copies of her observations interspersed with letters she wrote to Jakub while she awaited his return home.

One copy of the journal came with her to France. The other stayed with her eldest, Irina, who was also trained in the healer's art.

This letter which I am about to relay, shows when Agata realized she has "powers like Gaius." It was originally written in Medieval Moldavian. Pascaline translated the journal early in the 1700 century to French. It was translated again into English in 1952 by Norma, so forgive any strange turns of phrase. Agata says it is basically correct.

MEMORIE OF AGATA

09, July, 1509

My beloved Jakub,

I once believed that hell was terrifying pain and lakes of fire, but now I know it is the crushing, stony loneliness that dashes upon my mind over and over.

Six months ago, I died.

I might have thought I would be numb to the isolation by now, but nothing has changed. I seek out the tiny creatures for companionship: flies, beetles, moths. But they scurry away from me in terror, and I cannot keep them in the manor less they damage the wood and cloth.

I suppose it is natural I still ache for you and the children. Still, I did not comprehend how I would miss Cook's songs, Gavrilla, (Insertion: Gavrilla was Jakub's brother's wife and Agata's bosom companion before she was transformed into a vampire) and my weekly tasks of making and delivering bread for our town and the farmers who lived afield.

When I can sleep, I fall asleep dreaming of the balls at the castle, services at the fortified church, and the bustling market day in the town square. I miss the women I used to nurture as they brought forth life into the world. Did you know Gavrilla had a little girl and I wasn't able to be by her side?

I miss my cows. No sounds of gentle cows mooing to be fed or milked in the lower herdland. No calves bouncing through the grass, mud, or snow. The lower herdland have been emptied.

Artur and Petru sometimes move cows through the upper herdlands, but neither visits the manor. They never come close to the house. Even so, remember our boys always in love, for they need you so badly to be proud of them.

The leaded glass windows rattle from the summer wind coming from the mountains. Did they always? I can't remember. My hearing is much better now. The sound makes me think of our beloved children running up and down the halls. I wish I hadn't scolded them for such things now.

I try to sleep during the day as other vampires I met did, but I wait and watch for you or for Gavrilla's valet who drops supplies or our daughters when they bring me a basket of meat which they leave outside the door.

The summer sun protects them from me. I cannot

touch their soft, warm skin. Though I long to feel our first grandchild kick, I cannot chance to touch Irina's growing stomach. Nor I can I change to embrace Daciana. Because I can hear their beating hearts and smell their living flesh. I do not trust myself to touch them. I love our children too much.

I pray for the children daily. And when they come close to the pantry door, I call, "Thank you, girls. I love you both. Daciana, mind your sister and brothers."

Our girls always reply they love me.

As I instructed Irina, they always turn and walk away. Sometimes they weep. Sometimes they wait to weep until they are far enough away from the manor with the belief, I cannot hear them.

Last week, Daciana had a tantrum and wailed for me.

Jakub, you will be so proud of Irina, she has eternal patience for her little sister, but Daciana is so young. And if she cannot have a mother, at least she might have her father.

I long and fear for your return. I am dead. I have no hold upon you, and if you are to have any life at all, you must cast me out. I am not sure where I will go, but fear not, my beloved, I have been experimenting. Soon I will know how long I can stand the sun, soon I will know how long it takes silver to burn my flesh. I must focus upon my experiments. I must be ready to leave when you return. I will bless your future if I can. I know you must have a wife, not a walking corpse. And Daciana needs a mother.

Wait a moment, my dear, there is a knock on the

door. I smell someone. Who would come here? Wait a moment.

Jakub, my love, I have broken quarantine.

You see, I unlatched and peeked out the small window in the door and saw a dirty young woman, perhaps of eighteen. She smelled vomit, filth, and blood. She clutched a dirty shawl around her shoulders though it was a warm afternoon. She was too thin for health—except for her large stomach which stretched her coarsely woven le and fota.

There was no history or tales of love embroidered on her skirts or sleeves. Blood and water soaked the woman's stained and damp skirts. Her skin held a layer of greasy dirt, which had seeped into her pores. Her dark hair was stringy. I wasn't sure how I knew, it wasn't my experience as a midwife; it was something darker. The darkness inside of me knew her water had broken awhile before. She should have called for a midwife hours before now.

"I am sorry, but this house has been quarantined..." I told her.

"Please, you must see me," she cried.

"My daughter, Irina, sees all mothers."

"She won't see me." The woman screamed with a birthing pain and leaned on the porch post.

"Irina will help you. You can pay her whenever you can," I said.

"No, I cannot. Please," the woman begged. Her eyes were scorched with agony. "There will never be..... You don't know, you don't know."

"My daughter would not set you aside."

"I never said she would," she gasped as she rambled. "Forgive me, Lady Agata, you must let me in. There is no one else." The woman screamed again as she bent over.

I did not know the woman or the woman's husband. Perhaps he was a bully who refused to pay for a midwife. I thought perhaps she was an apostate or a Jewish woman or for some reason unable to go to the nuns. If she felt her only solution was a vampire, she must be in dire need.

And, Jakub, I broke quarantine. I opened the door all the way and stepped out onto the porch. Hopefully, you will think kindly upon me.

"Why can't you go to Irina?" I asked.

She wobbled on her feet. "I can't show my face in town. I can't."

"Why?"

"Please, just help me, milady."

"I will help you, but I must know what I'm working with."

She flinched as I pressed my hand against her belly.

This close, I feared the smell of blood and sweat might drive me mad. The woman's heartbeat was fast, but the baby's was fairly regular. Fresh sweat coated her skin. I wanted to lick her. I wanted to bite into her tender flesh.

She is not meat. I thought. Perhaps my urges were written in my complexion because the woman whimpered. *She is not meat.*

"Hold still, dearie," I ordered. She did.

I waited until I could feel the contraction. Once it finished, I began to count. Two hundred seconds later, another. A bit over three minutes between.

I wrapped my arm around her. "Come into my hall. Take a deep breath after each contraction, and as it begins, that's a good girl."

Though my birthing equipment was in the kitchen, in truth, I did not want to bring the woman into my sanctuary. I feared her life might taint my resolve to remain quarantined from the children and the rest of our family.

I settled her on a dining bench. I brought in the birthing chair, the basins, and lay out fresh hay on the hall floor.

"How many moons have you been pregnant?"

"I'm not sure. At least four... but longer obviously," the woman said.

"What do you feel?" I asked.

"My legs have been cramping. And I have so much pain... for the past week." She grimaced as the birthing pain took her.

"Undress, please, and sit in the birthing chair. I need to check how close you are to delivery."

Once disrobed, I observed the woman's body. Her back bore scars where she had been whipped. The flesh of her wrists had been rubbed raw. Around her neck was a ring of rough skin from an oxen's yoke or some sort of collar? **No: Stocks**.

"These marks are from the stocks? You are a criminal?"

The woman opened her mouth, but no sound came out.

"It's all right. I will still help you."

The woman wept in relief. Her heartbeat fluttered.

She is not meat. She is not meat. She is not meat. I repeated in my head.

I checked to see how far the woman was along. Her cervix had dilated. She would deliver within hours.

Hours. I wasn't sure how I would survive the temptation of her blood. *Just because I hunger does not mean I must indulge. I am not an animal. I ate my cows, but I also nurtured them. I didn't think of a steak or leathers when I brushed their fur or delivered their calves. A human is no different.*

"Every woman's labor is unique, is this your first?" I asked.

"My second, but my first was stillborn. I'm so afraid something is wrong again," the woman said.

I compelled myself not to smell the sweat and blood in the woman's skirts. *She must be cleaned.* It would help her and the coming babe. She was a mother in need, not meat. If I could help her, it meant I could return to being a midwife. And if I can midwife, Jakub, my beloved, you need not fear for me. A midwife can support herself comfortably enough.

I told the woman to step on a grate. With a clean sponge and herbal soap, I scrubbed the woman's dirty flesh. I ran a strigle over her skin to push the soap into the basin below and combed a heavy oil through her hair to kill any lice.

"Hold your nose, honey." I dumped a bucket of warmed water over her skin.

I wiped her face with a hot and wet towel dipped in rosemary oil. The pungent herbs concealed the smell of her flesh. I ran the oil over her.

I moved the woman to the birthing chair. I massaged her calves and gently applied pressure to the knots in the muscles until the woman relaxed.

"Hold the cross and pray with Mother Mary," I said.

"God doesn't hear my prayers," she murmured.

As you know, my beloved, I did not believe that, but one should never argue with a woman in labor.

"Now, breath with the contractions, dearie. I will be right back," I said.

I dashed into the pantry and sucked on the dry meat of this week's last rabbit. I was still hungry. I chipped a piece of salt off my saltblock and pressed the chip onto my tongue. I filled myself with well water and put on a kettle. I pulled Cook's abandoned tin trough and old pallet into the hall.

The woman's heartbeat called to mine. Refusing to listen, I sang a birthing song and massaged the woman's extended stomach. I sang so loudly, I feared the woman thought me mad.

She cried out in agony as the contractions took her body. I stroked her hair and wiped sweat from her brow.

Wanting to assist her from the pain, I thought of Gaius and how he forced his will upon me when I was at the fort. Perhaps, I could do that too, but to take away pain, rather than give it.

"Did you know, dear, cows almost never feel much pain in birth."

She screamed again.

I thought I failed, but I kept talking in a gentle voice:

forcing my will over her and covering her like a soft blanket.

"Certainly, it's uncomfortable for the cow, as it is for you, but there doesn't need to be in pain," I explained.

The woman cried out once more. Still, she did not hold her head, as I once did, as if a million insects crawled inside her skin. Her eyes glazed over. She sobbed how she saw the cows and calves frolicking in the lower herdland. They were not there, of course. But she saw them. She saw them because I was showing her!

"All right."

I showed her a birthing cow—a cow who had more than one calf—and whose body understood what it was supposed to do.

"Do you see the cow?"

"Yes, Lady."

"Good. Now you must push."

The woman bared down.

"All right, dearie, you must push more gently. I see the head. Just look at the cows."

The woman cried when the baby's face was exposed. One more push and the baby's head was freed. The rest of the baby's body followed.

I cleared the babe's airway, and he took in air the first time.

"The babe is a boy."

The woman shivered. This was a good sign.

"The placenta will be coming soon," I told her. "Look at the cows. Look at that calf, able to take his first breath on his own."

I dipped my blade in boiling water and cut the

umbilical cord.

I gently pulled on the umbilical cord. The placenta fell into the birthing basin. Observing the pile of bloody filth, I realized with delight I could take the bloody mass away which I did. I set it in the cold pantry beside my rabbit meat.

I poured steaming water into the trough and rebathed the woman in order to check her injuries. She dipped herself inside and relaxed. I rubbed in a healing poultice first into her face to soften her skin, then her neck and wrists for the rash from the stocks. She dozed off then.

I felt as if I were a wolf looking down at a sleeping deer. I shook the thought away. I nudged her shoulder. "Do you wish to hold your baby?"

I helped her from the bath and onto Cook's old pallet.

I instructed her how to make the babe latch on, which took her a few tries. Very normal. The babe did and began to drink from his mother.

I found some old clothing left behind from our valet. I even found one of Cook's discarded skirts for the mother. I diapered and swaddled the child and set him in a basket beside his now exhausted mother.

Fearing I might do harm, I hurried into the cold pantry. I ate the placenta, I delighted in the fresh blood. My tongue was coated with pleasure, and I felt more alive than I had in months. I heard the newborn cry and my stomach growled.

The child would more tender than a suckling calf.

They are not meat, I told to myself and focused on

the placenta.

Then I seeped chamomile in water. I have almost no food in the house, but I set aside a jar of honey and a sack of herbal lozenges for the woman. She can sell them if she must, but I hope she takes them as they will strengthen her milk.

Then hot cup of chamomile in hand, I returned to my window and my journal to breath in something besides the mother and child.

How I long for your arrival. There is little doubt that I have become a monster, Jakub. No matter what happens, you must promise to never let me near the children.

I will love you through eternity, Agata.

After her signature there are several scrawled sentences: *They are not meat. They are not meat. They are not meat.*

If Agata had remained with other vampires, she might have had a more abundant knowledge about her gifts. Of course, if she had, she might not have had an adventure with Jakub. Of course, if that didn't happen The Paper Flower Consortium might not exist at all.

As most initiates have realized by now: When Jakub returned, he told Agata to transform him. They left Moldavia together and settled in France for a few centuries, than England and then America. In March 2020, they celebrated their five hundred and twenty-eighth anniversary. Seventeen as humans and five-hundred and eleven as vampires. They had five human children, four whom survived to adulthood. Agata had two vampire daughters, Pascaline and myself. Jakub had two vampire sons and together twenty-eight grandprogeny and four greatgrandprogeny. And several more in the initiate program.

A WORD FROM OUR SPONSOR:

MYT Clothier

Vampires, Do you dislike ripped denim, thin fabrics, and how well-made modern clothing is covered in labels? MYT Clothier creates handmade custom clothing in accessible styles for all body types from all eras—including this one! We use the best quality handwoven silk embroidery from China, Damask from France and Italian Embroidery and Leathers, and other fine fabrics. And if you wish to look like you stepped out of time or even reality with fantastical designs, we can make that happen too. At MYT Clothier, quality is our style. Call for a fitting tonight!

INITIATE QUESTION:

FROM THE LETTER IT SOUNDS LIKE HER LADYSHIP, AGATA, DOES NOT KNOW IF SHE KILLED THE MOTHER AND CHILD?

Indeed it does.

When asked, Agata is pretty sure, after the woman woke, she sent her and the babe out the door, but she does not really recall. Five hundred years is a long time to remember anything. However, there is no mention of eating a human in her observations and experiments so that is probably correct.

LADY LORETTA, I AM CONFUSED. YOU SAID VAMPIRES KEPT THRALLS FOR BLOOD AND DON'T KILL PEOPLE.

Yes, modern vampires keep thralls, but Lady Agata and Sir Jakub have existed for over 500 years. The enthralled were not even a thing back then.

As the letter reports, her daughters were bringing weekly rations of meat and her sister-in-law, the Countess Gavrilla, was sending other supplies until Jakub returned from war.

LADY LORETTA, THOUGH YOU CALL THE GIFT, "MESMERISM" THE STORY DESCRIBES MORE OF A STATE OF HYPNOSIS.

Ah listener, you were not listening close enough to be so pedantic. Agata was stroking the mother's hair and bathed her. There was touch and spoken word, however, if you would like to call it hypnotism, glamours, or enchantment, I don't think anyone would care. Languages change.

We call it Mesmerism, primarily because that was the term in England during in the 1790s when Jakub and Agata, Pascaline and I fled France. Charles had already left for America at that point and Derrik was not born yet.

Though we all still spoke French at home, Jakub especially did not want to stand out in England during the decades we were there.

LADY LORETTA, IT SOUNDS LIKE AN INITIATE CAN CHOOSE THEIR GIFT BY CHOOSING THEIR MENTOR?

To a certain extent that is true, especially in the modern era with the coven system. However the next story tells how my Fifthborn, Marion, surprised us all by having Clairvoyance even though Agata, myself, and all my offspring until Marion had Mesmerism.

Have a good day and sleep the sleep of the dead.

INTRODUCTION

Beloved Initiates,

Last time, I spoke on vampire gifts and Mesmerism. Tonight, I shall speak about Clairvoyance and how gifts can be elusive. As I mentioned: in our experience: when a vampire is reborn, the progenitor's most potent gifts seem to be passed on to the fledgling, but that isn't always the case.

We once believed we could anticipate which gifts went to each progeny, but we learned as we expanded it is not always the case. There are theories of why certain gifts are passed while others are not. One such theory is the gift past has to do with the amount of adrenaline in one's system when one dies, to ensure the fledgling's survival. A similar theory speaks of hormones. Another theory is that vampires do not choose gifts; gifts choose the vampire. I personally think this last one is hokey, however it is a common idea in elder vampire circles.

Let us begin by discussing the progeny of Lady Agata and the gifts they received.

In 1509, Agata was reborn gifted in Mesmerism.

Agata has created three vampires.

The first was Jakub. As Jakub was her husband in life, he was also her husband in death. They knew very little of vampire traditions when she transformed him as they had no mentor. They learned however, Jakub was talented in Clairvoyance, is the ability to locate people or objects, which was good, because the pair needed to know where people, resources, and shelter could be found. Moreover, to become a knight of France, Jakub killed a legendary monster for Louis the 12th, so the uncanny ability to locate things was quite useful.

There is one more aspect to Clairvoyance that Jakub found quite accidentally. While most vampires see their bloodline only when they are transformed, once appropriately trained, a Clairvoyant can also use the skill to see and move through the bloodline. This allows the vampire to contact ancestors for help—especially those with the same abilities. And though our relationship with Gaius has been complicated, he has been willing to answer questions about offspring. And at times even helped us. At least in our bloodline, vampires more ancient than Gaius do not seem interested in us at all, or the going-ons of Seattle or even America.

The next vampire Agata created in 1686 was my sister, Pascaline. Agata's gift for Mesmerism was there, but it was a lesser gift. Pascaline was gifted in true Celerity: which not just speed, but the athleticism and agility to use it. Though she was a lady of the French court, she was reborn physically as strong as Jakub. This is one of the reasons our coven believes in the adrenaline theory. Because Pascaline died with rage in her heart and wanted vengeance on the soldiers who killed her husband and daughter.

I also wanted vengeance, but at the time, I was only sixteen and though I was a woman of that era, Agata and Jakub refused to transform me until I was Pascaline's age. By that time, Pascaline already had her vengeance. And like Agata I was naturally skilled in Mesmerism.

Jakub passed Charles his Clairvoyance. And Derrik surprised everyone by being reborn with Telepathy. After we were settled in Seattle, it was obvious that Agata wanted her offspring to produce offspring. My first born, Xiao was gifted with Mesmerism. Pascaline's only child, Alice, also is talented in Mesmerism, though she also had some gifts in Celerity. So it seemed Agata's daughters were passing on Mesmerism to their offspring.

In the 1950's, I began sharing my blood as it became obvious that the coven needed to grow. My next three daughters were also proficient in Mesmerism.

So we were sure my fifth Reborn, Marion Betsy Crabtree, would be gifted with Mesmerism. In fact that is why she wanted to become a vampire.

But now I find myself in the middle, when I should be at the beginning. I will not be repeating Marion's accounts verbatim, because of the police lingo and coarse, at times derogatory, language. The world was a different place in 1969.

Marion worked as what is commonly referred to as a beat cop. She had held this position for seven years after getting her degree at UW. She had always wanted a career in law enforcement. However, unless directing traffic, her sexuality and gender was constantly challenged by her colleagues, victims, and perpetrators of crimes. She heard common derogatory words for female homosexuals several times a night. She had been given the common moniker of Crabby which she wasn't crazy about.

In the era, the police forced used teams of two for safety reasons, as their radios were only in their cars. Her partner, an older police officer with twenty-two years on the force, Ralph Henry, was often teased too about how Crabby had a bigger male sexual organ than he did. Though the "jokes" angered her, Marion always laughed it off. She felt she had to be one of the guys to garner their respect. Moreover, rank was everything. She felt if she could just earn her detective's badge, they would respect her. So she sought some way to solve crimes more efficiently. She was, and still is, highly detailed and organized. Ralph was not.

Do not misunderstand me, Marion always spoke highly of her partner, Ralph Henry. The citizens and business owners on their beat loved him. What he lacked in paperwork skill, he made up for in how he served the community.

Part of their beat was the waterfront district. Restaurants sometimes passed extra food to Ralph, and they delivered it to a group of hippy street kids who lived under the viaduct. Though sometimes they were called pigs or narcs, the kids still took the food. Homelessness was a problem in Seattle, but not the problem it is now.

July 7th, 1969

Marion saw something that shifted her reality.

As she and Ralph walked southward on the waterfront, a young woman ran toward them crying for help. The girl's feet were bare, with her heels in her hands. Her toe poked out of her ripped nylons.

Marion put her hand out her hands. "How can we help?"

Tearful the woman related in a slurred voice how she and her boyfriend were coming out of The Polynesian and tripped over "a dead seal or something".

Her boyfriend was hurt. They went out for the night and maybe they drank a little too much for good sense, but neither were really drunk. They were supposed to take the streetcar to a club on the other side of the waterfront.

Marion and Ralph followed the rambling young woman to just south of Pier 51, where the young man sat with his head in his hands. (Insertion, For anyone who is confused, in 1969, Pier 51 was not one of the Washington State Ferry Terminals, but rather housed a restaurant, The Polynesian.) Beside him was a slimy creature, which smelled like a thousand rotting salmons.

Marion had heard of mermaids, of course. Every Seattle Police Officer knew an old-timer who swore up and down about arresting a drunk mermaid when they came to shore to seduce a sailor. But Marion wasn't ready for the sight or smell of one.

The creature was not a pretty human woman with a fishtail and waves of gorgeous hair. For that manner,

Marion did not know for sure the gender of the creature anymore than she could have known the gender of a porpoise. No hair covered any part of the amphibious beast's body. Webbed fingers ended in sharp black talons. Shimmering scales clad strong, wiry muscles. Spines emerged out of their back. Their upper body was covered in what might be natural marking, might be tattoos. Deep in her heart, Marion was glad the creature was dead, she did not want to see it move on dry land with an undulating crawl. Stretching and contorting its body as it reached for its victim.

Ralph bent down and helped the man to his feet and walked him a few feet away "for hygienic purposes."

Marion radioed in a "123 for a deep slashing cut, 4 inches long...and a strange-looking DB. Possible need animal control."

The dispatcher asked a few questions and eventually said, "Detectives Thompson and Taylor enroute."

Hearing those names, Marion felt trapped by Alaska Way Viaduct's thick concrete posts which rose above them and the drone of cars which drowned out the lapping water.

Marion did not like James Thompson who openly took bribes, and never failed to speak in a crass, derogatory manner. She didn't know much about Harold Taylor. He was a quiet man, but it was whispered Harold Taylor could find out anything about anyone. Marion didn't know about that. What she did know is Thompson wasn't reprimanded in '66 as many were when the newspapers exposed a payoff racket. It was said Harold Taylor got him off, somehow.

The detectives got out of their car. They didn't

question the young woman or his beau. Thompson growled at Ralph.

"Get them out of here,"

Taylor quickly bandaged the scrape and helped the young man to his feet. Then snarled: "It's just a scratch. Grow a pair and take your girl dancing."

Ralph helped the couple to the streetcar station. Taylor radioed in a few acronyms that Marion didn't know. He murmured something Marion did not understand, but she was sure he said "Child of Poseidon."

Seeing her study Taylor, Thompson impolitely suggested, "Beat it, Crabby."

Ralph and Marion did.

As they patrolled their beat, Marion tried to speak, but Ralph said, "Look, Crabby, I got a family! I saw nothin' and you didn't either. Crap rolls downhill."

They finished their shift. Marion went back to her apartment but tossed and turned that day. She couldn't get the image or smell from her mind. She couldn't stop thinking that there were many things beyond her reality.

When she arrived at work on Sunday night, she checked the report which read Officers Henry and Crabtree discovered the body of a female victim, possible transient, drowning. Tangled in fishing gear. No witnesses. No identification.

Case closed.

Marion entered the morgue. She hoped the assistant coroner would allow her to examine the strange body.

The assistant coroner asked, "What strange body?"

She showed him the report.

"Oh, that. The body was released to the family."

"On a Sunday morning?" Marion said.

"Look, I just work here," the assistant coroner said.

Marion returned to her desk.

When Ralph arrived, she explained to him about the file and how the body had been released.

Every night of his twenty-two years on the force showed on his face. "Leave it be, Marion, I have a family to take care of. It is best when any weird stuff happens to ignore it."

"Wait, you've seen…"

"Look. Get yourself a husband and a couple of kids. Then you'll know what's important. It's certainly not an unidentified dead body."

Over Ralph's shoulder, Marion saw Thompson and Taylor climbing the stairs. In the station's light, she saw how tired Thompson looked, huffing with every step. Age was catching up to him. Though they looked to both be around 50, Taylor was not out of breath.

Ignoring Ralph, she hurried to catch up. "That… strange…"

"Wasn't that strange. Once the coroner arrived, we realized it was a fishing accident," Thompson said.

Taylor said nothing.

"But those spines…" Marion said.

"Mother of God, this is why women make terrible cops. You're too hysterical," Thompson said.

Heat rose to Marion's cheeks. She thought about throwing a punch. She wanted to scream. She did not. She would not prove Thompson and all his ilk right. However, anger set on her shoulders like a weight.

Marion and Ralph drove from the precinct to their beat, checked on local businesses, the homeless kids, and the elderly. There were a few drunks and a robbery. Otherwise, it was a quiet Sunday night.

However, the image of that strange body was an itch worming its way through her flesh, digging deep into her brain and setting up a life of its own. Marion found herself listening to her police scanner for anything that sounded strange or unusual. She didn't hear anything right away.

On her night off, Marion ordered two buckets of chicken with all the sides, which she delivered to the kids under the viaduct.

The hungry gaggle surrounded her and grabbed at the food with dirty hands.

"I need to ask you guys something?" Marion asked.

"We ain't no narcs, man." One of the older boys, nearly a man or a very young man still with boyish features, said between bites of chicken.

"I want to know, do you ever see anything scary—or perhaps, just strange--down here?"

"Like your friend?" One of the younger girls said.

The older girls shushed her.

"You guys aren't scared of Officer Henry?"

"No, your other friends. The one with the monster," A different boy said.

The elder boy punched the other in the shoulder. "The detectives?" Marion asked.

The elder boy passed the younger boy the coleslaw. "Go, eat your vegetables. Your eyes are broken." He pushed him away.

Marion had been a cop too long to be fooled by the act, but she needed to keep this casual.

"What kind of monster is the detective?"

"Look, Officer Crabby, we like you, and Officer Henry," The older boy said, "But sometimes people disappear. Some of them are just kids. They don't care. They don't investigate. Protect and Serve, my butt. They only protect and serve their wallets."

Then he fell quiet. Marion knew she would get no more out of him.

It wasn't much to go on. Marion could not stop listening to the police scanner. And one night she was rewarded.

"Two DB: It's strange. Possible wild animals. 2nd and King."

She drove to 2nd and King and parked down the street. As she suspected, she found Thompson and Taylor over two large, hairy creatures in the middle of the street, their motorcycles on the ground. They told the officers to beat it. Just as she and Ralph had, the officers did. The detectives closed the intersection.

Detective Taylor radioed someone. Thompson wrote out notes until a blue truck pulled up.

A slender brunette slipped out of the driver's seat. She politely said "Hello, Detective Taylor, Detective

Thompson."

She looked a little too young to be driving, a little too young to be out alone this late. Younger than some of those hippies under the bridge, but there was something old in her face and world wary.

The girl handed the detectives two envelopes. Marion knew a payoff when she saw one.

The girl studied the strange hairy bodies entwined on the ground which seem to be shifting and molting. She did not seem shocked at the naked man's exposed organs. A girl that size shouldn't be able to lift the hairy bodies, but she did with the assistance of a hand truck. Then she covered them with a dark-colored tarp which she tied down. She pulled out a broom and swept the street. Then she mopped up the blood until all that was left was the trace of bleach in the air.

The detectives reopened the intersection and got into their car. The girl got into her truck. Marion wasn't sure if she should follow the girl or the detectives.

She chose the girl.

The girl drove south. Marion tried to stay a bit back and even let a semitruck get between the girl and her car. The girl sped up and slowed down, always the legal speed limit. She went in circles a few times. Marion feared she would lose the truck on the twisting streets. It was a clear night, but she felt trapped in a maze. She wanted out. All the houses looked the same.

Then the taillights on the girl's truck disappeared.

Marion pulled over. She tried to listen for the sound of an engine on nearby streets. All she heard ships. She was confused, unsure of what part of Seattle she was even in other than knowing she must be near SODO. She turned and drove until she found a main road that headed north.

Unwilling to give up, Marion confronted Taylor and Thompson at their habitual diner, not because they loved the food but because they did not expect to pay.

Marion slipped into the booth beside Taylor. The waitress brought her a coffee.

"I saw you with that girl," Marion said quietly.

Thompson made a few threats, but Taylor just tilted his head as if Marion was the most interesting person in the world. His coffee-stained teeth looked a little too sharp. And this close, something was off about him. She thought about how those kids called the detectives monsters.

A cloud passed over her. Her coffee cup seemed too heavy. She surprised herself by saying: "I want to be a detective," Marion said, unable to think. "But you stole my body."

"Take the class and pass the exam," Taylor said.

"I need to be allowed to take it." Marion said. "Perhaps a recommendation?"

They did not answer.

Marion glanced over her shoulder at the waitress helping some truckers at the counter. "My vic was a real mermaid?"

"Yes," Taylor said.

"Last night, those hairy creatures."

"Werewolves playing chicken," Taylor said.

"Kids of all races, man, they do stupid things." Thompson took another long drag on his cigarette.

"The supernatural can't cry to *The Times*," Taylor's jaw seemed wider than it should be.

How many teeth do people have? He seemed to have too many.

Thompson took a long drag on his cigarette. He laughed, but his laugh was hollow. "All right. I'll give you a recommendation, but people will say we're having an affair. Worse for you than me."

"I doubt that. Everyone thinks I am a lesbian," Marion said.

"Hey, I don't care if you are a lesbian." Thompson tried to be lecherous; instead he sighed. Again Marion thought he seemed tired, worn down.

"If those asses at Seattle Times hadn't done their expose in '66, I'd still be haunting the scene with my hand out and my eyes closed. We got kids to feed."

"Your kids are grown and your hand is still out, Detective. Who is the girl?"

"That sweet little piece is Norma Rollins, but be clear, Crabby, you speak a word of this, and we will expose you."

Marion was creeped out by Thompson referring to a young girl "as a sweet little piece" more than his threat. Thompson was a dirty cop and a disgusting pig through and through. She no longer cared that he seemed tired.

"What is she?" Marion asked.

"A vampire, obviously," Taylor's jaw clicked a little too hard with each syllable.

"Any reason a vampire couldn't be a detective?" She looked hard into Taylor's eyes to see if he gave anything away.

His eyes glittered. "None that I know of, assuming you plan to remain on the nightshift."

His words were smooth and Marion had the feeling he was undressing her, no, skinning her with his eyes. "If you want to know about vampires: Paper Flower Consortium is in the book."

Thompson suddenly looked sad.

She thanked them for the information. She was glad to leave.

Marion lied about the reasons she came to the coven. It was so obvious a lie; I gently mesmerized her and asked, "Officer Crabtree, why are you really here?"

She went under easily. "I want a better way to get perps off the street," Marion said. "I want to know if that Dracula stuff is real."

By Dracula stuff, she specifically meant she wanted to dominate a perp's mind---not to entrap, but to get to the truth without violence. Since manipulation was considered a feminine skill and she already worked nights, she figured being a vampire could help her career.

Some people may judge her immoral for wanting this, I do not. I have seen too much in my existence and this is a good enough reason to be a vampire, better than many I have heard.

Marion began her initiation education. She worked nights as a police officer and came on her night off. And if this was a film rather than an instructional lesson, this would be time for the montage with a snappy song showing Marion working, studying, occasionally helping Taylor and Thompson out, taking the detective's class and exam, and passing. However, the final scene would show her being passed over for promotion due to budgetary reasons.

She was disappointed, but she focused on her vampire studies, believing if she could learn to mesmerize, she could be promoted to detective.

After the initiation period was complete, I transformed Marion. Though the steps were the same as my other children, something felt different when she died a. I told myself it was because the world was so changed. Marion did not need to be a vampire; she wanted to be one. There were no prayers—at least not from Marion, who is not particularly religious—though Agata, Pascaline, Charles, Derrik, and I prayed silently. Perhaps others did too. Even so, I knew it felt different.

After her transformation, on her second night of her undead existence, Marion tried to dominate her thrall.

"Look into my eyes," Marion said.

"Gladly." Her enthralled opened his eyes wide and peered into hers.

"Be serious," Marion said.

"All right, I'm serious."

"I want the truth." She looked the man in his eyes.

"About what?"

"Why did you come here?" Marion asked.

"To find a beautiful woman —who will be beautiful for eternity," he said. That was the truth, but it was a truth Marion already knew.

"Do you want to be a vampire?"

"No. I want to worship you."

"Later," she said annoyed.

They were interrupted by a phone call from Taylor. "So you died but came back. Excellent. I look forward to seeing you at work." Then he hung up.

More than a little unnerved, Marion tried to dominate her enthralled again. She failed again. She stormed into the library and accused me of weakness. I was not afraid of my daughter's tantrum and told her perhaps she might need practice.

Marion threw the lamp from my desk. It sparked and shattered against the wall.

Then she apologized and swept up the mess.

She tried and tried but could not dominate her thrall – even though he wanted to be dominated.

On her first night back on her patrol, Marion and Ralph checked up on a robbery complaint. After catching the man in the act and cuffing him, Marion tried to mesmerize the suspect. She failed.

He responded with derogatory names and laughter. "I ain't saying anything till my lawyer..."

Furious, Marion slammed the man's head into the hood of a car.

Ralph grabbed her arm. "Hey, Hey. Don't sink to their level."

That's when she sensed the detectives Taylor and Thompson were nearby and watching. Thompson's pulse was weedy, but she could not hear Taylor's pulse at all.

She quickly and calmly put the perp into the backseat

of the car.

On the drive back to the station, neither she or Ralph said much.

Then they heard over the radio: Thompson in pursuit of a suspect with a knife. Back up requested.

Then radio silence. Marion felt a sinking feeling.

Since they had a suspect in their car, they had to continue to the precinct. But there is something terrible when you know you cannot help someone in danger, even if you don't like the guy.

Taylor's report read that Detective Thompson died from multiple stab wounds, pictures of Thompson's chest did not look like it had been cut by a knife. Instead, it looked like a motor or something which dug deep into the flesh. These lacerations exposed heavy lung tumors and blood clots. He had been a dying man.

Taylor pretended to care as people gave their sympathies, but Marion sensed no pulse under his smooth, lying tongue. His heart was wrong. It was not like a human's—or a vampire.

She tried to confide in Ralph, but explaining her hunches just confused her explanation.

Ralph told her gently: "Shut your mouth unless you want no career at all. You should have never become a vampire."

Marion knew Ralph was correct, but she also needed to understand why Thompson was dead. And every time she thought about Thompson, she saw Taylor working through his shift, drinking coffee of the greasy spoon, or sitting in his bed at his efficiency lodgings.

After a few more days, Marion followed her hunch. There he was in the stripped pleather booth, just as she suspected.

She walked over to the booth and sank across from him.

"Thompson?" Marion asked.

"Don't make his mistakes, Crabby. He grew old. You won't," Taylor said.

"What do you want..." she said.

"It's time to clean up this town..." He listed a few public servants, few well-known minority leaders, and a list of monsters who he wanted to take out, including a few vampires.

They left the diner together.

She wondered how she was going to get out of this situation.

She tried to dominate one last time: "Taylor, Look into my eyes..."

An intense blistering hot pain entered Marion's left leg. She fell to the concrete, gasping. A gunshot won't kill a vampire, but it, certainly, hurts.

He dragged her into his car. Her leg became an achy numbness. "I won't kill you, but I can make you suffer for eternity. Do not do that again."

Furious, Marion threw herself into Taylor. She pushed him against the driver's door.

Her lips burned as they pressed against his flesh of his throat. Yet, it didn't feel like flesh, stiffer like rubber from a shoe . Unlike the salty deliciousness, she had tasted from vampires and humans, Taylor's blood tasted acrid and bitter. She spat it out, her lips blistered.

He punched her.

She unloaded her gun into his side and stomach.

He laughed as gore pored onto the bench seat. "Bullets can't kill me anymore than they can kill you."

She stumbled out of the car and tried to run down the street.

She didn't want to call for help, but didn't know what else to do. The sun would be rising. Where is Norma when I need her!

And in her mind's eye, she saw Norma in her truck. She limped to a phonebooth and called the coven switchboard. Marion slid down to the dirty, urine-soaked concrete floor.

Norma showed up in less than ten minutes. The older vampire gently assisted Marion to her truck.

"They might come after me or the coven," Marion asked.

"No, Just tell me if you want to disappear into the coven or remain outside it," Norma said. "I make magic happen. Do you have Taylor's home address?"

"If you could take Taylor out, why didn't you!" Marion shouted.

Norma just smiled.

Marion wanted to slap that smile off her face, but she did not.

"Better the devil you know," Norma said. "But you were the last one he was seen with...so I must know your plans."

"I can't dominate anyone," Marion said.

"No, but have you considered clairvoyance?"

"Charles and Jakub aren't of my bloodline," Marion said.

"But Gaius is," Norma said.

She counted out on her fingers: "You, Loretta, Agata, Nicheola, Gaius and whoever older than Gaius."

"You said his name. That's pretty insensitive to Agata," Marion said.

Norma snorted when she laughed. "I'm pretty sure you've heard how everyone says: Poor Norma, it's a shame what William did for her."

Marion saw that world-weariness, the deep sadness that Norma could not hide.

Marion didn't say anything right away, the dull achiness was making it hard to think.

Norma said, "We need some salt and a glass bottle. But mostly salt"

When they returned to the coven, Agata removed the bullet and gave Marion a few mouthfuls of blood in order she might heal quickly.

Then Norma and Marion went after Taylor.

Norma won't say how they did it, but somehow, they trapped him into a glass jar.

She always smiles and winks and claims "Trade secrets."

Though one night, I am sure she'll feel up to sharing it.

They packed the jar in rock salt and very carefully

placed it in a silver urn which was locked and taped shut. Then they put the urn in a salt-lined box. Agata took it from them and hid it away.

I've seen the box and sometimes if one listens closely, one can hear scratching and moaning.

Marion was not ready to leave the world, so Norma made sure that it looked like Taylor took off, but his paper trail ended in Yakima where he dumped his car and bought a new one with cash. His sidearm was found in the Yakima river.

The bill for Norma's services was high, but reasonable, considering she saved my daughter's existence and career. As for Marion, though disappointed about the Mesmerism, once she accepted her Clairvoyance, she used it fully. She earned an uncanny reputation to always know where a perp was hiding. When the next round of promotions came around, she became a detective. She retired after her lack of aging had become apparent. As the city was growing, coven security became paramount. I am very proud of my fifth reborn daughter, the head of coven security.

A WORD FROM OUR SPONSOR

Smile Forever Dental

Vampires, your teeth may be eternal, but your dental work is not. Without proper maintenance cracked fillings and crowns can cause centuries of pain, Dr. Scott Hanson uses state of the art technology to match your old dental work and restore it like new. Remember to keep you fangs pearly white with regular brushing and flossing and twice-yearly cleanings from Smile Forever Dental.

Initiate Questions:

Lady Loretta, this story did not quite tell us what Taylor and Thompson were?

Well, my beloveds, the names I give them would not give you a full sense of it, but Taylor was a demon and Thompson was the "wizard" who summoned him. Thompson was dying of cancer and Taylor looked for another person to keep him in this realm. Marion was a young woman and her interest in vampires made her extremely attractive to him.

Once Marion became a vampire, if Taylor had bound himself to her, he might have stayed in this realm indefinitely.

Forever Knight was about a vampire police officer, did Marion, or maybe Norma, find that show entertaining or sordid?

When I received this question, I searched what *Forever Knight* was. Thankfully, Norma had it on DVD. Marion watched all three seasons. She thought the show was fun, but went a little off the rails in the third season. It was a show obviously made for humans since

Nick wanted to be human and of course, like many TV vampires, Nick had practically every power. Now Marion loved that Nick used his vampire powers to solve crimes as she did back when she was on the force.

The only other thing she wanted to add—and this is the same for most police programs—precincts in every city of every size have strict budgets and crimes don't stop because the police are busy, so officers and detectives cannot work at one case at a time, no matter how important and they don't have the budget to research or investigate every crime, especially minor crimes.

I hope you found this lesson useful and educational. Next time, I shall speak how some gifts like Telepathy, can be a benefit and liability.

Good Day, beloved initiates and sleep the sleep of the dead.

WAS IT LOVE?

INTRODUCTION

Hello, my beloved initiates,

The final ability somewhat common in the Paper Flower Consortium is telepathy.

Telepathy is the ability to read minds and emotions. Gifted telepaths can even speak to each other without speaking. Many people have the misconception all vampires can read minds, but that is simply not true. Most vampire's hearing is excellent, they learn to perceive living creatures, including human's, involuntary reactions such as heartbeats, food digestion and pulse. This helps vampires seem telepathic and other worldly, True Telepathy is a rare and dangerous gift. Because telepaths can hear people's secrets and wandering thoughts alike. And it is up to the telepath to decide what is important and what is not. They often become overwhelmed and only with intense training are they able to learn to control that gift.

While Mesmerism can force someone to take a specific action and even plant memories, a talented telepath can break another's spirit with their thoughts. And telepaths who have known evil can pass on this evil—

as we saw with William. That is a story for another time. This is the story of his progenitor, Derrik Miller. He was born with these inklings which became telepathy when he transformed.

Derrik was and is a gentle soul and unready for the pain of ages which we pressed upon him. .

Let us begin by telling you a bit about him when we met.

An uneducated, orphaned lad of seventeen, he answered Jakub's help-wanted ad for an able-bodied man in the fall of 1842. We needed someone to assist the family in traveling to America and meet Charles who was already here.

Derrik could read a little and he matched up the address on the ad. However, he had no functional handwriting to speak of, though he could print his name. He had mostly survived by what he called his "inklings".

He felt guided by these strong feelings which he believed originated from his late-mother looking down upon him from heaven.

However, if anyone suggested he was a telepath or a witch, he would have laughed. He didn't believe in such things.

One of these inklings drove Derrik to skip his shift, and risk a beating, perhaps, even lose his job all together to meet with Jakub. In some ways it is logical, a situation in private service for an aristocratic family sounded better than his apprenticeship in tin factory.

Due to the overpopulation and lack of jobs in London, Jakub must have interviewed a hundred men, and a hundred more were left waiting when Derrik entered the parlor. They spoke of knights and vampires and going to America.

Now Derrik thought Jakub might be a little crazy, but it was a good job. He accepted the job. And after a time, this happy situation became happier because Jakub asked Derrik if he would like to train to be his son. Now Derrik had an unusually long instruction period of a little over nine years. Derrik's first years were spent on basic instruction, reading, writing, and two years as a clerk's apprenticeship.

As this was in the 19th century before current guideline, Jakub offered to change Derrik after his clerk apprenticeship which a clerk's situation was a position where he could support himself and perhaps even a wife. However for Derrik, vampirism was an escape from poverty. Being a clerk wasn't enough. He refused to be transformed until he was an attorney with a solid roster of clients, both supernatural and human, and a trusted human secretary for day errands.

It had also become apparent during his law apprentice; a family man would have greater opportunities than a single man. Derrik asked Jakub if Pascaline would find him suitable—her rank and his being what it was— before he tried to court her. We did not know Derrik's anxiety of such things would haunt their marriage.

At this point in time, the six of us lived in a four-room cabin outside the city of Vancouver in Oregon territory. (Insertion: Just to clarify, though Vancouver would become part of Washington territory, in 1852 and Washington State in 1889, at this point it was the Oregon

Territory.) Near a dairy farm who sold us old cows from time to time. We also had an American hired man, named Sam, and a dog named Dash who came from England with us.

Though we knew Vancouver was not to be our final home, our family needed a liaison with human leaders, the nearby werewolf congregation, a vampire coven and the few rogue vampires who sometimes sought us out. As a pretty noble-born widow, Pascaline had found it inconvenient in America not to have a husband. She was often prepositioned, proposed to, or simply not taken seriously, in a town surrounding a military fort.

Pascaline was strong and fast enough to get out of any scrapes that came her way, but her training as a courtier ensured scrapes never escalated.

Though they married for convenience, the two are well suited in each other's company, Derrik found the opportunities he wanted and Pascaline had greater social prospects in both human, werewolf, and vampire circles. Though condoms were expensive, in Vancouver they were readily available for use in the line of brothels, so Derrik was not worried Pascaline might accidentally transfer vampirism too early. (While sexually transmitted vampirism is rare, especially from female to male; it can happen.)

When Derrik felt enough of his dreams had come true, he emptied his office schedule in order to be transformed on June 21, 1851.

Now it is important to hear some of this from Derrik's own words, dictated directly to me by my brother-in-law a few nights after he was transformed. Please forgive my brother-in-law for being snappish, but as I've said before, transforming into a vampire can be difficult. Derrik obviously was quite upset. And Jakub had wondered if he should kill Derrik and get the energy which he had given the younger man.

STATEMENT OF DERRIK MILLER
June 24, 1851

"Why are you questioning me, Loretta?" Derrik snapped from his coffin where he lay with Dash, her snout nestled in his neck.

"I need your statement for coven posterity," I replied.

"Leave me alone. Dash is the only one who I can abide. She loves me fully. Why are you writing that? You're so annoying!"

Dash whimpered in concern and wagged her tail slowly, obviously not enjoying Derrik's raised voice. I was not afraid of a vampire born only a few nights prior, especially not my brother-in-law. I waited.

"Fine. Since you won't go away, I'll talk to you. I dreaded the rite, and it hurt to perish of course, but it was less painful than I feared," Derrik said.

"It was afterward, when we prayed in thanks for my transformation, a pain pulsed with my heartbeat. Impressions, opinions, and recollections pushed into me from the other vampires, Dash, Sam, and even the cows in the field.

"Imagine ripping the layers of curtain off that window and permitting the sunlight in. But instead of burning you alive, it fills you with boundless scorching thoughts. My mind is finite, and the information flooding into me is ceaseless.

"Have you ever wondered how a dog thinks?"

I shook my head.

"I know now. I should burn in eternity forever, losing my temper with such a sweet creature. I grow colder as your thoughts drifted into me. Memories drifted past. My wife loves another man."

"She only ever loved you and Andre," I said.

"I know." Derrik snapped.

"He's long dead," I said softly.

"That Andre is dead doesn't matter. After all, I am dead now too...

"After I died, all of these emotions flew through my skin, my bones, my organs, my brain. Before I could appreciate what was happening to me, more hollow impressions flooded me. I couldn't breathe. I was dead. I didn't have to breathe. But I want to breathe.

"I vomited. I remember looking at the blood-stained wooden floor of our cabin and realized I had lost control of my bladder. Thankfully I already had relieved my bowels before the transformation. Is my humiliation the type of history you need?

Derrik rolled away from me. It was obvious he hoped I'd go away. I did not. I waited, knowing he would speak.

"Why are you just sitting there, Loretta? Why are you still writing? Leave me be. Are all sisters-in-law so annoying?"

"I wouldn't know. Are all brothers-in-law so petulant?"

He sat up to look at me. He ran his hand over his face and huffed.

"In all the stories you told me over the years: you never spoke of befouling yourselves. Jakub and Charles are so brave and strong. I know they did not foul themselves. Yet I did. I am not worthy to be a vampire, or Jakub's son ...or Pascaline's husband.

"If you must know for posterity, you should write that I am a dishonest four-flusher. I ought to be in England with a scarred back and factory-damaged muscles but here I am... I am something else."

I took his hand. "What happened?"

Derrik sighed. "I don't remember exactly what happened after I was transformed, but from far away, I heard, Jakub ask, 'Are you seeing other places, son. Come back.'

"I think I said. 'I—I'm here,' I remember the taste of Charles's blood as he opened his wrist for me."

He met my eyes. The kindly man he was disappeared. "If I could I would eat your husband. If I could, I would kill you all. I know what you've done. I know everything."

"Lady Agata and Pascaline must have helped me undress. I think I remember Pascaline removing my socks. Gentle hands caressed me and rubbed a salve into my shoulders, my chest, my feet. I think Agata mesmerized me to sleep. And Pascaline helped me into my coffin."

I nodded. "They did."

"Pascaline tried to kiss me, but I turned my head away from her so her lips brushed my cheek. You see, Pascaline wasn't thinking of me. She remembered Andre—how she lost him. And she feared she would lose a second husband. The world I had so carefully built was crumbling, yet nothing had changed.

"Then Dash jumped in and snuggled beside me before my wife closed the lid. I do not know how long I remained in my coffin, but the thick pine boards of my coffin muffled the sound from all of you. Yet, I still could touch your thoughts and memories.

"I know I married a widow, but I obsess over every detail in my wife's head. I could not help but notice how tall and beautiful Andre had been--especially in French court clothing. He had been the perfect gentleman in all things like Jakub. Andre had fought in wars; I had run from the press gangs and street sergeants. And he gave her a child...."

Derrik trailed off and met my eyes then. I observed his pain.

"Pascaline loves you, Derrik."

"Perhaps she does, but it doesn't matter. I witnessed their precious little girl through Pascaline's eyes. The joy of holding her baby overshadowed the pain of her birth. Pascaline rocking her in her special Italian enameled brass cradle. Celeste's baptism. Celeste suckling her wet nurse and how Pascaline hid her tears when her own breasts were heavy with milk that no one would drink. Her sad, loneliness when Andre insisted, she remain in confinement with the baby, rather than return to court.

"Celeste crawled at nine months. Celeste had a

smile to warm a vampire's heart. How soft and gentle are Pascaline's thoughts toward Celeste, how much agony was buried in her shredded heart even after 167 years.

"I replay her memory and yours of the last night you saw Andre, half in court dress, pressing her, the baby, and you into a carriage with the other women. How can I ever compete with a brave marquis?"

"No one expects you to," I said.

"I left my previous existence behind, and even though I am an attorney, a gentleman. I am still a commoner. My common blood won't leave me no matter how much blood I drink! And I can never give my wife a child. Talk to your sister—tell her this. She deserves a better husband.

Derrik stopped speaking and wept. Dash jumped out of the coffin and brought him a well-chewed leather ball. Derrik tried to ignore the dog, Dash brought over a stick, then a bone. At that point, he rose, because no one wants a dog-drool-covered cow bone in their coffin.

Sitting beside me, Derrik continued his account. "Last night, Pascaline and I left to hunt. We raced towards the water, yet she was restricting her pace to mine. I struggled to keep up. I know Andre was a just human but I kept thinking, he would have been able to do this. If he hadn't die, he would have been her match for eternity."

He gestured at the two bodies hanging on the north-wall, former loggers. "They were drunk, but they had so much love for each other. I was glad we were going to eat them. I want to destroy their love because I knew Pascaline loved Andre.

"Pascaline took her victim down. It took seconds.

"I sank my teeth into the neck of the second, but as I drew in his blood, a numbness spread from my right cheek and down to my feet, creating a lasting pins and needles wherever it touched. I was in the flurries of thoughts. But instead of vampires, it was this human, it was my victim.

"My arms and legs twitched with my victim's terror. Suddenly my jaw shifted open. He escaped. I stood there stupidly, still experiencing his horror.

"Dropping her comatose victim onto the ground, Pascaline bolted after mine. 'Think of the others,' she had shouted.

"I couldn't move. I gazed upon my wife, desperately helpless. This was not my dream of eternal life, eternal love: the world which I created collapsed around me.

"My wife drop him in what seemed like seconds. Silently, Pascaline sank her fangs into his neck until he collapsed, convulsing. At least, as the man lost consciousness, his horror subsided.

"Pascaline reached for my hands. Her fangs were stained with crimson and her cheeks were flush. And she was so lovely and delicate. 'You need more blood, Derrik. Drink from him,' Pascaline had said.

" 'If I can't hunt, perhaps I shouldn't should eat,' " I had said.

"Pascaline shook her head. 'It doesn't matter, if you can't kill them, I will keep you fed. We should bring them back for the others' "

"As a gentleman, I should have helped her with the bodies, but I stormed off and returned to my coffin. I felt her return. I felt the tingling ache when the family ate the first logger.

"I sensed Jakub wonder if he should throw such a weak vampire in the sun. Jakub created me, but he created me for Pascaline. It was always for her. Not me. I was only his son-in-law. He wondered if I was a mistake--a long investment that wouldn't pay off.

"Jakub and Charles went outside and I lay listening as they discussed what ought to be done with me," Derrik said.

"Are you frightened," I asked.

Derrik shook his head. "While I've some concern, mostly I miss my mother because I understand my inklings were not from her. Fearing my mother might not be in heaven, I felt as if I lost her all over again. I prayed for her soul, but with the knowledge, I can't ever be reunited with her because I will not die.

"Then I realized if Jakub killed me, I might find my mother in heaven and my sweet, lovely Pascaline could be free of me...

"Enough, Loretta, have pity on me. It causes me pain to drive these thoughts to my mouth because I am not sure which thoughts are even mine. You are never quieted because it is not your mouth that is speaking. It is your minds."

I kissed my brother-in-law's cheek. "Don't lose hope. We will take care of you. I love you as my friend and Pascaline loves you as her husband."

Derrik's sobbed.

I patted my brother-in-law's shoulder. He shrugged me away, went to the outhouse, and returned a short time later to his coffin. Dash lay beside him, nudging his arm and whimpering.

Charles and Jakub split watches throughout the day when Sam was out running errands. And though Charles was awake, Derrik ignored him as he rose at noon. He stared at the leftover corpse hanging in the north corner.

"Would you get off the pot, brother? You have to eat, or you will go insane with hunger," Charles said behind him.

Derrik turned from the corpse. Wrapping himself with a woolen blanket, he sat beside the fire and looked at the burnt heads of the used matches.

Charles dug his knife into the body and pressed the man's muscles so drips of coagulated blood fell into a bowl below.

Derrik's focus remained on the matches. They did not make sound. He rubbed two together. Creating two studs, he stacked the rest together and placed glue on it, and formed a wall.

"What are you doing?" Charles asked.

"I don't know. Building something," Derrik said. The movement soothed him. "I need more matchsticks."

"Eat first, for Pascaline's sake," Charles said.

Derrik broke a matchstick as rage overtook him. "Loretta loves you with a full heart, and Agata has only been married to Jakub. How can I be sure if Pascaline loves me when she still loves her first husband?"

Charles tried to hand Derrik the bowl. "How can you

be jealous of century-old shadows?"

Derrik did not know, but he was jealous. He refused to take the bowl. Charles set it at his feet.

Derrik told us later he had a tiny urge to kick it over, but a Victorian Gentleman did not make an unnecessary mess. Instead, he glued the two pieces of matchstick together and set it aside for it to dry.

And Charles did his best to comfort his brother. "They had a child, Derrik. Pascaline didn't come back from death for him but for her daughter. Time may have made that Marquis soft in Pascaline's memory, but the man wasn't perfect."

"You didn't even know him," Derrik snapped. He finished his wall of burnt matchsticks because he realized concentrating on the matchsticks helped him filter out the thoughts around him.

Though Charles wasn't done speaking.

"No, but there were little things Loretta said to Jakub that he repeated to me before he allowed me to court Loretta. The Marquis kept her confined long after her pregnancy. Why would a man keep his wife—a wife who understands politics—away from court?"

Derrik shrugged. "Pascaline believes it was the cost of new court fashion. Or the dragonnades."

"Perhaps," Charles said. "Or he was simply resentful she was shrewd. Or such a beauty such might be courted by a Duke, a Prince, or even the King. Which means he was hardly a man, not even a patriot. Loretta thought so little of her sisters' and her parents' marriages, she sought to be a mistress rather than a wife. I'm lucky she changed her mind."

Derrik could read Charles's memories and mine and Jakub's, so he knew Charles spoke the truth, but he still couldn't drink the blood at his feet. He had felt the man's fear.

"I know what Loretta dreams about," Derrik shouted.

Charles shrugged. "I am glad I don't know everything in Loretta's head. But I know this, our wives are adventuresses. New Women. And you married Pascaline knowing that."

Derrik lips trembled, "Do you think my mother is in heaven?" He gestured at the corpse in the corner. "Are they? She was murdered, just as I murdered these poor souls." He sobbed so hard, he choked on his tears. "No. It's worse. These men were murdered randomly, my mother was murdered by him, and now I am just like *him*."

Charles did not know how to comfort Derrik. He clasped his hands together. "Do you want me to kill you? So you can go to heaven?"

"Yes."

"Be certain. Because if I destroy you, even with your permission, I will destroy the great love and happiness between our wives.

"Pascaline may only love you in her way, but you are her husband. She will not forgive me for destroying you. And Loretta will be forced to choose her bosom companion or me. She will grow to resent either choice.

"Still, better I do it than Jakub. If Jakub killed you, it would destroy the entire family. I swore to protect this family when I became Jakub's son. Of course, so did you, but if you are too weak to keep your vow, I will end your torment. And though we will mourn you, the family will eat you."

Charles said his peace and waited. He could see that Derrik could see he goaded him.

And Derrik felt Charles's resolution as if it was a physical presence surrounding him. Charles picked up the bowl and handed it to Derrik's trembling hands.

He drew his hunting knife and checked its sharpness.

Derrik had a choice. Be a vampire or meet final death, there was no going back to humanity, but eternal existence was his decision. There was never going back to the time when his mind had only inklings rather than full-blown telepathy.

Derrik lifted the bowl of blood to his lips and drank.

A WORD FROM OUR SPONSOR

Untidy hunt? Congregation-wide blood feud? Unsolicited worshipers? Puddle of blood staining your carpet. Don't worry! Norma's Cleaning Service tidies all kinds of messes in the greater Seattle area. Depending on the circumstances: Guaranteed to solve your problem or ensure you never have a problem again! Licensed and bonded private investigator and house cleaner.

Call or download the App!

INITIATE QUESTIONS:

Before I get started, I must answer a question after the last lesson because the answer pertains to this lesson.

•WHY DID MARION SEEM SO ANGRY —ESPECIALLY WHEN DEALING WITH NORMA?

Marion was angry, because nothing was going as planned. Also she had just been shot and was in a great deal of pain. As a young vampire, she needed to remain in control of her bloodlust and all of this took her energy.

Moreover, as soon as Norma got Marion into her truck, Marion felt as if she was drawing out information which is one of the reasons the conversation was hard to follow.

We love Norma, but dealing with a vampire with telepathy can drive a reasonable vampire to irrationality. And Norma is much worse than the average telepath. Norma thinks fast, talks fast, and while she is talking, she slips into people's minds and unearths what she needs to solve problems.

Then she skips ahead.

As I said in her ad, she always resolves any difficulty, but that doesn't mean she isn't a challenge to deal with at times.

LADY LORETTA: SOME SAY TELEPATHS CAN COMMUNICATE WITH THE DEAD. IS DERRIK OR HIS

OFFSPRING ABLE TO COMMUNICATE THOSE WHO HAVE DIED?

If you mean those who died and were reborn vampires, zombies, ghosts, or ghouls. Yes. Derrik and offspring can speak to the dead. As long as the undead speak English or French from the past century or current conversational Spanish—though Derrik's Spanish is not fluent, and he may request a statement or two to be repeated. It's so hard to learn languages as an adult. Now Norma also can also speak Spanish more current French, and Mandarin and while I don't know why it would come up, Ryan is also fluent in Latin.

If you mean the final dead, the answer is no. They have gone beyond our realm.

Lady Loretta: Is it true all of Derrik's offspring been gifted with telepathy?

While Derrik's offspring have all been gifted with telepathy—there isn't a big enough sample size to know if Derrik is gifting his offspring. His sons, William Caruso and Dr. Ryan Jones, were both reborn with telepathy. William passed telepathy to Norma. However, after research, the coven is pretty sure all three had latent gifts.

You see, our ancient ancestor, Gaius has made thousands of vampires in 2500 years, but only saw true telepathy with one other vampire. Phillipa was the fourth vampire, Gaius created and he wouldn't realized how rare her gift was until a few hundred offspring later. He explained that Phillipa had always been a witch. It was how she made her living. After she was transformed, he also warned us Phillipa needed quiet and routine, or she became overwhelmed. And in her long existence, she, too, rarely hunted for herself.

During William's initiation period, he admitted as a boy, he sensed things, but whenever he tried to tell someone about what he saw, his father "whipped the devil out of him" so he learned to stop talking about it.

Ryan had a strong connection to animals as a boy, which drove him to be a marine biologist. He admitted his grandfather sometimes had trances.

I must also point out that though William was a romantic attraction and Ryan is a platonic one, Derrik claimed he felt a magnetic attraction to both of them.

Now Norma could not confirm any prior gifts. However, she didn't know her maternal relatives, and her father died in World War II, but she confirmed sometimes she knew what her mother wanted before asked or knew gossip before someone told her. But then she said: there was a lot of routine on a farm and Issaquah was a very small town at the time.

Lady Loretta: So if I want to read minds…

Due to her low death weight, Norma has been forbidden to transform anyone, but you can approach Derrik or Ryan for mentorship if they agree. But as I said in the last lesson: gifts are elusive.

There is no guarantee, you will receive telepathy, but on the bright side you will still be a vampire unless you fail to thrive.

Good Day and Sleep the Sleep of the Dead.

INTRODUCTION

Beloved Initiates,

Over the last few lessons, I spoke of vampire powers in the bloodline of Agata, but for you to decide if you want to be a vampire, you must also know our weaknesses.

There are plenty of myths and legends about vampire's weaknesses: surrounding water, silver, gold, crosses, obsessive- compulsive natures. Though I don't doubt that some of them may affect a vampire or two, there is only one species-wide or near-species-wide weakness: the sun.

Vampires are creatures of the night. Our sun will consign our flesh to ash. However, there are many stories of mythical day walkers so it is possible our allergy to the sun may not be species-wide either. Speaking of the sun, I must clarify a horrid point. If a vampire faces capital punishment or if a vampire is tired of existing and chooses suicide, they may walk into the sun. They do not do so fully dressed.

Movies love to show vampires fully dressed, and Norma explained that is to ensure a R rating or better. However, that is a stupid way to burn. Clothing, especially layers of linen and wool, offers sun protection! Exposed body parts may begin to smoke, burn, or blister, but it can take days for a healthy vampire body to fully burn. Even weakened vampires take hours.

Assuming they can get an infusion of human or vampire blood—they will heal on their own – even if they are badly burned. As shown in lesson three when I described Alice and Derrik caught in the sun.

Many people, especially in Western cultures, think crosses stop vampires, but that is just colonist foolishness. There are hundreds of religions.

Other than Jakub, all the founding members are Christian as are most of the second and third generations in our coven, so we look at crosses, statues, and paintings of Jesus, Mary, or the Holy Family all the time. We certainly aren't afraid of them.

We also have shown no pain at looking at Buddhist symbols and statues: my beloved Xiao, Michelle, and Mi Young have a lovely, shared shrine and prayer room, as well as their private shines within their condominiums.

We do not have any Muslim or Hindu Vampires, though we do have enthralled humans from those traditions. Their relics don't bother us. But there are members of those religions within Strawberry Fields, our sister coven in Bellevue. They have never complained of looking upon their religious artifacts or ours.

Even the apostate, agnostic, and atheist vampires

don't seem to mind relics. Jakub never forgave God for allowing Agata to be attacked and murdered, but as he might have lost his land and title, been tortured, or burned as a heretic or an apostate, he never denied Catholicism until we came to America. Jakub has been to thousands of services during the centuries.

Marion skips services but shares in our Fellowships. And Norma, much to Derrik and Pascaline's sorrow, simply doesn't care about God (or Gods) as she is sure God (or Gods) don't care about her. Still, on the nights, Derrik invites her over, she quietly attends services with him and Pascaline.

However, the need for Coffins and Earth is very real.

Sleeping the sleep of the dead is essential for the vampire's long-term health. Our modern existence depends on the sleep of the dead. This is why we teach vampires to sleep in their coffins long before they are transformed into vampires.

As vampires age, we are blessed and cursed with unnatural strength, speed, and stronger hearing and eyesight. Due to the energies our undead bodies expend, we must sleep the sleep of the dead. When we commonly say, "Sleep the Sleep of the Dead," I am wishing you Good Health or Or Blessings be upon you. The sleep of the dead heals us. It ensures our minds are clear. A vampire with a mind fogged with exhaustion becomes short-tempered and dangerous.

Our condos were designed to hold heavy stone sarcophagi with firewalls between each unit and strong beams between each floor, but realistically since we don't have an elevator, we rarely see vampires who want to use stone coffins.

While some prefer an older wooden coffin, most prefer a newer casket. It's all preference. Regardless, during the initiation period, it is expected the initiate will buy themselves a coffin in the first year and begin using it to get used to it. Those with less financial privilege will often test a few other vampires' coffins in order to decide what works for them.

Most modern vampires find the back support of a well-built coffin as good as any firm mattress. For us older vampires who did not live with modern mattress technology, our coffins were the best sleep we ever had.

Inside, most coffins are lined with velvet, satin, cotton or linen. The fabric of the vampire's choice. Quilts, blankets, and pillows for comfort and deadening outside noise.

Some younger vampires line their coffins with memory foam. I personally find foam a bit too warm for my taste, but I sleep beside my husband each day.

Some long-term couples sleep in one larger coffin, such as Charles and I, while some long-term couples sleep in individual coffins, such as Pascaline and Derrik. Just like materials, It's all preference. Honestly, Derrik's love for Dash, God rest her sweet soul, was one of the reasons they never slept in their coffins together once Derrik was transformed as a vampire. Between Dash and Derrik moving around in their sleep of the living, Pascaline was pressed against the side a few too many times for comfort, and she started sleeping in her old coffin again. The two have a happier marriage because of it.

Due to many modern movies and books, there are myths that make some vampires fear the coffin. The most frightening myths surrounding coffins are vampires are helpless within them. To a certain extent, that is true. Many species are vulnerable when they sleep. However if when one opens the coffin's lid, it is quite likely the vampire inside will wake because the real reason to sleep in a coffin is to deaden the sound outside the coffin and sleep in complete darkness.

Beyond a coffin, there is also a need for Earth, it doesn't have to be of our homeland, but it needs to hold our memories. Norma has shown me films where vampires line the coffins with dirt. That is just foolishness. In my experience, vampires are fairly fastidious creatures of the night, so we put the Earth in jars near our pillows to ensure sweet dreams.

Humans and animal pets sleep the sleep of the living, and some choose in coffins as their vampire sponsors do, though some sleep in beds. It's a personal choice.

In tonight's history, we will be returning to the 16th century.

Agata had not had a good night's sleep in ages. Part of it was she was a vampire, and switching to sleeping during the day was not easy. Of course, there were several years of adventure, traveling to France with Jakub, learning the ways of the French Court, while Jakub was asked to kill monsters to prove his loyalty to France and his noble blood; Agata was a courtier. This was centuries after the inquisition in France, so Jakub told her not to fear as they were Catholics, but Agata feared being called a heretic. She feared the sun, the flame, and torture.

After her adoptive father-in-law died and Jakub was the lord of the manor. His stepmother, Maria, still lived at this point, but she had asked Jakub to find her another husband as she was too young to be a widow. Jakub and Agata obliged her, and she would go on to bear a son and two daughters for her second husband. Then Agata and Jakub were alone in the manor, but Agata could still not sleep. Let us go now to the Kingdom of France under Louis XII.

MEMORIE OF JAKUB

Seventh of January in the year of our Lord 1512

My Agata still does not sleep the day. Trying not to wake me, she paces the halls, careful not to step in the sun. I would do anything to ease her hurt and fear, but nothing seems to help. She is a God-fearing woman though God doesn't deserve her. Only touching her Moldavian Earth gives her relief, though then she is flooded with memories of our children. How she misses them—especially Irina—who is now a mother herself.

I also miss our children but sometimes wonder if Irina's light words bare the truth or are those the words to ease our distance.

Was Irina as gentle as she seems?

Is she truly her mother's daughter, who happens to be gifted with my eyes? Is Artur as brave as a soldier should be? Did Petru want to be a spice merchant, or was it simply a good option? Will Daciana throw off her sister's teaching as a midwife and go to war with her brother as she wishes? Who knows? They are but strangers to me. And they will be forevermore. Today's events have proven that to be true, if nothing else.

Worse, now, I must be satisfied with my wife's unending pacing as it gave me a warning. We have been so careful these past years. Since we have been settled, we had not seen even one vampire until now.

At dusk, when I rose, Agata wrung her hands, and her brow was creased. She informed me that while she was instructing the servants, she saw a hooded young lad creeping around the manor's north wall. Something about this boy chilled her. She asked our groundskeeper if he had hired the boy, but the groundskeeper had not hired anyone.

As Agata watched, she realized how carefully he was to remain in the shade and how he hid his face from the sun.

So she followed him until the vampire turned to face her. He was tall, but he looked to be a young boy of perhaps twelve, maybe a year or two older.

"Are you like me?" Agata called.

When the boy caught her eye, he scurried off.

Whether this is my vampire intuition or simply my training as a soldier, something deep inside me knew this boy is a scout. I wish I had not stabbed Gaius, and he was here to guide me in vampire relations.

We've killed vampires and run from them, but that was before we had a home. My lady will not be forced to tread the road again.

I have spent the dawn hours with the magistrate. The groundskeeper's son was taken from his bed and found drained of blood upon our land. We cannot let our village believe it was us, but it is obvious that another vampire is here. Agata tried so hard to save the poor moppet. Now she comforts his poor mother, who is beside herself. He rests in the chapel to ensure he does not awake because if he does, I will kill him.

Eight of January in the year of our Lord 1512

We have not seen the boy, but a local dog has gone missing. I searched the village, the valley, and the wood. There is no sign of the boy or the dog. I know he has taken him. When I find the lad, I will kill him.

Ninth of January in the year of our Lord 1512

I have seen our enemy in the wood, daring to cross into my hard-fought land. I would have preferred it if my lady had remained safely inside, but I could not force her to stay behind. Though a woman has no claim to land in France, this county was won by Agata's wisdom as much as my sword. It is hers as much as mine.

Agata rode her palfrey, Junette, beside me upon Castor.

I heard a whisper on the wind, a subtle shift in the farmland as those creatures approached.

"Do you hear that?" Agata whispered.

From Castor's saddle, I saw them slinking toward us in across the frozen ground. Twenty-seven vampires crawled on the ground as if they were animals. Some limped, dragging useless limbs, and under their dirty rags were boils and black tumors and pus-filled gavcollos.

The black death.

Though my Agata and I could not be touched by the Black Death, I must get rid of it. The villagers would fear the death. Moreover, they would fear those who did not die of the black death. They would know something was wrong with us, and the villagers would revolt. I could not help but think this wandering horde might have been my beloved Agata's fate if I had not come with her.

These warped creatures trapped in flesh and night were led by a vampire in a nun's habit. At least, she walked like a human.

I shouted Hail to her.

The nun looked up at me. I had seen them before. I recognized her from our early days in France. We ran from her horde then, but now I know I should have killed them.

"Lord Jakub, we have heard of your great deeds to the Crown. How you, among all vampires, have gained favor of the King. We beseech you to help us earn the King's favor."

Before my sweet wife might speak, I curled my lips into an evil, uncaring sneer. "You who have stolen food from our mouths when my wife and I ached with hunger. You who have killed one of my vassals and a dog besides. You come to me for aid?"

The nun put out her hands and fell to her knees. Behind her, the nun's followers fell to their knees if they were able.

"We left you in peace. I am Sister Sophie Marie, and these poor souls are my charges. We need food. And we can offer knowledge in return."

"What knowledge do you have, woman?" I shouted

"We know your wife wanders the day. And we know how to turn this village. I give might her a thousand children to warm her heart for those she has lost."

Before I could speak, Agata ordered in a cold voice, "Remove yourself from our land. We will give you goat's meat as alms, but nothing more."

My Agata has never been tempted by evil.

I added, "You will not turn a single person within our county, or I will destroy you all in the name of the Louis the XII."

Sister Sophie told Agata: "You are a great and noble lady. You must help us; we only ask for alms."

She held out her cross."We are the way we are because I made a deal. I don't believe it was Lucifer. It may have just been a vampire. And he left me with these others to care for eternity."

"You are nobleborn?"

Sister Sophie spoke of her merchant class parents

wanted her to marry, but she became devoted to God instead. But as she spoke sweet words, I sensed how her creeping fellows started to slink into a position in which to attack.

Most of these peasants were unarmed, not knights or even foot soldiers. However, we were outnumbered, and I did not, still do not, know their talents. I could not let the vampires surround us. Before they could come closer, I reared Castor. His mighty hooves slashed through the icy air. "Another step, lady, and I will slaughter you where you kneel."

One of the creatures, a boy, jumped on Junette. Using her small blade, Agata slashed his throat and fought him back to the ground. And once freed, Agata wisely moved back. Once Agata was out of the way, I decapitated the boy.

The cut was clean. The vampire's head rolled to the ground and begged to be restored to the still-moving body.

I picked the head up and threw it at Sister Sophie's feet. The others slunk back.

"Can he be revived from just the head? I need not kill him for touching my Lady if I can destroy the flesh."

Careful to use a gloved hand, I tied the body to a tree with a silver chain.

"I don't know, my lord. Please return his body." With each word, Sister Sophie's voice grew more panicked. "The sun will hit him! He is my Firstborn! His name is David!"

The others slunk further back.

"Tell me, woman, how long have you survived?" I asked.

"Two centuries since the last pandemic!" She rolled up her sleeve and showed us the blackened tumor on her arm.

"And do you wish to survive another night? Get off my land. And never return. To show you our goodwill, I will return his body to you at the border."

"But we must survive the sun."

I almost told her how I did not care for their fates, but sweet Agata said, "There is a grotto not a mile into the forest. Spend the day there. But no killing on my husband's lands. I want your word before God."

Sister Sophie slunk kissed Agata's crucifix and gave her word.

Listening to the women speak, in my annoyance, I could not find the words to articulate my thoughts. However, I have been a soldier too long. I would not turn my back on these creatures. Yet whatever else this lady, this sister, was, she was the leader of her people and at least once a woman of God.

Yet, we led them to the grotto. The boy's body remained unattached to his head, though I did bring it with us. After all, the last thing I needed was a commoner to find a living body without his head.

"In truth, I can help you sleep," Sister Sophie said. "I used to work in a hospital. We worked side by side with pagan healers like you."

Agata did not hide her annoyance. "I am a learned midwife. Not a pagan healer."

The sister shrugged. "We all have wisdom. And it was the pagan healer from Rome, Marcus, who taught me to drain the pustules. His techniques healed many people. The way he described things the world was almost magical and I admit to you I loved him. Though he scurried away at the sight of a visiting bishop less he be whipped or worse."

The women gossiped and I listened and discovered many things.

When Sister Sophie found pustules on her own arms and armpits, she tried to drain them, but they grew infected. The smell of rot emanated from her body and she knew she had days left.

She did not pray for herself, but she prayed with fervor for someone to come and protect her charges.

She went to the market to purchase lanolin, herbs, and wool for blankets. A man in a long peasant coat stopped her for alms. She threw him a coin, but he pressed her into the shadows.

She cried with joy. It was Marcus. But his nails had become blackened. His eyes smoldered with want. She hadn't felt such desire from a man in a long time, and she didn't deny that she wanted him. He kissed her lips and whispered how he could ensure our patients survived the Black Plague, but there was a cost to the gift of eternal life. We would never see the sun again, but we would be one with darkness...

She went on to explain how she enjoyed Marcus's kiss, and then he tore into her flesh. She died screaming. Then she awoke starving, habit stained with blood.

She returned to the convent, seeing more than she ever saw before. Seeing the world through Marius's eyes. One of the other nuns said a rude comment about her stained habit. Still hungry, she ripped out her lying gossiping tongue and boiled it until it was soft, then ate it. As any thrifty and practical woman, she saved the rest for later.

The sister said, "I heard Marius's thoughts in my head. He told me how to kill my Firstborn to give him life eternal. And I did, but my child was hungry. As I had only cut out her tongue, I put him in the room with the nun. David made short work out of the meat, but you know how lads are, always hungry.

"And the two of us created the others of the faithful and ate the ones without hope. That fat visiting bishop was a delicious treat we shared. But word must have gotten out because villagers and church officials burned down the hospital the next day."

Sophie took her charges and wandered France. But they knew how to hunt and to dig deep in the earth and sleep the sleep of the dead.

They knew that lying in a coffin could heal them in a way that even eating the fattened meat of a spoiled bishop could not.

"Now, please return my Firstborn's head to his body."

Agata took David's head and gently attached the head to his body. She sewed the flesh so it would stick together as it healed, and then she offered the patients a goat and a rope of sausage for the road.

"Is it human, milady?" David asked- a little too excitedly.

"No, more goat."

I warned Sister Sophie Marie and her convent of vampires to never to return to my land without proper introductions. "If you step foot on my land without permission or harm a hair on the head of any of my vassals or livestock, I will run your down and kill you."

Thankfully, they understood.

Agata and I returned to the manor. After caring for the horses and speaking to the servants, I took Agata and a jar of her Moldavian Earth to where my adoptive father lay. I opened the tomb of the man who gave me the name of Banquier and the claim to all his lands. I pulled out the dusty bones and rotten cloth. I did not want to desecrate his tomb. He no longer needed stone to protect his corpse; my sweet Agata does.

I swept the inside carefully and lay down some of our older ticking and a quilted blanket.

Without quarrel, Agata climbed inside. I pushed the stone lid over her. She fell asleep and remained asleep through the day and through the next.

Knowing this must be a temporary arrangement, less the servants talk, and the Crown or Church seeks our strange arrangement, I took the tomb of my adoptive father's father. I slept so deep, I heard the music of my bloodline in my ears.

So strong I felt, I left my body and followed my bloodline to Gaius.

He is still a mercenary for the Margraviate of Brandenburg with his vampire horse, Nix.

I told him what I learned and the vampires I met with the hope that we would no longer be enemies.

He just laughed in that strangely ancient merry way of his. And told me that he and I were never enemies.

I reminded him the last time we met, I stuck a sword in his chest.

He laughed again. "At least it was my sword." Then he said that even if we were on opposite sides of a battle, we would not be enemies, just two men who fight for different kings.

I shall end here, my beloveds, because the rest of the journal entry speaks of a further conversation with Gaius, but it has nothing to do with sleeping the sleep of the dead and a lot about horses. The vampire horse, Nix, and the living horse, Castor.

A WORD FROM OUR SPONSOR

Night Owl Extended Stay Inn

Are you a vampire, ghoul, shade, werewolf visiting Seattle?

The Night Owl Extended Stay Inn offers clean, comfortable lodging just south of the city for the undead and other species. The night is staffed by vampires and the day by humans so you can get room service or housekeeping 24 hours a day. Specials for stays over a week. Check out our free Wifi, laundromat on-site, fresh-squeezed cow blood in the minibar!

Initiate Questions:

Lady Loretta, Why was the vampire horde covered in boils?

It may seem strange now we can get any type of information immediately. However back then, the horde had no way to know the truth about the blood could heal new injuries after death.

And as an aside, remember the blood can not heal injuries which happened long before the transformation.

They were scavengers and fed off the weak and nearly or newly dead. They could not truly hunt anyone with strong blood.

Lady Loretta, You mentioned vampires can be dangerous, what happens if they don't sleep the sleep of the dead?

First of all, every vampire has a restless day or two; what I am speaking of is the chronic lack of sleep. They weaken, and in so weakening, there are several symptoms, including: confusion with memory lapses or the development of false memories, muscle tremors and headaches, malaise or simple irritably.

As for the danger in it, when Norma was actually fourteen, she threw, for lack of a better word, temper tantrums, which often led to full-blown panic attacks. She even fell into bloodlust. Fortunately, surrounded by adults, we could control her. However, when a vampire is alone, it can bring about violent behavior.

It is widely known that Charles was sent to America ahead of the family. He worked as a trapper until he lost his coffin and the earth of France. He lost his memory—though he knew his own name and how to hunt. He even knew he was a vampire or at least different from the human trappers. Jakub knew he was alive and felt snippets and images of where he was from time to time but couldn't track him through the bloodline.

So Charles found himself drifting from French fort to French fort, killing bear, beaver, and deer and selling their skins. Unlike many trappers, Charles did not waste the meat. Occasionally soldiers or other trappers would come across him sleeping during the day, hidden in the shade of rock shelters or the roots of trees. If they woke him, they did not waste their meat either.

In these moments filled with human blood, he would remember Jakub or me. He would find coins in his pocket and made a cache. He would mark these on a map in order to provide for me. However, as he was never safe, he could not sleep the sleep of the dead. Then he would forget again and wander.

So there is a difference when sleeping and when one sleeps the sleep of the dead?

Yes, Charles was getting some rest, but he was not getting a deep sleep of the dead. From one of my enthralled humans, I was told to say it's the difference between getting a cat nap in the afternoon, versus a full night's sleep. As I have gone over the Paper Flower Consortium's common vampire weakness, on our next lesson, I shall discuss a real weakness of vampires: an eternity of taxes.

Have a good day and sleep the sleep of the dead.

RECIEPTS

INTRODUCTION

My beloved initiates,

To become a vampire, you must die. I have gone over this in previous lessons, but there is one other certainty in a vampire's existence, and that is taxes.

The world's governments know there are vampires and they require us to pay our taxes. That we have died once does not permit us to forgo this obligation. As we are part of society, it is imperative that vampires file federal taxes, state, and local taxes. So many vampires, especially rogue vampires, get behind on their taxes, and their eternity becomes an eternal hell.

If you cannot imagine an eternity of paying taxes, you cannot imagine an existence as a vampire. And you must leave the initiation program. Some may feel I am being harsh, but the entire reason for this program is so you understand the true existence of being a vampire.

Tax structures change throughout the centuries.

The duty which Jakub owed in France weren't even paid in Francs but a specialty dye and, of course, men at arms, most eager to prove themselves to their kings.

However, The Paper Flower Consortium is an American coven so let us talk about American Taxes. At this time, these are required to be paid in dollars by Tax Day. Since 1955, for those living in the US, Tax Day has typically fallen on April 15. Though there has been special arrangements made for the Pandemic.

For tax year 2019, the IRS has adjusted income tax brackets for inflation which may impact how you prepare your taxes. Therefore I recommend to every vampire to get a good vampire accountant. These experts can pay for themselves as they take a longer view than human accountants.

And one of the most important benefits of a vampire accountant is they understand the financial ramification and the need for torpor and can be hired to represent you and file taxes during this time.

Let us define torpor.

Torpor is not the daily sleep of the dead, it is a long sleep which helps our mind in the long centuries of eternity. Every vampire needs torpor, though the time between torpors is individual. Most vampires don't take the first torpor until after a century or even two. However, the world moves so fast and I've seen younger and younger vampires need torpor more often.

One more thing: though some call this hibernation, there is an important difference. Torpor is involuntary, once the vampire's body begins the torpor cycle, the vampire only has a few nights before torpor begins, and if they have not already, they must make preparations for a long sleep. One of the most important arrangements you can make is your financial arrangement.

To illuminate my point, I shall tell an account based on real events in 1956. Though I was able to get permission to tell this story, the names in this lesson have been changed to protect the innocent.

Mortimer Robert Edwards, a rogue vampire, was a computer for the port. He had held this job since 1911. Before that, he was a clerk for a now-defunct shipping company.

You may wonder how he held the job without aging. He worked the night shift as ships came in and out at all hours. Though he had friends among his coworkers, plenty of men changed jobs or went to war during those decades. No one really paid that much attention while Mortimer steadily worked.

You see, in 1896, he was attacked by a vampire. He woke up and survived a few more days and then died. He was reborn with minimal understanding he was a vampire and did not need to fear death, though he did fear the sun and fire as we all do. To keep himself safe, he did not keep a thrall nor hunt humans. He bought large cuts of beef and kept a hutch of rabbits. His sustenance on animals meant that he had a long life and stopped aging in his thirties. Though he had gotten a bit stronger after sixty years, he did not know his vampire abilities at all.

He liked being a computer. This was before machines undertook the job of computing. It was a decent, although humble, occupation that allowed him to use his mind without a college degree. Mortimer was not a rich man, but he was content in his quiet little two-bedroom craftsman, which overlooked a park and was within walking distance to the house of worship of his religion. He was a quiet man and a good neighbor.

However, as he worked nightshift, his neighbors didn't know him well.

He started his vocation in faith, which meant he was a good man and a gentleman at that, but when companies turned their operations from commercial imports and toward the military shipyards, his calculations also went to war.

Still, as a computer, no one asked why an able-bodied man was not volunteering for the military. So he quietly remained. It pained him to lose many friends in WWII when they volunteered for the military, or worse, sent to the Japanese Internment Camps. Still, Mortimer's skills were needed at the port, and he would not leave his job.

However, once the war ended, like our own William, Mortimer felt his actions contributed to the wholesale slaughter of humankind. In this new age, he stopped wanting blood. He didn't want to drink blood from his rabbits. Instead, he freed them all. He spent the nights staring at his numbers. His work suffered. In 1947, Mortimer set his affairs in order through human legal systems. He climbed into his coffin and decided to sleep.

Seven years later, Mortimer opened his coffin, which was crusted with rat droppings and spider webs. His home smelled mold since this is Seattle, and it is often wet. Still, he felt freer than he had when he had lain down. He walked downstairs to the parlor. His house was empty as he expected it. There was a pile of mail as he expected. His power and water had been turned off, as he requested. He had plenty of cash.

He dressed in his suit.

Outside, the sidewalk was damp from the ongoing drizzle.

That was good. Even though it was daylight, he could leave his house. He could walk and consider his options. He would have to walk down the street to call to get power and water turned back on.

He walked across town. Cigarette butts littered the sidewalk. The street hadn't been washed and was stained with pigeon and seagull poop. As he moved through town, he noticed taxi drivers and doormen nodded or touched their caps at his approach. He felt he was watched in this new world. He wondered if they knew he was unemployed.

After being employed since age thirteen, he did not know himself as unemployed. He reapplied for his job at the port and was sad to see his old job no longer existed.

However, he met one of his former coworkers, who remembered him as a kind, hardworking man. This contact helped him find employment as a switch runner in the telecommunications room. And Mortimer was happy with this new challenge.

Unfortunately for Mortimer, there was an IRS agent, David Micheal Ackerman, who enjoyed searching old self-filed tax returns with early social security numbers and filed after long periods of inactivity.

Now this story is not to slander the hardworking people at the IRS. This agent was an evil man. Agent Ackerman was not a true vampire hunter; he had no interest in killing. He simply wanted to serve his own interests. And knew most vampires would pay rather than face a scandal.

As an honest man with a history in bookkeeping and math, Mortimer was shocked to receive an audit notification. He didn't worry. He was sure there was a simple mistake. He answered it and made the in-home appointment.

Mortimer did not like that he had to make a daytime appointment, but the cold voice on the phone gave him no choice. He collected his paperwork and identity information and opened the door to his small house for Agent Ackerman without representation.

Mortimer felt as if there was something bitter in Agent Ackerman's fake smile as the men shook hands. "May I get you a cup of coffee?"

Mortimer wished Ackerman had not followed him into the kitchen but did his best to remain polite.

He felt as if Ackerman's eyes were looking through him and landing upon his possessions. Trying to bring the man's attention back to him, he asked, "Milk? Sugar?"

"I take it black," Ackerman said. "Your account was flagged due to the long gap in filing your tax returns,

Mr. Edwards. Please explain why you did not file your tax returns from the years 1948 to 54?"

Mortimer handed him a cup of coffee. "I had a gap in employment during those years, so was not required to file."

"Why did you have such a long gap in employment, Mr. Edwards?"

He poured his own cup.

"A sickness. I had no income during those years."

Ackerman held a small compact in his hand. Mortimer thought, Did he know a vampire did not cast a reflection? Damn Dracula!

"What lovely cups? Are they antique?"

Mortimer shrugged. "I got them from Sears."

He didn't actually remember if he got them at Sears, but since he purchased most of his possessions from the Sears catalog, it was a good guess.

They returned to the dining room, where Mortimer had his paperwork ready. They both sat at the table. Ackerman did not look at the paperwork. Instead he stared at a painting over the fireplace. Mortimer did not know why. He liked it, but it wasn't valuable. He had purchased it from an unknown street artist at the farmer's market.

"How can I help you, Mr. Ackerman?"

"Do you have medical bills or anything to prove your illness?" Ackerman said,

"No, Sir, I did not keep them," Mortimer lied. "I didn't know I needed to."

Ackerman pressed his fingers together and leaned forward. "Then how did you live?"

"I live very simply, sir."

"Do you have any other investments?"

"No, sir."

Ackerman scuffed his chair loudly against floor as he stood over Mortimer. "I think you are lying. And you have no rights, Beast."

Mortimer froze as Ackerman opened his coat and pulled a knife. Without warning, Ackerman shoved the knife into Mortimer's forearm.

The pain didn't register as Mortimer tried to slap the other man away. All he ended up doing was spilling coffee across his dining room table and paperwork. Mortimer's tongue went dry.

The dull throb grew into a surging hot pain as the knife withdrew. Mortimer wasn't sure he felt the second time the blade sliced his arm.

What he noticed was Ackerman's pulse never rose. He wasn't even sweating. "It doesn't hurt you. Now tell me what I want to know."

Before Mortimer could decide what to do, his body moved in self-preservation. Knocking a chair over, the vampire ran into the daylight. The knife hit his back several more times.

The sun was out, but Mortimer ran to the park to hide under the trees. Panting in the shade, he realized he was hemorrhaging profusely, and blood soaked into his dark gray tweed coat.

He glanced around.

Agent Ackerman was not behind him. Mortimer didn't know what to do next or where to go. He didn't understand why Ackerman stabbed him. At that point, he was still thinking he made a major mistake and needed to get right by the IRS.

He looked at the open flesh and sliced muscles. Mortimer's skin was aflame as the knife wounds slowly crusted together. He choked on bloody vomit, which he pushed back down.

He needed blood.

He heard children playing a boisterous game of tag nearby. *I might...no!*

Fearing he might harm them, he gathered his strength and rose to his feet. He began to walk, doing his best to remain in the shade.

A siren made him jump. He lowered his hat on his brow and hid behind a tree.

He squeezed himself into a cafe's doorway. There was a seat at the bar. Hoping the dark tweed just looked wet rather than bloody, he took it and ordered a cup of coffee and a rare steak.

The waitress and other patrons' pulses inflamed his passion. He realized for the first time their blood would heal him completely.

He was so tired ...and they looked delicious.

I could...no!

No, he couldn't kill them. Not for moral reasons; he knew it was if he exposed himself as a vampire, the crowd would destroy him.

He flagged the waitress: "Miss, excuse me, do you have a phone?"

She gestured. "In the back."

Mortimer let his fingers do the walking to the coven's directory in the Yellow Pages and called the Night Owl. Thus the coven became aware of Mortimer's distress and of Ackerman's misdeeds toward our brethren.

Since the sun was up, the human staff sent a car for him. The driver found him still clutching the phone.

He moved jerkily with artless incoordination as he tried to pay his tab.

The driver helped him into the backseat of the car. And Mortimer wept the entire way to the coven, occasionally mumbling about his debt to the IRS. By the time they had crossed the city and the human staff checked him in. The driver was concerned enough that he called our apartment to wake Charles.

As Charles can be accidentally or purposely intimidating, I went with him to check on Mortimer.

Mortimer was reticent with Charles, his fear was written on his ashen face, but when he saw me, he looked around and offered me a chair. In my long centuries, I have seen injured vampires trying to hide their wounds too many times to be fooled.

"What's wrong, Mr. Edwards?" I asked with just a slight tug on his will.

"I can pay. I have twenty dollars on me." He said, "I can pay."

"Of course, My mother is a doctor; should I get her?" I asked him.

At first, he denied me, but I talked him into seeing Agata.

To be clear, this was before the bloodbank and the

cleaning service.

Agata took his temperature and stitched his wounds. She always has had a few what we now call polyamorous enthralled humans. She asked her enthralled human to give Mortimer blood to help the poor man heal. The enthralled obliged.

He took a gentle sip and screamed a thousand ear-splitting shrieks as flesh and muscles knitted back together.

Tears in his eyes and panting in agony, Mortimer told us everything that had happened. He still believed he just needed to get right by the IRS. In fact he believed that Ackerman had the right to stab him. Thankfully, he took our advice to speak to Jakub and Derrik.

The next night, Mortimer wanted to return home, but agreed that Charles, Jeffery, Pascaline, and Norma come with him.

As we feared, Ackerman had corrupted Mortimer's home. He changed it from a lovely place of security into a place of danger, and no vampire can sleep the sleep of the dead in a place of danger.

Searching for items of wealth, Ackerman left it in shambles.

Mortimer's coffin had been smashed, his stock of cow blood had been splashed on the walls and upholstered furniture, his china lay across the tile floor. Ackerman found a few antique snuffboxes, cufflinks and rings about $2,500 in cash which is close to about $24,000 today. However, Mortimer realized immediately that Ackerman also took his paperwork and identity. We would ultimately discover his savings account was drained.

At that point, the vampires collected what they could find in good order. A few suits, toiletries and towels, extra linens, a box of books, and even a few photos of Mortimer's human life. They were able to save his table and chairs as the furniture was solid wood. The rest was left behind.

Mortimer wept all the way back to the Paper Flower Consortium. Pascaline patted his hand, and Jeffery, a preacher by calling, spoke words of comfort. In the front seat, Norma kept her eyes open while Charles drove. They did not see Ackerman or a following car, but they circled the blocks a few times and took a less than direct route.

Mortimer gave notice at work. He realized if Ackerman wanted him, he had the address to everything. Due to the expenses of building a new identity and abandoning his home, Mortimer ended up in debt.

However, this story does have a happy ending. Jakub gave Mortimer a job in the bank and as the building was still mostly empty in the 1950s, Jakub rented Mortimer a coven apartment until he had enough of a down payment for his next home.

A WORD FROM OUR SPONSOR

Paper Flower Credit Union

Paper Flower Credit Union, formerly the Paper Flower Savings and Loan, reminds you that Tax Day is coming, and Personal Tax Assistance is still available to account holders.

Vera Montgomery and Jessica Carter are certified

public accountants in good standing. They remain vigilant with the yearly changes to the tax code to ensure your taxes are correct. And remember, beyond tax assistance, Certified Public Accountants are faithful advisors who assist individuals and businesses plan for taxes, reach their eternal financial goals, and offer representation.

INITIATE QUESTIONS

LADY LORETTA, YOU REALLY HAVE TO PAY INCOME TAXES EVERY YEAR?

Yes. You must file and pay any taxes due every year. Some years you might even get a return!

LADY LORETTA, WHY DIDN'T NORMA HELP MORTIMER?

Norma did help. She helped move furniture and pack boxes. But I assume you mean why didn't Norma clean up the mess? Well, in 1956, Norma's Cleaning Service did not exist yet. Norma was still at University, a sophomore. She still existed with Derrik.

LADY LORETTA, DO YOU THINK THE LIFESTYLE OF A COVEN VAMPIRE IS BETTER THAN THE LIFESTYLE OF THE ROGUE VAMPIRE?

Not at all. I just see the benefits of living in a coven and believe the benefits are worth the homeowner association dues that Charles and I pay.

This might be due to my past, but if you were thrust out into the world with your countrymen against you due to your religion--or some other reason--you might also feel this way. And if you had lived when vampires were hated, hunted, and feared, rather than sexualized, you might understand why I chose the more communal coven lifestyle with my husband and family rather than exist alone in the world at large, especially when it comes to torpor. In the coven, you are fairly safe during torpor periods. I have my husband and thralls to guard my body. The credit union to guard my assets. The coven building is strong and fire-resistant. There are plenty of vampires who do not see the benefits of a coven. One should always do a cost analysis at the cost of homeowner association dues and benefits.

CAN ROGUE VAMPIRES GET HELP WITH THEIR TAXES?

Certainly. Our Credit Union serves the entire paranormal community. Any vampire or thrall with an account with the credit union can sign up for yearly tax assistance, which is free for personal taxes and discounted business taxes. However, if a rogue vampire goes into torpor, they need to have an agent send the accounting staff the documents. That might be done by a trusted thrall or family member.

LADY LORETTA, OFF-TOPIC, BUT IT'S ON MY MIND DUE TO THE STATE OF THE WORLD. YOU'VE MENTIONED HOW THE SPREAD OF CELL PHONES

HAS CHANGED VAMPIRES. WHAT ABOUT SECURITY CAMERAS AND REQUIRED TEMPERATURE CHECKS?

Vampires do not reflect light, so all photography and video cameras take a lot of modest clothing or cosmetics to get a good photo. Moreover, since we like darkness, it is hard to get a good picture. Our image in photography and video is often blurry or seems like we are only shadow. It is why we have a photo studio onsite which helps vampires take all types of photography and our own DMV liaison for vampires who drive in order to get their license renewed.

Our body temperature is lower than that of a human's, so heat cameras pick us up, but we often seem chilled in comparison. As for business-wide, temperature checks due to the Pandemic, I suggest vampires remain out of sight as much as necessary. We do not want to spread the disease to our human and animal companions. However, I asked Norma how she has moved through the world these past months. She suggested taking a warm bath to get yourself to a comfortable 98 to 99 degrees Fahrenheit. Your body should remain warm enough to get to work and get your temperature checked.

I hope this lesson didn't frighten my beloved initiates, but it is important to know everything about being a vampire to truly know if you want to become one.

Have a good day and sleep the sleep of the dead.

INTRODUCTION

Beloved Initiates,

This lesson is based on the question I receive most often from initiates: *is eternal love possible*? To be clear, I speak of romantic love rather than familial love or friendship.

Though we receive this question all the time, we hold off on this subject as long as possible as vampires are often romanticized and even sexualized in Gothic and modern novels.

I am not saying we are not sexual creatures because most of us enjoy regular lovemaking, even though that is not how we produce offspring. But lovemaking is only part of our existence: as you must realize by now, we have careers, homes to maintain, clothes to launder. As everyone knows, like taxes, laundry is also eternal. If you don't or won't understand this, you will hate being a vampire.

However, so much fiction portrays our existences as gravitating around starry-eyed fixations or worse. Many come to us hoping for an eternity of love, but they don't want real love. They want a never-ending honeymoon.

Some may think it may have started with Bram Stoker's *Dracula*, but in truth, these stories are older than that. One of the first known works to touch upon the subject is the short German poem *Der Vampir* (1748) by Heinrich August Ossenfelder, a man is rejected by a maiden.

He does not respect her decision. Instead he pays her a nightly visit, drinks her blood by giving her the seductive kiss of the vampire. The vampire taught the woman the ways of love.

Sound Familiar?

That poem is centuries old and written in a time when women had less standing than men. But even in modern love stories, especially those which feature vampires, we rarely see people of equal standing.

The characters act with jealous obsession and worse. And don't get me started on vampire erotica.

Many vampires who are fictional vampire fans deal with problematic narratives by writing what is now known as fanfic. They take the beloved characters and making them more vampiric.

In modern vampire society, there are no alpha vampires. (And if you are curious, I have never met an alpha werewolf either. There are only CEOs or Presidents of Werewolf Congregations.) Older vampires are treated with respect due to their wisdom and experience, but unless they are jerks, they don't order younger vampires around, and certainly don't ravage humans kind enough to donate their blood.

Though fiction often brings in both enthralled

humans and initiates to the coven, we find many depictions of our lifestyle problematic. The characters act very unvampiric and focused on short-term gain. Worse, the narratives end with death, rebirth, marriage, the birth of a child, or another existence event. However, we don't end. We continue.

We don't go into relationships due to infatuation or pretty much forget anything you've seen in a RomCom. And societal expectations are non-existent in a vampire relationship.

Most of us cherish the companionship of another vampire and multiple trusted enthralled humans.

Since humans die, vampires rarely fall in love with our human companions and rarely monogamous with them. However it has happened once or twice and afterwards the human begins the initiation program or leaves the coven. However, Derrik Miller and Scott Hansen are the rare vampires who have one enthralled human at a time and stay with them for their lifespans or until the thrall wants to leave.

Derrik chooses a thrall whose lifestyle and morals align with his own to keep the down the random thought arguments. Scott permitted me to say he is asexual and only connects via biting. Though both men confess to be quite fond of their enthralled humans, neither loves them. Derrik romantically loves Pascaline and before Willam's exile, William. Scott claims he loves no one in that manner.

However, between vampires, we have seen several love affairs which have lasted longer than a human life.

It is hard to generalize since every relationship is a

little bit different, but love that lasts is filled with mutual respect, fidelity, trust, and serving each other. They stay by each other's side in times of hardship and trouble.

Often the vampires are within a few centuries of each other or have hobbies or other shared interests in common. Some relationships are monogamous, some are what is now called polyamorous. The vampires involved set the rules, not the coven, not the council.

In the Paper Flower Consortium: Agata and Jakub have been married for over five hundred years. They were a political match decided by their human fathers, but they fell in love and remained in love. Death could not part them.

In Strawberry Fields, Hitome and Kanae originally met in their native Japan during the tenth century and immigrated to America in the 18th Century as midwives. They have lived as lovers for over one thousand seven hundred years! As midwives they were independent and well respected, first in Japan, then in America. Though in America they were unable to marry due to Human Law until 2012.

Will these love be eternal? I cannot answer that. Both couples I mentioned seem happy.

However, we also have known a relationship which ended after 2500 years—and ended badly—due to Gaius's short-temper with younger vampires in his previous coven. Gaius still loves Phillipa, but after self-reflection respects her enough to leave her alone after she usurped him.

Unless there is a true problem, vampires rarely get divorced. We have a less than 1% divorce rate. Both out of habitual cohabitation and the inconvenience of tearing existences apart as well as deep attachment, harmony, and trust.

I want to say my husband, Charles, and I will be together forever, but I cannot know that. I know I love him and can't imagine him to act in a manner which would make me despise him. After three hundred years, how could we easily disconnect our existence?

Since I am speaking of love I shall explain how Charles and I met and how I realized I loved him and wanted to be with him.

But I warn you, tonight's story will not be a romantic narrative of boy meets girl, one acts stupidly and they break up, boy regains girl's affections. And it will not be a story of a love-struck boy who was ignored until he won my affection by some idiotic action. Because life and undeath is not a romcom.

This is the type of story which tends to be romantic to vampires. It is about the insignificant details which mean everything. It is also the story of why and how Pascaline and I changed as humans, how we were forced into maturity, and ultimately became vampires.

King Louis XIV, who was also known as Louis the Great, or the Sun King, built Versailles and tried to keep his nobles housed there. As some may know, unlike his predecessors, King Louis XIV enforced Catholicism as a national religion, in order to strengthen the authority of the Crown.

Before we were the daughters of Agata, Pascaline and I originated from a Huegonaut family.

My childhood was happy enough. I was the youngest of seven surviving children. I adored my mother and elder two sisters—especially Pascaline. I loved my sister-in-laws much better than I knew my brothers. My father and four brothers were practically strangers to me. My human father, Jean deFabron, had one goal for his three daughters: that we were given enough nutrients and care to be beauties and discover our womanly talents so we might enhance his fortune and standing through marriage and court intrigue. In all honesty, my brothers also had little choice in their lives, they just didn't have to worry about being a beauty while doing what our father commanded.

Like all sixteen-year-olds, I believed I understood the world. I was engaged to a wealthy commoner whose father wanted his son to marry a noble girl and whom my father wanted to enter a business with. I cannot say if my promised was a good or a bad man. I never met him. I tell you all of this because I believed if romantic love actually existed, it was only merchant class or peasants who might enjoy it.

I was and am talented in music and trained in courtly behaviors. My father and future father-in-law trusted me to become popular and, when I married, assist my husband in gaining a Court appointment.

Since I did not know my betrothed, I secretly planned to use my time to become a mistress of a Count, Marquis, Duke, perhaps even the King. As long as my lover was high-ranking and favored, it wouldn't have hurt my upcoming marriage. Moreover, I figured I would be safer in such an arrangement. After all, according to my mother, my father's mistress was treated better than she. And my sister-in-laws faired no better.

During my betrothal, I resided with Pascaline in her husband's townhome outside of Versailles so I might debut. As I've said in the sixth lesson, Pascaline loved her first husband. She was married at eighteen and was pregnant within a year. She had just turned twenty when Celeste was born. And Andre, a decade older, was the perfect gentleman of that era. He had seen battle but also understood poetry, art, and other genteel pursuits. He allowed me access to his library, the dailies, and kindly answered my questions about Court and having the perfect debut.

Neither Pascaline and I can say if her feelings of love her for her husband were returned, but we would both say Andre was a good man. We are pretty sure he did not keep a mistress because Pascaline managed the household accounts in Paris. There was nothing unaccounted for. Moreover, he was very concerned with having a son, as their firstborn was a girl. Thus he returned home to his wife each night. Though Pascaline looked forward to returning to Court, she was mostly concerned with becoming pregnant and bearing a son, as was her duty.

I will pause to clarify a point: In France, land and certain titles could not be transferred to a daughter. Andre loved Celeste very much, but he was in want of a son to cement his legacy.

However, dreams of Court and future children crashed upon us when the Paris house was occupied by the

King's Dragonnades.

The troops forced conversions by whatever means they wished. They killed the men and infants of a household, raped the women, then murdered them.

Once Andre got word they were coming, he pressed the women and children of the household in the carriage. He told the driver to go to our family's chateau. We rode off into the night. Pascaline embracing Celeste. The nursemaid sitting beside them. The housekeeper beside me. The two young chambermaids on the roof.

We never saw Andre again. He died to get us out, believing we could find a way to our family's chateau.

Many churches burned and we found no sanctuary. Most of our hardships is a tale for another time, except to say with the limited funds on our person, we were unable to care for the household servants, including the driver who took possession of our horses and carriage. We were quickly abandoned and cast along the road.

For months, Pascaline, little Celeste, and I roamed France. We were hated for being Huguenots, but at least we could hide our religion. Our noble names and titles were reviled when the populace was famished. It didn't matter, we too starved. Every movement, every soft word practiced for the King and Court, betrayed us until I learned to mimic them. I pretended it was just another form of singing.

We witnessed violence among the commoners, but there were also acts of devotion, sacrifice, and loyalty. Sometimes, I watched lovers holding each other against the cold, the darkness. Some were happy, some were not, and I learned that even commoners married who their parents commanded or someone from the same guild or class.

I also admit I entertained thoughts of suicide or running away and joining the opera, but I would not leave Pascaline and Celeste. They needed me.

One night, Jakub came upon us, hiding in the forest which was part of his manor lands. Poor little Celeste was coughing, so he assumed we were pilgrims seeking Agata, who never turned away a mother or child.

Agata took us in.

I was undernourished, but healthy. Pascaline and Celeste both suffered from pneumonia.

While my sister and niece were convalescing, I observed how Jakub treated Agata and the servants and commoners of the village which surrounded his chateau. He listened to Agata's concerns both about the manor, us, other patients, or what was going on at Court. I had never seen a man act with such respect to his wife.

I remembered how my father would strike my mother if she gave him an opinion on anything a lady should not know and even Andre would snap at Pascaline if she spoke on politics too long. My brothers were no better to their wives. And I hated them irrationally. I wanted to remember them, but I couldn't.

Jakub did not keep a mistress nor did he even cast a lustful glance upon women who were not Agata, especially not "girls in peril." Though that was more due to his "condition" than any other reason.

When asked Jakub spoke of a French Knight, long dead, who spoke on laws of Chivalry. Honestly, he was like no nobleman I ever met. He was a man from a love song:

brave, gallant, and kind.

And in every way Agata was his match. And there was love. I soon realized their condition was that they were vampires.

When Pascaline and I spoke on this we decided they were lost innocents. To call them vampires was the same as to call them fairy-folk. Pascaline and I knew what lay beyond Jakub's manor lands and we grew quite protective of them.

Watching them together, I had begun to believe that love might exist, but still did not believe such a thing would ever happen to me.

Jakub and Agata were from a different era when love and chivalrous knights existed. And France was no longer a place for that. I had not been trained in managing a manor as Agata once been; I had been trained in intrigue to know when I might twist or manipulate to the betterment of my family and my family's lands. I had been a pretty puppet for my father, who could play the harpsichord and the harp and sing. I no longer wanted to be a pretty puppet. Moreover, my family, except Pascaline and Celeste no longer existed.

We learned that Agata and Jakub were being pressed to return to Court. Unlike most of the girls in peril whom Agata assisted Pascaline and I knew how to help them and protect their innocence.

Jakub laughed at this as he had been to war, but I argued even that was the war of another century. And Pascaline and I knew the 17th century.

Though this news will break the hearts of listeners,

my niece, Celeste, died from pneumonia, which racked her tiny body for many months. Agata could not save her.

I cannot describe my grief which was nothing compared to Pascaline's fury and sadness. Pascaline wanted to die. But before she did, she wanted vengeance and was turned, but I was told to wait.

We traveled to Versailles in the Winter, so Jakub and Agata had more hours in which to function. Even so, the hours at Court are long and rigid. People who romanticize the gowns probably don't fantasize about standing in one for ten hours. As Jakub's rank, as his daughter, I was not allowed a stool.

Now Jakub was out of favor. We were assigned a tiny room in the north wing that four people could barely turn in and smelled of mold. But outside our room, there was so much beauty. I still remember the first time I walked behind Agata through the glorious Hall of Mirrors. Thousands of candles were lit and thousands more danced in the reflections creating a corridor of light and art. Emblazoned with thirty tableaux, the entire room depicted Louis XIV's epic achievements and aspirations. One even showed him as Zeus, which Agata barely hid her disdain.

Still, I will admit that my debut and Pascaline's second debut as the daughters of Jakub and Agata was even more exciting than I expected. Jakub presented us to the Queen, who nodded at us. The King also inclined his head. Except for one thing, King Louis XIV was older than my first father, older than Jakub. A dark wig, furs, and gracious manners to the ladies didn't hide a wrinkled face. Though outwardly I kept my composure as I had trained to do, I cringed inwardly when the King referred to Pascaline and I as lovely country roses of France.

Even that first night, several men approached Jakub to procure Pascaline or my company. Though I had come to idolize Jakub as my true father, this brought deep terror in me as my father had the right to marry us off as he will. He turned them all down. To me, he promised he would never bind us to someone without our and Agata's permission. Not even the King could have me unless I wanted him.

I was to be Agata's Secondborn, and that made me his daughter too. Then he reminded me Agata and Pascaline would happily murder anyone who hurt me.

If love were to exist for me, I wanted a knight, someone like Jakub, who spoke to me and asked my opinion and who didn't live by intrigue. I had begun to hate the world which I had been born into. These thoughts preyed on my mind as I did my duty to Jakub and Agata.

I spent the next months on my feet, surrounded by finery and splendor. But every word, every request had several meanings, and I needed to parse all of them. There were also rumors of scandals that I listened to, though Jakub would not use them for his own gain. My aching legs were tired from the unceasing standing and waiting.

There were surprises and fantastical splendors for the eyes surrounded by the constant smell of urine and ammonia. Thousands of voices awaited the King and the constant murmurs of voices who didn't dare speak to the King.

Still, when Court was released in the middle of the day, I was left alone with my own devices for short periods. I was not important enough to be invited to eat in the dining room. I discovered walking provided relief from tired knees and feet. I often walked in the gardens both to listen to the rumors and enjoy the majesty. Then I would find a quiet place to read as Jakub and Agata allowed me both novels and treatises.

One day, in early spring, I watched sparkling water leap from the fountain of nymphs and flow over detailed animals. I thought about how when I became a vampire, I would never know such pleasures again, but I would have the freedom my elder sister had. Agata had.

"Mademoiselle deBankier?" A deep rich voice spoke behind me.

I turned and discovered the voice belonged to a large man with spiraling dark curls tied back with a silk ribbon. Even in this modern era of vitamins and cheap nutrition, Charles is tall, but in the seventeenth century, he seemed to be a giant among men. He towered over me, though he wore unfashionably flat shoes.

His red justacorps were embroidered with glittering golden thread, which brought out golden flecks in his eyes. His white lace sash was peerless, but by the way, he held himself, I guessed he was unused to wearing stays. I could see the edges of skin, which had been tanned from the sun peeking out from underneath the painted ivory and his scars.

He was undoubtedly a soldier.

Still, I thought him handsome. I liked the steady way his soft brown eyes looked upon me without coyness or pretense. But in Versailles, I could not bring myself to trust anyone at first glance.

"Forgive me for being forward, I know we have not been introduced, but I have a message from my ...father."

I simply asked: "Yes, monsieur, and you are?"

"My name is Charles Onfoy, but my future father is called Gaius Soren, and he wishes to speak to your future father."

"I don't know what you are referring to." I stepped away. "I am the daughter of Jakub Christian deBankier."

He followed me closely, not daring to raise his voice. "I also walk among the undead. Though I still live.

"I comprehend why your family sleeps during the hours of the sun and why you act as their representative at Court. The King knows it too." His voice became firm and protective. "Be careful how you step, Mademoiselle."

Using the moment to collect my thoughts, I asked, "Who is your future father, monsieur?"

"Gaius Soren." Charles spoke without hesitation, yet, I sensed there was fear in his eyes when he spoke the name.

"I have never heard of this Soren, though my mother was created by a man named Nicheola created by a Gaius Severus."

"Yes. The same. You must tell your father: Gaius Soren seeks him and your mother under the Zeus tonight.

You must not fail in this message. He set his eyes upon you last night after the sun went down."

"I don't care what Monsieur Soren set his eyes upon, nor will my father," I said. "But I will tell him."

"Take care, Mademoiselle. We walk in dangerous times. Moreover, Soren has seen you, and his Firstborn has seen you. Soren will use you as bait, but the son enjoys the blood of pretty young women."

"Thank you." I backed toward the palace.

Charles stammered. "Mademoiselle, who keeps you company when your father sleeps?"

"That is none of your affair, monsieur."

He bowed again. "I also keep my own company when the Sorens sleep. I would be deeply honored if I might continue this conversation—even though I have no more business with your family." He bowed again. "May I walk with you?"

I admit I found his unease charming. It would not do to sit with a man, but we could walk together.

Today the age difference of a decade would have raised eyebrows. Back then, it did not. We were both of marriage age.

I looked him in the face. "I shall do nothing to bring a scandal onto my household."

Charles hid his scars under a lock from his wig. "I will not harm your reputation in any way. I swear it as a Frenchman, newly arrived in my homeland after so many years abroad. I will swear upon my honor if you wish, but I was not born a noble. I am, was a soldier of the French Royal Army. I can get the family's page."

"Did you serve in a Dragonnade?" I asked, refusing to allow rage upon my countenance. "Forcibly convert..."

"No, Mademoiselle, I served abroad as a grenadier." He said. He glanced around to ensure that no one was too close.

This didn't surprise me. Nowadays, most soldiers are taught to throw grenades, but in the 17th century, this specialty skill was only taught to the strongest soldiers.

"I understand what you ask and swear I have only killed men on the battlefield," he said.

"I walk the Grand Canal. You may walk with me, Monsieur Onfoy."

"Yes, thank you, Mademoiselle," Charles stammered.

Now Charles is the grandson of a knight. This meant his family though petty noble with a small estate and no transferable title. And as a younger son, Charles had no lands or estate of his own. He had no political standing or even the ability to speak to the king on his own, but he acted with true grace that day. We walked close enough to speak but not so close someone would say we were acting scandalously.

In this way, being the daughter of a low ranking nobleman was preferable, as while everyone surveyed everyone looking for a way closer to the King, few really paid that much attention to me until I started to climb the social structure on my own.

"Is it a fancy of mine, or do you not love Soren as I love my father?" I asked him once we were out of earshot.

"Soren is no a father to me," Charles said. "How can one love them?" His voice was still soft, hiding the undercurrents of anger.

"Monsieur and Madame deBankier sheltered my sister and I in their home. They loved us as if we were their natural-born daughters. My sister has become their own, and once I am twenty-two, I shall also be turned. I love them dearly."

"Then you are blessed," Charles snapped.

He spoke so abruptly, for a moment, I thought he would take his leave. But a loud boom from two small sailing ships in mock battle rang out across the grand canal. The assembled nobles clapped and cheered.

Charles wiped his brow, smearing the cosmetics into his hairline into his justacorps.

I handed him my handkerchief so he might dab his brow.

"After my unit was captured by the Prussian government, I was sent to work in Soren's mine. I suppose I was lucky not to be shot outright, but the mine was just a slower death sentence. Many of our countrymen died in those mines. He needed a Frenchman, so I am a messenger, but I am not his son. Though he claims I shall be someday."

Looking at the sun glittering off the Grand Canal, I whispered: "Do you wish for eternal life in the darkness?"

"I don't know," Charles said. His eyes were filled with sadness. I felt he wanted to say more, so I waited.

"Soren only allows warriors to be his sons. I suppose I should feel grateful to be chosen and for my freedom. I am grateful to see France again. And I am happy to be at Versailles."

"Do you wish you might see your birth family in the

crowd?" I asked.

"That would be unlikely," he said. "I don't even know that they still live, perhaps my brother does, but I do not know how to find him."

Then he looked as if he had said too much. I saw his eyes glance at my hand.

"What were you reading?"

"The libretto of Cupid and Psyche."

"What's it about?"

Charles did not interrupt me as I spoke of the libretto, original myths, and what was changed for the opera.

He told me his Godly mother once read Roman myths to him and his brothers. However, he had forgotten the facts, so he asked me to continue.

In truth, I did not think I loved Charles at that moment, but I liked the way he spoke without pretense, and nothing he said seemed to have two meanings.

I informed my family about Gaius's message, and also told them about Charles and me walking the gardens. Apparently, I could not stop smiling when I spoke of him because Pascaline gently teased me about it.

Agata and Jakub said nothing, but Jakub met with Gaius that night.

It is not my place to even tell you what they spoke about though the battles are an ancient memory now. Or even how Charles was right to warn Pascaline and me about Gaius's Firstborn. All that is important to know is

Charles and I spent all the time we could speaking in the daylight. He listened and spoke to me and listened when I spoke of all matter of things.

After a few days, and I went to Jakub and Agata and told them if Charles asked for permission to court me, give him permission.

Since both of my vampire parents knew of my previous plans, they were surprised, to say the least.

Agata lectured how though one day I would be a vampire with a vampire's freedoms, I was still a human woman and must be careful not to cause a scandal or catch syphilis which would mar my beauty or get pregnant. Agata reminded me if I came to be with child, I would not be turned until the child was grown.

Though assurance caps, which were that era's condoms, were known, they were not readily available as birth control was considered immoral by the Catholic Church.

She told Charles and Gaius something similar.

And Jakub made it very clear to Charles what it was to live in deBankier's household. And that I was his and Agata's beloved and we would not be married until I was transformed and set the date.

Though Gaius was disappointed by Charles's decision to leave him, he did not fight us when Charles left Gaius's service to become Jakub's Firstborn and, four years later, my husband. I was twenty-two when I was transformed, and of course, Charles had remained twenty-eight. We have had our struggles like any married couple; overall we have been happy.

A WORD FROM OUR SPONSOR

The Law Office of Derrik Miller

Derrik Miller has assisted people of the paranormal community in the Greater Seattle area for over one hundred and seventy-five years with the formation of a new business, the closing or sale of an old business, and prevent disputes through fair and ethical contracts. Call tonight for an appointment.

INITIATE QUESTIONS:

INITIATE FERN: LADY LORETTA, YOU MARRIED YOUR FIRST LOVE? AND BECAUSE HE TALKED TO YOU? I LIKE CHARLES, BUT THAT SEEMS LIKE A PRETTY LOW BAR.

Today people have OKCupid and meetups for every passion, but we did not and as I said before, ladies didn't date in the 17th century. The truth is Charles speaking to me without an introduction in itself might have been treated as a scandal if our parents did not have business.

I picked Charles, because he treated me the way Jakub treated Agata. Jakub agreed with my assessment of his character and transformed him to be my husband.

Gaius did not want a young woman who was not a soldier among his legion, so he allowed Charles to be transformed by Jakub though he did request Jakub and

Charles's services from time to time.

Initiate Cleo: Lady Loretta, Absence makes the heart grow fonder. Do you, as in vampires, ever have to take an extended break from each other? How do you do that in a coven setting?

This is definitely a modern question.

For most of our, elder vampires' existences, we worked such long hours there was only limited time for enjoyment or romance. And even if they lived and worked in the same place, they were working towards something: farming, trapping, etcetera.

We also didn't have cars or airplanes, so travel was limited. Also, being alone was dangerous. Even vampires needed other people around for protection.

When we were in Versailles, Jakub and Agata rarely saw each other. She was busy being of service to higher ranking ladies, including as a midwife. Jakub followed the King's chancellors around while Pascaline and I represented the family in other ways.

As I mentioned earlier, Hitomi and Kanae worked and lived together. They said there were still many times that one traveled to a nearby farm to spend the day with a family. So separation was built into their lifestyle. When I see them, I always see them together, though I know they have separate parlors in their home in Bellevue.

Jakub left Agata several times to serve different kings in battle during the early modern period, and he used to run the credit union on his own. Agata was a midwife and ran the manor. Now she is a doctor and runs the coven. She always seems to have a million things to do on her list.

Charles and I were separated for fifty years when he got lost in America. And I missed him terribly. Due to his anxiety of losing his mind again, he doesn't leave me during the day now. But he does have his office over at the Night Owl when he needs more space, and I have my library, and other than Sunday mornings, the parlor is empty, so I can play my harp all the time.

However, holidays are a tradition now for young vampires, and some take separate vacations to gather a little space. Charles fourth born, George, goes to a golf retreat every year, and his husband, Charles sixth born, Michael, spends that time visiting other covens or going on vampire-run tours to exotic locales.

Well, not this year. This year they are missing their vacation.

And there is always torpor. Vampire couples generally don't torpor at the same time as the other is taking care of things like running the household and filing taxes.

Have a good day and sleep the sleep of the dead.

INTRODUCTION

Welcome back, my beloved initiates,

Due to a recent Dracula mini-series, some people believe a vampire can simply drink the blood of a modern person and learn their language and contemporary lifestyle. If only it were that easy!

In the original novel, Count Dracula kept English books and newspapers in his remote castle. Meaning he taught himself English long before Jonathan Harker arrived. In fact, he asked Harker to help him with

intonation. We have seen this with our own population of vampires. Staying current with language takes so much time. Even if you already know the language.

For example, our own Derrik Miller spoke English, of course. He was born in England. And even in the 1850s, most Americans loved a posh English accent, but Derrik was born in a low-class neighborhood in London. He forcibly abolished his cockney accent when we came to America. He, and everyone else, felt it sounds uncouth. He mimicked Jakub and later the lawyers he had apprenticed under, and then Xiao helped him.

For decades, he had the transatlantic accent of a radio announcer, and then when that disappeared from modern usage, his accent also toned into the West Coast American accent, which you hear today. And not only accents but slang and words also change through time.

Some people believe vampires are intrinsically formal creatures, but the truth is keeping up with modern slang is difficult. We tend to speak in words and phrases we know well, which makes us sound stuffy.

So many words change from generation to generation. "Dude" used to be a slight insult when we learned the word.

When I was a girl, God, or perhaps the King, gave people a sense of awe. But once that word, "awesome" has lost its meaning of wonderful and terrifying at the same time.

Now people call chicken "awesome," and I am never sure if they mean this literally and therefore should eat said chicken or if it is just good.

There are a few ways we keep up with languages and technological changes. The way others do -- through the consumption of media. We also have torpor when we need a rest from the changes. And finally, we have the re-education fund paid for with coven dues.

While the coven dues go to maintaining and upkeep of the building, garbage collection, water heating, and temperature control, there are a few line items that are only found in vampire covens. One of which is a re-education fund. All vampires of the coven have access to this fund when they need it. This can be used to pay for university, technical, or vocational re-education.

Centuries ago, perhaps it was possible a stagnant vampire could live in a small coven, ignoring the outside world, but the world doesn't work that way, especially in this world of computers, instant communication, and videos.

By keeping current with language and developing new skills, and learning new things, eternity is not only endurable, but it also becomes pleasant.

Most vampires want to have a job or at least something to fill their time. With a job or a career, a person can earn money. If you can earn money, you begin to have freedom of choice. All vampires must have freedom of choice.

There is another misunderstanding about the education of the vampire, which has to do with work and wealth. We were once asked, why don't we just sell some of our gold doubloons instead of work?

Because gold doubloons were Spanish coins, and I

have never been to Spain. Nor has Charles.

However, stockpiling gobs of cash and coin will not bring happiness, and vampires do not exist in suffering. We never have so much that we hurt others and certainly not enough that we can be idle and exist in frivolity for centuries. I will not pretend money doesn't buy happiness because it is proven that money brings security. This security allows one to relax and be happy.

Like most Americans, most vampires' wealth is in our homes and the land which surrounds our coven, but we do have several added expenses due to our night-hour existence and allergy to the sun. We cannot often work during the prevalent business hours.

We all know about generational wealth, which grows, but also waxes and wanes. In my existence, we have moved several times. In the last Great Depression, much of our liquid wealth disappeared. And I assume it will happen again.

That being said, after a few centuries, most vampires have some wealth.

Still, there are other reasons to work: older vampires work for self-fulfillment and challenge as well as money. It also makes one happy to contribute to one's community.

Jobs are essential as it gives something for the vampire to do with eternity. Yet even vampires must know that their jobs will change or at least transform during their existence.

And I will tell the story of my beloved First Born, Bai Xiao, a relatively young vampire of one hundred and thirty-two years who has already gone through three career changes.

It is my sorrow that Xiao came to us in grief. Charles and I found him kneeling in the brush in February of 1886 outside the coven, which at that point was just a barn. He looked like a frozen deer, his eyes wide, his heart racing.

At that time, Georgetown was its own town, not part of Seattle proper, but we knew of the violence against the Chinese residents. We understood he was scared.

Back then, the night was dark. Only stars and the moon offered any light. And, of course, most humans fear the pure dark for its lack of any visual stimuli. Xiao simply could not see what was around him.

Every shadow might be a man who might hurt him. There was no way to know if every footstep was a friend, foe, or wild animal. I don't know now if it was something in his eyes or if I had a momentary telepathic connection, but I remembered my own childhood as a Huegonaut in a Catholic country. Suddenly, I knew he had witnessed small aggressions in the past years, which had become many offensive, cruel actions and assaults towards his people in previous days.

I didn't speak any Mandarin. In fact, I still only spoke French and Italian with any fluency, but Charles had been speaking Broken English and Chinuk Wawa since he came to America.

(Chinuk Wawa or Chinook Jargon was a pidgin – a mixed contact language used for trading. Now it is a creole language as it is spoken as a primary language of the Grand

Ronde.)

We tried to see if we could help him and hoped he understood us.

Xiao was born in Seattle twenty-six years prior. He had all races of clients at his parents' herbary. And many people were still speaking Chinuk Wawa quite often—sometimes even as a way to prove how long their families lived in the area.

I put out my hands and told him not to worry, and Charles translated as best as he could.

He was terrified. Moreover: Chinese culture has many ghosts and supernatural creatures. And at first, Xiao thought we were souls of wicked humans who were reborn as demons. Plus, we were European Americans, and it was white people who started this riot against the Chinese.

We soon learned he lost his parents and younger siblings somewhere in the wood. He didn't know where. He had two younger brothers, who were eighteen and nineteen, respectively. They had moved faster than the others. His parents and siblings, who were still children, had disappeared behind him. Xiao had slowed for a moment. His brothers disappeared in front of him. There was so much shouting. He tried to go back to find his parents but found himself lost in the darkness.

We offered him shelter in our home. He wouldn't accept it. We offered him a blanket and a bowl of cow meat—which Charles cooked in front of him, so he knew we weren't trying to hurt him. He accepted that.

We went to get Derrik, who was able to pry his family's image out of his mind. He and Charles went to look for them, thinking they too may be hiding nearby, but we did not see them.

I never expected to turn him, we actually hoped that we would find his family, but we didn't. He went out to look for his parents every day. We had heard many Chinese people had taken shelter with the indigenous peoples. He checked there, and though he found some families he knew, he did not find his.

Xiao returned to the barn. We fed him and offered him soap so he might remain in cleanliness. One night, it stormed, and he came inside. Once he was inside, Agata cared for him as she once had doted upon Pascaline and me, upon Derrik.

Xiao remained in the coven for another few weeks. He already knew Chinuk Wawa, so he already had a basic knowledge of French. Still, I was surprised at how quickly he spoke French to us. As he was born in Seattle, his American English was cleaner than Derrik's, which was a bit fussy, and Derrik listened carefully to eradicate the last of his accent.

Once Xiao felt it safe, he reopened the herb shop though it was more focused on confectioneries as he had found that to be a profitable business. Derrik and Jakub popped in from time to time with legal documents that needed translating.

Eventually, translations and simply writing letters home for loggers and miners became the more profitable business as there was very little overhead.

Since he lost his first family, I thought he might marry and have children of his own, but instead, he grew closer to our family. Xiao visited me often. He claimed he felt my worry about him.

When he asked me to transform him, I did. Obviously, back then, there wasn't the initiation training there is now, but we did ensure he understood his sweetshop would close if he couldn't be open in the daylight. We told him to collect a large jar of Earth from the shop to hold his memories of his first home, family, and siblings.

After he became a vampire, it was a natural progression to translate full time. Xiao was a dutiful son to his human parents. He worked their shop without complaint. And he is a wonderful firstborn to me and very much my beloved. He learned several more languages: Cantonese, German, Japanese, and Arabic. Moreover, he also learned to understand the strands of interconnectedness that languages have and how they developed. He mastered several aspects of language that the layman does not understand.

I believe my firstborn was happy until the 1960s.

In the nuclear age, Charles and I had begun growing our family. Charles had successfully transformed Jeffry, and I had Michella and Vera. Not that anyone was trying to exclude him, but Xiao told me he felt ganged up on by his coven siblings. He felt closer to us rather than them due to the generational difference. In fact, I am so thankful to Norma, who understood this better than any of us.

He wanted to travel. He had a little money set aside, and I told him he should. He collected his Earth and packed a bag.

Charles has had vampire guests from a coven in

New York. He had introduced Xiao to them, and Xiao planned on visiting them. He made it to Seatac with a reservation on a red-eye to New York and loose plans. He didn't know where he would go, but he had Gaius's number in Hamburg and Sophie's in Paris, and we had sent Phillipa a letter of introduction if he made it as far east as Romania. And we figured Gaius has contacts all over the world, so if Xiao wanted to encircle the globe, there was no reason he couldn't.

However, when he disembarked the plane in New York, it felt as if something broke inside him. He felt as if something was going wrong with his blood. He felt as if his body had begun to fail. Perhaps he had started aging again. He sat down on a bench. He felt as if everyone was staring at him, as if they knew he was a vampire. Instead of calling our friend in New York, he had Norma paged.

Norma answered the page within minutes.

He tried to speak, but he saw words slipping out of his mind and lost his ability to think critically or in English.

He was so afraid that someone would hurt him. Norma told him not to worry. She informed him she was calling their friends in New York to give him shelter, but he wouldn't leave the airport. He said he couldn't figure out the time, and he knew the sun would rise in the east, and he was on the east coast.

Thankfully camera technology was not as it is now, and he did not attract the wrong type of attention as he went to hide in the bathroom.

In disguise, Norma flew to New York. They stayed the day in a nearby hotel and took a flight home.

By then, he had lost his power of speech. We assumed he needed torpor. We got him into the sanctum. His affairs were largely tied up since he had planned on going on an extended vacation anyway, but Derrik and Norma did the final walk-through of his apartment to ensure cleanliness. And Derrik aired his apartment once a week, so things didn't get musty.

When Xiao emerged a decade later, he still wanted to travel, but the personal computer was beginning to become common and marketed to consumers, and Xiao saw his next passion.

Most home computers were sold already manufactured in beige plastic enclosures; Xiao sought out a kit to teach himself the inner workings of the machines. He was nervous about heading out into the city, but he had Norma, who never left the world, and now Xiao had three younger sisters who had lived in the past few decades and encouraged him to go with them into the growing city.

Seattle was different but the same in many ways.

And Norma suggested he still try to take that trip to New York.

Xiao did spend a week in New York with our friends who exist there, then he rented a car and drove through a few neighboring states. Afterward, he flew to Paris and spent a few nights. Apparently, he met up with Gaius, who played tour guide. He went to see Jakub's old Manor Lands. He sought out other places we had told him about.

He felt the history of those places, and he touched

the Earth that we once walked and felt our memories. He collected extra jars of our Earth, so we might know what has happened in those places in the centuries we have been gone.

Then he came home.

Using the re-education fund, Xiao attended the University of Washington and, after four years, earned a degree in Computer Science along with several technical certifications. He learned the inner workings as well as several computer languages. He was recruited towards some of the startups, but especially after his trip abroad, his goal was to work for the coven.

It became apparent to Xiao that our coven would need someone to ensure the security and function of our computers as more of our businesses were computerized. He brought up the need at an HOA meeting, and we all agreed. (And it goes without saying all vampires and thralls who work for the coven are paid fair market wages.)

You see, Xiao was not the only vampire of our coven taken in by our new world of technology. Derrik, Jakub, and Vera had already shifted away from using typewriters to using computers. And Norma was an early adopter of all communication technology. Even so, none of us knew how it worked. As far as we knew, there were little elves in the boxes.

Xiao knows. He has kept up with computer technology since then. Now the coven has grown, he manages a staff to assist him.

I don't know when Xiao or any of us will shift careers again, but there is a fund for us to do so.

A Word from our Sponsor:

MYT Clothier

Vampires, Do you dislike ripped denim, thin fabrics, and how well-made modern clothing is covered in labels? MYT Clothier creates handmade custom clothing in accessible styles for all body types from all eras—including this one! We use the best quality handwoven silk embroidery from China, Damask from France and Italian Embroidery and Leathers, and other fine fabrics. And if you wish to look like you stepped out of time or even reality with fantastical designs, we can make that happen too. At MYT Clothier, quality is our style. Call for a fitting tonight. And werewolf friends, we have a wide variety of double woven stretchy materials for those quick transformations. If the cloth tears when you transform, we'll fix or replace the garment for free! Call for a fitting tonight!

Initiate Questions

Lady Loretta, Did boredom or generational gaps cause Xiao to go into torpor? Or were the two events unrelated?

Torpor happens when a vampire needs to rest between generations. And I believe it was the sudden influx of new vampires into our coven. Xiao had not experienced that yet. This was the first time he really had to think about his existence.

Before the Great Depression, most people joined the coven almost accidentally. The world had failed them in some way, and they were escaping poverty, racism, sexism, etc. We fell into vampirism as a way out of our situations.

However, Derrik's Firstborn William came to the coven wanting to be a vampire. Afterward, we saw a subtle shift in all the initiates. They had the same problems, but they came to know more about vampirism than anyone thought possible—due to written fiction and film.

When Charles and I began growing our family, Xiao keenly felt this generation gap. This shift set off Xiao needed to know new words just to get by, and he was trying to know them in ten languages.

In human terms, he is closer to Derrik's age than anyone else. And though once he and Alice had been close, Alice was working on her own issues at the time as she felt the age of Aquarius was just around the corner.

It became too much. And his body was telling him to slip into torpor. I just thank God that my beloved Firstborn faltered before he left the country, though Gaius or another ally would have no doubt helped us if he had been in Europe.

Have a good day and sleep the sleep of the dead.

COCONUT
WATER
FAT FREE

INTRODUCTION

Welcome back, my beloved initiates,

We must have blood, and human blood is preferable. We have discovered around two pints of human blood a week keeps an average size vampire rational. Smaller vampires need a little less. Larger ones need a little more. But that two pints is not enough to sustain us. And we must consume something with blood nightly.

Humans are delicious, but they are not the only source of meat and blood on this planet. Most of us enjoy at least two meals in any 24-hour period, some of us enjoy three, and some of us are grazers.

Now we have heard of some vampires consuming only human blood. While it sounds like heaven, it is an expensive way to exist. You would have to move from one place to another constantly and live in the shadows.

By eating several common livestock species and not only relying upon humans, we do not require the death of humans. This means we can live more modest lives and be part of society.

Some believe we cannot eat dead flesh. Or drink dead blood. We absolutely can. We have the ability to eat the flesh of humans as well as animals. With modern cooking methods and refrigeration, we can actually kill a cow and feed several vampires for weeks. Some of our number who live near water prefer fish. Many hunters in rural areas love venison. And of course, Americans do eat a lot of beef, pigs, and chicken along with smaller amounts of more exotic animals. We can also consume rotting carrion and coagulating blood, but fresh tastes so much better.

I'd like to claim fresh food is healthier, but there is no evidence to back that claim or disprove it. Before there were enthralled humans were common, plenty of vampires consumed dead flesh.

Though we are carnivores, we can eat other things, but not all foodstuffs are palatable to us. I shall speak in generalities here, but vampires tend to be allergic to wheat, rice, corn, and other grains, including ancient grains. Some can digest some grains and not others. We also tend to struggle with legumes and other densely fibered foodstuffs. It generally tastes like ash in our mouth as a warning not to eat it.

We do drink water and eat some fruits and vegetables as long as they don't have too much fiber. Most of us enjoy alcohol, juices, or sodas as special treats. And Seattle vampires, especially those who changed after the 1970s, love coffee.

We, older vampires, still enjoy a hot cup of bullion on a cold winter's night. Though apparently, that drink has fallen out of favor with young people. Jakub and George have sweet tooths and love hot chocolate. Gaius, after 2500 years, has an old Roman herbal blend that he still drinks for the "health benefits."

Though many fictional vampires don't seem to have the need because we eat and drink more than blood, real vampires evacuate our bowels and bladder with regularity.

A word about coconut water as this always comes up. As veganism has expanded, vegans have come to the coven claiming they can survive without blood, but we turn them away if they are unwilling to drink blood.

The reason why is we simply do not know what would happen, but we have seen vampires fail to thrive and waste into wraiths, and we have seen them lose their ability to think and reason due to hunger. And a hungry vampire is a dangerous vampire. We live with humans and will not risk them on a vegan vampire experiment.

Now the basis of this idea is that coconut water is "identical to blood plasma."

It is not.

The truth is those making that claim are generally companies selling coconut water or Internet memes.

There is anecdotal evidence that it was successfully used as an emergency hydrator in World War II when there was no saline available, but that does not mean it is identical to blood plasma.

While we can drink some coconut water without ill effects. As a drink, coconut water can be refreshing. Many enjoy the taste of it, and from what we have seen, it is considered a healthy beverage. If the shell has not been cracked, coconut water even can be regarded as sterile.

Scientifically, coconut water is not identical to blood plasma. It is more acidic and does not have the same sodium, calcium, magnesium, and potassium ratios as blood plasma, so to claim that it is identical could be dangerous.

As a side note: please do not assume everything on the Internet is true, especially if it comes from a meme!

If you are a vegan or otherwise concerned about eating brute animals, then just stick to consenting humans. Enthralled humans have many benefits, plus enjoy the sensation, and since you're eating local, it probably even lowers your carbon footprint. The only possible disadvantage is it might get fairly expensive depending on your obligation to your enthralled humans.

Tonight, I almost told you how Charles lost his mind in the deep forests of the Pacific Northwest, due to the loss of his earth and surviving only on animals which made humans incredibly hard to catch and kill. However, I decided the lesson is even more illuminating if I tell you how Marcus Faccio's misadventures when coming to America. If you do not remember, he is our brethren from Strawberry Fields and now spouse to Pascaline's First Born, Alice Monroe.

I first heard this story in 1952 when it was told to Norma to distract and entertain her after her species test by the council. I asked if I might record the story for posterity, and Marcus agreed. And when I asked for permission to retell it for this lesson, he was absolutely thrilled.

Now before I get started, You see, Marcus has

one other distinctiveness. He is the only vampire in our acquaintance besides Norma, whose species was challenged. He wanted to ensure Norma had an ancient's protection during the bloodline testing—which she needed.

Trying to calm her, Derrik sat with her and told her one of her favorite stories. I believe this story made her feel closer to him, knowing he was once a teenager in a coven—even if he was still a human.

And Marcus was especially impressed that Derrik and Jakub successfully crossed the Atlantic with three sleeping vampires and only the deaths of three sheep, And so Marcus swore allegiance to such a great strategist.

Jakub answered, "Yes, a thrifty wife makes all the difference. Agata's planning kept us safe. On this venture, I was simply her and our girls' and Derrik's protector."

So impressed, Marcus told us his history and eventually how he crossed the seas to America. He admittedly did not plan as well as he ought.

HISTORY OF MARCUS G. FACCIO

Marcus Grecus Faccio was born in Naples when Naples was part of the Rome Empire in the 2nd to a merchant family. Now in Naples, a femminiello is a legitimate and long-standing third gender, but this lesson is not the place for drawn-out gender studies, so forgive me if I oversimplify. In general, Naples used the pronoun "he" for the femminielli and in general, Marcus had male privileges and responsibilities. Marcus said he used he/him for centuries and probably won't change now, but he might some night, who knows?

Though he lived as a homosexual in Naples, he is not exclusively anything in eternity. He enjoyed the company of all genders. In Naples as now, he doesn't always dress as a woman; he doesn't always dress as anything.

The most important thing to know is a femminiello was considered lucky, and sailors loved to take them gambling. One night, the sailor happened to be a vampire, and Marcus was transformed.

He never knew much about the man who transformed him as he sailed off the next night. Though in the past centuries, they have met from time to time and are now friendly.

After all, other than taking blood from willing men, Marcus felt his life did not change that much. He was a night owl, and he still lived with and cared for his widowed mother until her death. In these early years, Marcus did not know his gifts. He almost never killed; he simply took a little nibble when he was close enough to do so.

As a gender, the femminello were also considered good with children. Mothers tossed coins for blessings on their newborn babies. Indeed, he did like children, so Marcus learned medicine of this time, and so not only did he bless children, but he was able to prescribe herbs, sunlight, or lemons to keep them healthy.

He remained in Naples for many centuries but dropped his family name when it became cumbersome and went by Marcus the Medicus.

When doctors and others like him were hated, he became an actor and found the love of the stage. He danced at times, and sometimes he just returned to selling his luck as a femminello to sailors or blessing children.

He roamed Europe for centuries and took on different occupational names. Sometimes people called him vindecător or healer or Herbman or Herbson. He has created offspring. As you may remember, he is the creator of Sister Sophie Marie. However, though he enjoyed the company of others for short periods of time, he felt too many vampires would bring the wrong type of attention, so he tended to wander alone, making his way, trying to remain ahead of those who hated vampires and in later centuries those who hated pagans.

Eventually, he went to Spain primarily because they were crossing the sea to America.

Marcus didn't want gold; he wanted freedom from Europe's obsessions with heresy. So he paid for a private cabin and pretended to be seasick, which is why he only stepped out on the deck in the night air.

He had brought along dried meat, but, unfortunately, the ship was caught in foul weather. He did not have enough for the journey, and too soon, he was purchasing sailor's rations. The sailors' rations, at this point in time, primarily the proteins were fish, chickens, and eggs yet there was not enough to keep him from hungering. Though he choked down dried bread to keep himself full, it also caused him to feel queasy.

Marcus caught the eye of a handsome sailor who joined him in his bunk as it made his journey easier and passed the time. Then one night, in a fit of passion and hunger, he bit the sailor too deeply. Blood squirted across the tiny cabin. His lover's screams echoed across the deck, across the sea. It didn't take long for the sailor's crew to find them.

Fearing rabies, illness, or perhaps vampirism, who really knows, the sailor and Marcus were thrown overboard. People may imagine being cast off on a lifeboat. But, no, they were just thrown into the sea.

His lover knew how to swim and showed Marcus how to float on his back. Marcus did as he was told, but he knew the sun would rise, and he would burn. But waves crashed around him. Marcus felt the agony as his lungs filled with water. He spat it out and more splashed in. His eyes stung, and his fingers grew numb in the cold Atlantic as his body dropped to the temperature of the sea.

Worse, his lover was bleeding, his wound open, every drop of precious blood floating away. Marcus could hear the panicked heartbeat, the thrashing limbs before his lover's heart finally gave out.

Marcus refused to waste the corpse. At first, he tried to hold on to it and sank into the abyss.

He tried to ration the corpse as he did not know how long he would be in the sea. Soon the body bloated. It rose back to the surface.

Marcus realized it would keep him somewhat afloat, but the corpse attracted fish and other predators. The fish nibbled on Marcus too, but mostly they were interested in the easy prey of the rotting bloated body. This was not like it is today, with the seas overfished and filled with plastic. Back then, the ocean was alive.

Marcus knew he would need to take shelter under

the body when the sun rose, which he did.

His chest screamed as his lungs and heart went through the pain of drowning, but there was nothing to be done. He didn't chance to surface as he could see the sunlight filtering and changing direction in the water. Worse, fish nibbled on his ever-shrinking shelter. There was nothing to be done but get his own bites in.

At night, he tried to kick in what he thought might be a straight line, but the sun would rise behind him, and each day his lungs went through the pain of drowning again until his lover's body had been nibbled enough that all the internal gas escaped and Marcus sank again.

As he sank, he dragged the mostly-eaten sailor down with him. He didn't want to let his lover go, though eventually, there would be nothing but bone.

He was always hungry, but his stomach didn't growl, or if it did, he couldn't hear it. His head ached from the pressure in his ears.

And Marcus wandered alone in the profound dark. Without the moon, stars, or guiding light. He feared sharks and other beasts moving in the murky water, but he was safe from the burning sun.

He did not know if he headed west, though he continued to the American continent.

Most fish were too fast to catch, but he could eat sea cucumbers, shrimp, and other bottom dwellers. Sometimes he watched ships fall to the bottom of the sea, and he ate the corpses if he could get them from fish. Sometimes he leaped towards the surface and snatched scraps from whales and sharks.

His vampire senses and instincts grew more intense in this world of the abyss.

Marcus didn't really know if the merfolk knew of vampires, but they left him alone and shut their doors to him, or they chased him away from their villages.

His clothing quickly wore to nothing. His skin became covered in algae and slime. His once lush dark curls were stringy and tangled. His body hair was coated in dirt, salt, and plankton.

Sometimes barnacles would attach themselves, but he would pluck them off and eat them. His flesh was mutilated by the enormous pressure and lack of it. At some point, his eyeballs and eardrums exploded in the deepest depths, only to regrow again when he came across the body of a whale that he used as shelter and food.

He mimicked the sea creatures moving as they did. Though he was not as fast, he learned to reach into a school or take them from behind. And he learned direction in this new environment and to feel the pressures of the depths. He sensed where it was deep enough for the sun to not burn him but not so deep that the pressure would destroy his features again.

The first thing he forgot was his name. In fact, he barely remembered being a vampire, much less human. At some point, he lost time. His memories floated away from him. He could not imagine any future point. There was only the present.

One night, Marcus found an empty boat on its side on the seafloor. Its ropes and sail were mostly intact. It caught Marcus's attention because he thought a fish might be inside, but then on a strange reflex, Marcus pulled it from its grave. Tugging it along with him, he swam toward the surface, feeling the sunlight. Once above the surface, he dumped most of the water from the hull and hid under the canvas using it as a shelter from the sun. Following the currents, he drifted with the innate knowledge that he would find himself somewhere.

He felt the agony as his lungs and bowels released the seawater, which had been there for months. Yet he knows he did not return to the sea to escape the pain due to some powerful instinct to survive. In fact, he might have had the instinct of a newly formed life crawling from the sea for the first time. No doubt, that was also painful.

At night, he watched for birds, fish, sharks, and seals. He was driven on errands he did not understand. He only knew he had to eat whatever he could catch, and he must remain with the boat.

Marcus saw land, the barriers islands, in the distance. He let the currents drive his boat toward them.

One night, he came across another fishing boat. He heard the heartbeats of the fishermen. With the hunger of a shark, he left his shelter and swam to the boat. He claimed he had no thoughts, just craving and instinct. He ambushed the first man, incapacitating him by draining him of his sweet blood. Then he attacked his partner.

Both fishermen died screaming.

Feeling safe, he remained in this new place as it held a tiny cabin to rest from the sun and a bounty of fish in its nets, which he consumed. Perhaps he was like a hermit crab climbing into a new shell.

Marcus found a small stash of coins, and a compass. He bit into each item but did not remember what to do with them as they were not edible or warm.

He came across other small boats, he ate other small crews and their fish. Sometimes he remained on the new boat. Sometimes he returned to his older one. He found more shiny treasures. He remembered woolens would keep him warm, so he began to strip his victims and take their clothing.

One night, he found a watch in the pocket of his newly found vest. And looking at it, he remembered that humans counted time and had names for the nights, days, hours, and minutes. He pondered on this point for several nights.

And he remembered other things like candles and matches.

Once he had the power of light and fire and time, he finally risked the trip to the land.

Like many Europeans without means, Marcus worked his way across America. It was easier to travel as a man, so he became a man. In this era, there were plenty of Italian Immigrants who were shortening or anglicizing their names for ease of English speakers. Marcus became Mark Smith.

He told people how he was a fisherman who lost his boat and crew, which is why he had no identification and never wanted to go to sea again.

He met an Italian calico merchant who sold fabric to general stores across the country. He was careful not to let his species be known, but worked a night watchmen for the man and learned English or at least a close enough approximation.

When he met his first vampire somewhere in Kansas, he left the merchant to live with our kind and find his memories again. They assisted him in this by getting Napoli Earth sent to the coven.

Yet he could not remain there long.

He moved west coven to coven, trying to find himself and trying to find friends. However, most vampires feared the ancients and were aloof to him. He found his way to Spokan Falls in 1893 (This city would later be changed to just Spokane)

He remained there for a few years, But there was some ugliness. Spokan Falls are the ones who challenged his species, hoping to kill him.

Due to his nomadic nature, most of their questions were to ensure he would be safe around enthralled humans after so many years of wandering alone.

Marcus admits he was an ancient around younger vampires, and he could be strident.

He was not physically harmed though many questions were harassing in nature and these vampires were not kind. This was one of the many reasons, he was not comfortable around them.

He wandered Eastern Washington for a time and eventually crossed the Cascades. Instincts drew him to Strawberry Fields, the home of two ancients.

Hitomi and Kanae are true ancients as he is, so he felt quite at home in Bellevue. He changed his name to Marcus Faccio and returned to his medical studies.

Shortly later, he met Alice. While we honestly believed this relationship was just a dalliance on both of their parts, Marcus and Alice enjoyed each other's company for nearly eight decades before Alice moved to Strawberry Fields where they married and combined their households in the 1990s.

Of course, they have all of Paper Flower Consortium's blessings. They seem to be truly happy in each other's company, and no vampire can ever ask for more than that.

A WORD FROM OUR SPONSORS

In this modern world, everyone, even vampires, need to carry an ID. A badly time traffic stop or a visit from ICE can end your eternity.

The Paper Flower Consortium was the first coven in the United States to ensure vampires had proper identification.

Even if you were reborn before photography, Photos Evermore, can ensure you are documented. We have a finely skilled painter on-site to capture your likeness. We take photos of impeccably detailed portraits so perfect that no one can see the difference.

And our Credit Union has liaisons with all government agencies to ensure vampires and other long live species have all important documentation. We can even schedule nighttime driving tests with the DMV!

And if you need religious documents, our pastor, Jeffery Conway, has contacts with many religious organizations as well.

So if you need identification, call the Paper Flower Consortium tonight.

INITIATE QUESTIONS:

INITIATE ROBIN ASKS: LADY LORETTA, YOU MENTIONED THAT TWO PINTS OF BLOOD KEEP YOU RATIONAL BUT DOES MORE BLOOD MAKE YOU MORE SUPER-POWERED?

Unfortunately, no, it does not give us superpowers. Human blood does heal us quicker than other animals' blood. This might be because once we were human. Vampire blood heals us even faster. That is why I mentioned young vampires are often given the blood of their coven when they are first reborn, and one of the first things Derrik and Xiao did when they got Norma home was give her their blood.

INITIATE LYNN ASKS: DO VAMPIRES NEED TO WORRY ABOUT DONOR BLOOD TYPE?

I have been a vampire for over 300 years, and I have consumed the blood of every race from every geographical location I have existed in and have never felt ill effects from the blood. And it is illogical that my victims and enthralled humans all had the same blood type.

In fact, we only learned about blood types in 1900, due to the experiments of Karl Landsteiner of the University of Vienna. He mixed red cells and a serum of each of his staff members. He demonstrated how the serum of some people joined the red cells of others. He identified three blood types, called A, B, and C. (C was later to be re-named O). AB was discovered a year later. Landsteiner would later receive the Nobel Prize for his work.

Of course, we do not know why some vampires fail to thrive. Perhaps blood type is part of that. This was one of William's experiments out in Issaquah, but he was never able to prove or disprove the theory. And as a rule, vampires love their offspring too much to do such experiments upon them.

Have a good day and sleep the sleep of the dead.

INTRODUCTION

My Beloved Initiates

Though it is possible for a vampire to survive wandering from place to place, most vampires need a safe place to lay their heads each day. And the modern world makes that even more important.

Some vampires do not wish to deal with an HOA, and that is understandable. However, many find benefits to existing in a coven so let's explain them.

Now many people, even initiates, expect a vampire coven to be stuck in a perpetual Victorian age. (Once again, thanks, Dracula!) We have many modern amenities in our condo building. Admittedly, our building is a walkup as we splurged on air conditioning rather than an elevator. However, vampires get stronger as we age, so as long as we remember to lift with our legs rather than our backs, we can carry anything or anyone who needs to be carried up the stairs.

Many enthralled humans come to the coven and spend their entire lives here. For those less abled, we have installed a chair lift and a manual freight lift.

However, most often, vampires just carry people up the stairs in times of illness or injury, or aging.

Admittedly, sometimes human men struggle to accept this assistance from their female or agender or pangender or third-gender vampires—even though we are more than capable of carrying them. If the chair lift is busy and when such things come up, Charles or one of his male offspring have often been available to step in and assist.

Safety and security are always concerns of the vampire, both modern and ancient. And our buildings employ double-bricked firewalls and a fire suppression system. All windows have interior wood shutters. And as long as the vampires do not remove the shutters, homeowners may hang whatever curtains they like over them.

Our HOA dues are a little higher than a comparable human building of our size without an elevator, but they cover electrical, water, gas, garbage and recycling, hazard insurance, and the maintenance of our building. And there are also many vampire-friendly amenities such as our re-education grant and torpor sanctum. Additionally, our Business Owners Association also covers the 24-hour security of our buildings and the upkeep of our network.

Our HOA works to ensure we are always in line with current Washington State Condo laws. Our HOA and Business Association financial documents are audited independently once a year. We schedule yearly maintenance as well as large building improvement projects using our reserve study as our guide.

The coven building has always been open to everyone—as long as they are a vampire. The Paper Flower Consortium Credit Union offers mortgages, some with century-long terms, to ensure that all vampires who want to exist in the coven can afford to do so. There are also no-fee extensions for vampires who lose their employment or find themselves in another calamity.

Vampires must feel overall safe at home in order to sleep the sleep of the dead and exist in health and general contentment. The coven tries to provide in both physical surroundings and friendship and society a place to do that.

HISTORY OF THE
PAPER FLOWER CONSORTIUM

Tonight's story won't quite be a story, more of a history of how our buildings were constructed over time.

We (Agata, Jakub, Pascaline, Charles, and I) existed in France when we decided we would eventually come to America. There was so much civil unrest and so many people starving, and King Louis XIV was a spendthrift. We, vampires, knew the Kingdom of France would fall. (Though that didn't happen until Louis the XVI) As you are well aware by now, vampires plan ahead.

In the early 18th century, Charles journeyed to America as it was easier for a man to travel alone at that point in time. He lived in the barracks of several forts of Hudson Bay Company and saved money, hoping to set up housekeeping for the family. But as I have said before, he lost his earth, and he ran into the deep primordial forests.

My heart was broken to lose word from him, but we waited as long as we could. Before France fell, we fled to England, where we would remain until the wealth to safely cross the Atlantic.

Agata, Jakub, Pascaline, and I came with two men, Derrik, who obviously one day join us in undeath, and Luc, Jakub's elderly manservant, and enthralled human. We also had with us Luc's sheepdog named Dash. She was very sweet and good-natured. We miss her. We had brought three sheep, which we ate.

We landed in Philadelphia as it was a smaller port and easier to get through the border. We set up housekeeping in a hotel and tried to get our bearings in this new place. Derrik and Jakub traveled briefly to New York to speak to the people at the Hudson Bay Company. They told the men Charles was last seen outside Fort Vancouver. So the family traveled there by ship, train, stage, and wagontrain.

We first settled right outside the city of Portland and thankfully found Charles. As I mentioned before, Pascaline was our liaison and when she returned home, she would tell us stories of what was going on in the vampire world at large. Even back then, things were changing. The old ways, the existence as an eternal predator, was dying.

During this time of education for Derrik and rest for Charles, Agata and Jakub began planning their eventual goals for our coven. We sought long-term stability for us. On the business side of things, Jakub wished to offer long-term mortgages for vampires and to ensure vampires had proper identification. In fact, we would be the first American coven to specialize in such things. Still, we had to be careful and plan where to go and have secondary plans if that plan fell through.

When the coven in Vancouver asked us to move on, we moved into what is now known as Georgetown. Our first building was a dairy barn constructed the year before, which we purchased from a family of dairy farmers. We split the large open space into rooms with woolen blankets. The old barn is no more than remnants of wood that line our walls in the chapel. Still, this building holds a place in my heart, as Xiao, Alice, and Walter were reborn in this building. And it is our sadness that Walter failed to thrive. It was cozy and functional for most of our needs but not quite warm enough in the winter for enthralled humans.

We built on another larger building around the old barn. This space is now the chapel and public parlor of the new building we exist in now. We had gas lamps and a good well. Eight vampires and several enthralled humans lived in these buildings for two decades. But we knew if we truly wanted to expand the coven, to exist as people of the twentieth century had begun existing, we needed to build even more.

In 1906, we purchased the land from the dairy farmers and began constructing our third building had modern plumbing and bathtubs and electricity. We moved the coven in there and now had our own rooms. This felt like a true luxury at the time. William was reborn in this building.

This building now houses the Night Owl. It goes

without saying that the old electrical and plumbing systems have been replaced and brought up to code over the years, but the Night Owl still serves.

Our current building's foundations, underground garage, sanctum, and the first floor began in 1935 and the first phase of construction went through 37. Though we had all lost money in the Great Depression, the eldest vampires, Agata, Jakub, Pascaline, Charles and I, were well enough established financially, we were able to hire many local contractors and keep them in work. But in '38, we heard the rumblings of war in Europe, and we had to build the roof over the structure we had.

When America joined the war efforts, work halted completely.

As some of the more historically inclined among you may know, we hid several vampires of Japanese and German ancestry during WWII. In fact, we took in any vampire who felt the need to hide as we did not know who the government was coming for, only that they were coming. These vampires went into an early torpor and slept in the safety of our sanctum under guard. Honestly, this helped the coven as the vampires and guards' presence also ensured the new building wasn't scrapped for the war effort and ensured rodents and other pests didn't take it over.

We knew this atrocity to US citizens would end with the war did, and it did

Once the vampires in torpor had awoken, the work on our current building was restarted in 1946 and completed in '47. William used this project to focus his pain after World War II and worked closely with our human architect to manage such an undertaking.

Though the building does have a bit of a late art deco feel of its era on the outside and in the public rooms, the spacious apartment are decorated as the occupant decides. Some vampires love antiques or decorate from an earlier era, but there are plenty of vampires that like modern architecture.

Now there is one other major difference between a vampire coven and a regular human HOA. In a standard HOA, most condos are one vote per unit, but in a vampire coven, all vampires have a single vote in the HOA meetings.

So families may choose what living arrangements work for them. Unlike a standard condo building, there is the ability to sell the condo back to the coven as a whole if a vampire's arrangements change.

There are two- and three-coffinroom units to be purchased for vampires to exist in. Each unit has two bathrooms. There are also several studios and one-bedroom to be purchased by vampires for their enthralled humans. These units have one bath.

Charles and I have a larger three coffinroom unit and own two studios for our enthralled humans. (We have three enthralled humans total, one lives in our home, the other two live in the studios.)

Before they were married, Charles's sons, George and Michael, each had separate units, but when they married, they sold their units back to the association and bought a large 3-room unit.

Other families have different arrangements. Derrik

and Pascaline bought two two-coffinroom units to live side by side, because they can never agree on how to decorate. They also own one studio, which houses Derrik's thrall's aging mother. (Though thralls have lived there in the past.)

Single vampires make these decisions that work best for them. Norma just owns a studio, but she rents that studio to any vampire who needs the extra space. Currently, Initiate Fern lives there. She is also a member of the business association, but she also owns and exists in an offsite condo in a human building in the downtown core. Mostly due to her love of dance halls, films, and live theater. Before the pandemic hit, she went out every week.

After when the pandemic hit, she came home. Since she rents the studio to Fern, she is staying in her old room at Derrik's side of Derrik and Pascaline's units.

Though she has left a few times to protest for human civil rights, she mostly has been running errands for the coven to ensure our enthralled humans' health and security. Honestly, in these troubled times, everyone is pleased to have Norma under our roof.

And it helps Derrik especially sleep better knowing she is in the next room rather than in a city whose police department used tear gas on its own citizenry. Forgive me if that offends you, but I am documenting this year very closely, as it has been a hard one for us all. No doubt will be bringing more people into the quiet vampire lifestyle as things open up again.

And this leads me to the final benefit of the coven.

On the night of their rebirths, coven vampires are offered a jar of earth from the bowels of the Paper Flower

Consortium. While we never want to part, if there ever is a reason which we do separate, this earth can remind us of all of our histories: our mistakes and our triumphs.

Sometimes families or lovers will share earth. I will be speaking more on how vampires use their earth next time, because the truth is home is not just the buildings of the coven, but the people as well.

A WORD FROM OUR SPONSOR

Sirens of the Salish Sea

Ladies, Honored Individuals, and Gentlemen Vampires, You may be forever the age you were at your turning, but that is no reason to neglect your skincare routine.

To help you look and smell your best in eternity, Sirens of Salish Sea produce perfumed skin-nourishing soaps and lotions using all-natural sea salt, non-invasive species of kelp, cedar, berries, and grasses held together in delightful amalgamations of discarded sea serpent scales and the blood of careless sailors which are collected, manufactured, and bottled from our own local sea and shorelines.

Our main store is still open every day, and satellite store in the Paper Flower Consortium, Suite East B, is run by vampire staff and open every night from 9 pm to 6 am. Come on by!

Initiate Questions

Lady Loretta: This building is now almost ninety years old. Are there plans to replace it, and how does that affect mortgages?

No. Though it's a vintage building, it has been well maintained and systematically updated to remain in code and in good working order. So there are no plans to replace it, nor does that effect mortgages in any way. Also, the land is not available in the area as it once was. When it comes to time to replace it, it is likely we will replace the Night Owl first and, even then, build skyward.

Lady Loretta: If one buys into the coven but wants to renovate their condominium right away, how do we do that?

The HOA regulations which govern renovations are under Section J, Rules 5-10. Basically, you must have licensed contractors do the work and submit your plans to Agata and Jakub, who will ensure they are not impeding your neighbors' quiet enjoyment of their homes, and then you must notify your neighbors in a timely manner. If you are doing major renovations, you will need the legal permits to do so.

Most human contractors don't want to mess with vampires, so we have a list of vampire and other supernatural contractors with who we have never had any real issues with renovations.

The only paperwork delay that I remember off-hand is one time a homeowner was told to use a higher-rated soundproofing layer under their new floors rather than the one her contractor regularly used. But that only added about $100 to the whole budget and did not cause any actual construction delays for the contractor.

Have a good day and sleep the sleep of the dead.

INTRODUCTION

Beloved Initiates,

There are many myths about the importance of Earth to a vampire. Some credit Bram Stoker for coming up with this myth as a plot device to heighten the tension of capturing Dracula. Others claim this is just a development of myth dating back from when it was believed vampires and other undead returned to their graves every morning.

All the vampire myths hold a little truth and a lot of fiction.

By now, you should have realized that we do not need to sleep on the earth of our homeland. I already told stories of when and where the vampire did not have the earth of their home and existed.

However, it is so much easier to sleep the sleep of the dead when a jar of earth is near your pillow.

As I said in our seventh lesson, we do not line our coffins with the earth as that would get our pajamas dirty. We just use little jars. Also, as a coven, we also have redundant supplies of earth—just in case. We keep a large jar of earth for every coven vampire in the security of the sanctum and another in a secure offsite depository.

The earth of one's home is important, but not for the reasons myths may have you believe.

We exist so long we often forget things, but the Earth holds our memories.

Like any other being, we grow and change with time passes as well as the era, but we still must remember where we came from. Our memories also ground us.

As supernatural creatures, it is easy to, how shall I say this in the modern parlance, it is easy to believe our own hype. We may be vampires, but we are not all-powerful. We still must peacefully coexist with humans and must recognize allies, or we will cease to exist.

Sometimes we have felt, and I admit even I have felt, it might be for the best to forget something, but that has not ever held to be true even in sorrow. Our memories shape us. Knowledge is power. Without these memories, we might shift in personality or principles and can be destructive.

Vampires without earth struggle to sleep the sleep of the dead.

This is not the story I will tell tonight, but during her first winter, Norma kept asking to see her mother, but Derrik and Pascaline always said no. Norma never asked for earth though she knew about Derrik and Pascaline, and all of us had jars of Earth. I don't think she considered she needed Earth. We didn't consider it either. We never met a vampire who needed earth from a childhood home. We all thought she was simply homesick.

But she kept going into Derrik's closet during the daytime and squeezing herself between Derrik's shoe rack and the wall. We couldn't figure out why. Even Norma didn't know why. Obviously, she had been traumatized, and there were times she wanted to hide in a closet or other small space, but she had her own closet. No one could figure out why she was bothering Derrik in the middle of the day?

It was Derrik's former enthralled human, Mary (God Rest her Soul), who suggested Norma might be trying to get closer to the bricks in the firewall created on Cougar Mountain. In fact, the places Norma tried to hide were nearly all against the firewalls.

Her mother's farm and William's barn were both in the valley in between Cougar and Tiger Mountains. She was born and reborn there as was her human father.

The truth is that no one ever knows when another undead person or artifact will bring us into the past. Norma needed her Earth. It's hard to explain to those who aren't vampires because Earth doesn't just hold our memories, but it holds our memories with others, both vampires and all our other friends, enthralled humans, clients, and other relationships.

Moreover, other vampires can also hold our memories which is why vampires share small jars of Earth when they love each other. And in fact, the mixing of Earth is one of our marriage rites, but to be clear, this is not only during romantic love: Pascaline and Alice shared Earth before Alice moved to Strawberry Fields.

And the night Norma moved out of Derrik's home

and into her own, even though her first move was only two floors up. It was a big change for them. Derrik had what is commonly known as empty nest syndrome.

Finally, earth does not only hold the memories of our existence but the memories of the long past.

Remember what Dracula claimed to Harker: "There is hardly a foot of soil in all this region that has not been enriched by the blood of men..."

I say in non-sexist language: there is hardly a foot of soil anywhere on this planet that has not been enriched by the blood of humans, animals, insects, and birds. And not just blood, but the cells of flesh, bone, and hair.

We can see all of them. We might even see the unicorns and dinosaurs which roamed the earth if we sink deep enough into the Earth's memories. We don't always understand what we are seeing, but we can see it. We see the history of the world and know our place in it. By seeing this, the vampires never forget to care about this planet, this world we are all in.

Apparently, there is a myth or theory that some humans have this sense too, or perhaps you all do. It may be a latent ability, but regardless this ability becomes active once one becomes a vampire.

Before I tell the story, I shall say not all vampires need Earth.

Jakub does not sleep with a jar of earth. He does not need it as long as Agata is nearby. As Agata is not only his wife but also his creator, he can always ensure she still exists and not in danger, by peeking through the bloodline. Jakub has gone on several errands for several princes and kings. He does not bring Earth. Rather, he carries a small talisman that Agata created for him. Jakub believes when he is not home, he must keep his mind on their errand in order so he may return home, but they cannot be distracted by home or memories. He wants this stress.

Another vampire who doesn't need Earth is Gaius. Gaius was usurped and tossed out of his castle. He did not collect much earth, but he had his charger, Nix who is also a vampire. Note: Nix was changed over two millennia ago, so he is a legacy vampire.

Wherever Nix is, Gaius is home. If he must leave Nix, he carries a small bit of his mane in a locket.

For Jakub, it is Agata who is his home, for Gaius it is Nix. And for other vampires, there are other vampires who also hold the ideal of home. Without them, our existence is not complete.

Now I shall tell the story of Laurence Roch, a friend and former employee of the coven. Before I begin, please remember this story is set in the eighteenth century. The morals of that century are not the morals of this one.

HISTORY OF LAURENCE ROCH

Laurence Roch was born Lorenzo DaRocco, the fifth son of a landed merchant who ensured the family's survival during the political upheaval of the Napoleonic era by trading favors or lending money. Young Lorenzo never considered the family estate his home. It was just the building in which he spent the first sixteen years of his life. But he was quite fond of his younger sister, Caterina, whom they all called Cate.

When Napoleon created the Kingdom of Italy, his family's money withered away as Austrians scurried out of Venice, leaving debts unpaid. As their fortune declined, so did his mother's health.

On the last day of her life, his mother bestowed gifts upon her six children with the only wealth that was left from her dowry. She gave Lorenzo a silver ring which he still wears to this day.

Lorenzo may not remember what was gifted to his brothers, but he remembered Cate's gift. Because after his mother breathed her last breath, his father ripped that rosary from his sister's hands and informed her: "Such wealth is wasted on a nun."

Cate had no idea their father planned to send her to a convent. She expected to be married, but her father refused to play the dowry.

Everyone obeyed their father, except Lorenzo, who shouted, "You're a landed peasant."

After a vicious row in which nothing was changed or accomplished, Lorenzo left the estate with red welts lining his back and a broken finger, but his father failed to recapture his silver ring.

He found a merchant ship and lied about his age to a magistrate to indenture himself to the captain, an American. Lorenzo signed his slip as a weak, untrained seaman. The captain's wife and children shaped him into an able-bodied sailor.

She understood the sails, was a fine cook, and a better teacher. She showed her husband Lorenzo's fine handwriting and sketching ability and encouraged him to learn to read and study English, so he was even more useful. His indenture slip was never resold. And his mother's silver ring remained on his finger. This is rare. Most indentured were not so lucky.

Six years later, at the age of twenty-two, Lorenzo DaRocco entered New York State, a free man with $100 and a letter of recommendation. In order to assimilate as quickly as possible, Lorenzo changed his name on his church records to Laurence Roch, as his former mistress suggested.

He found a job as a clerk in the Hudson's Bay Company. His shoulders grew tight hunched over a desk for twelve-hour days, but he enjoyed it well enough. It was easier than sailing.

He made friends with the other clerks in the bachelor's quarters and sent his sister a little money for her comfort. He was happy to learn Cate found contentment at the convent. Frequently, she wrote letters about making jam, beekeeping, and caring for orphans who often came to the nunnery sick and malnourished.

Laurence was satisfied until a letter written with a trembling hand informed him Cate had died of cholera. The rest of the bachelor's quarters faded far away from him as Laurence grieved for his sister.

His friend, John, set a mug of beer in front of him but otherwise left him alone. All the bachelor's quarters knew of his sorrow. There was hardly any privacy in communal living.

In his letter, Laurence apologized to his father for his

arrogance and willfulness. He spoke of his sorrow for Cate and begged his father and brothers to come to America.

Chewing on his quill, Laurence reconsidered. His father and brothers would call his work beneath them. His father's insistence on holding onto the quickly disappearing feudal systems was why Cate dead. Perhaps even why his mother is gone.

He burnt the letter in a candle flame. *If I'm to see Father again, I must be as a wealthy man.*

Another of his friends, Tom, touched his hand. "I suppose you and your father don't get on much?"

Laurence met his eyes. Tom had read the letters over his shoulder and had the gist of it.

"No, we don't."

"Then we'll drink to Miss Cate's memory tonight."

Laurence tried to stop that. "She was a nun-in-training."

"All that means is your stories will be filled with sweetness. Unless perhaps, you want to pray for your sister's memory instead?" John said.

Laurence said, "Drinking will be fine."

The men drank much too much beer, but the thought of becoming a wealthy man, impressing his father, lingered on Laurence's mind. He set aside part of his pay for his nieces so they might not know his sister's fate. Still hungover, he volunteered to travel to Fort Vancouver, which offered a chance for even greater advancement.

The train ride was cold and uncomfortable, but no more than his time at sea. Laurence did not sense the danger until the train made a water stop in the windswept Great Plains.

Hungry, he disembarked to get a greasy sausage, beans, and coffee when something white, dancing over the never-ending grasses, caught his attention. He thought he heard a strange unearthly voice. However, with only twenty minutes before the train moved on, Laurence purchased his meal and hurried aboard.

Taking his place on the hard wooden seat, he couldn't shake the cold, uneasy feeling of being watched. The only people around were other passengers heading west, eating their own dinners, or tucking in for the night. He choked down less-than-satisfactory beans and sausage, wrapped his coat close to his chest, and closed his eyes.

He awoke, unable to breathe. A narrow white face stared deep into him. Her eyes were iridescent and sparkling. Flowing white wiry hair strangled him. The Strega kissed him, pressing her tongue into his mouth. He bit down on her flesh and tasted blood as he choked.

She shrieked and backed away. Scarlet dribbled down her chin. She sunk her teeth into his wrist. Now wide awake, he kicked and screamed as he tried to push her off of him, but she was so strong. The world spun in front of his eyes as her hair tightened around his throat.

Laurence started screaming in Italian. Then the Strega disappeared. A man from China with calloused hands was helping him to his feet and patting his back.

He realized the man could not understand him and

said in English, "Where is she?"

"Who?" The man said.

Laurence couldn't explain the Strega myth in English. It is sounded too stupid. "A woman...she was choking me."

"I didn't see a woman choking you," the man said. "You had a bad dream or perhaps a good dream?" He laughed.

Laurence did his best to laugh with him, though he was still shaken.

A woman with a tanned careworn face poured a shot of whiskey. "Give him this. Just a nightmare, young man. A nightmare. Probably spoiled beans," she said. "You boys ought to know not to eat at the water stops."

From the next row, a man agreed. "Listen to the woman's wise counsel, Boys."

Laurence apologized profusely. The Chinese man sat beside him and introduced himself as Li, a translator for the railroads. Laurence told him he worked for Hudson Bay. They spoke of the land of opportunity late into the night until Laurence's fear and embarrassment subsided. Li was a good companion. Eventually, they fell asleep beside each other.

They awoke when the train stopped.

A sheriff boarded a first-class cabin. Two men carried a sheet-covered stretcher.

The old woman, the one who offered whiskey, asked the conductor, "What happened?"

The conductor said, "A man died in first class. Looks like a heart attack."

Other passengers whispered about the young man with prophetic dreams.

Even his new friend Li seemed nervous, and their conversation was more stilted. Still, they spoke the miles away. When Li's stop came, he hurried off the train and waved goodbye. He had promised to write but never did.

At Fort Vancouver, the strangeness of his trip was quickly forgotten. Laurence enjoyed the work, the daily company meals, the fellowship he found on Sundays at church, and the company of the other clerks. They were much like the friends he left behind in New York whom he wrote often.

However, a month after he arrived, the sun began to irritate his eyes. Irritation developed into burning, which eventually became so intense that it felt as if two nails fresh from the blacksmith were being plunged in and out his eyes. He requested a desk away from the window.

Bread became distasteful. He ingested only meat, pushing a random potato around his plate, pretending to eat. He struggled to sleep and paced the bachelor's house at night, which annoyed the other gentlemen in residence. He fought to remain awake during the day. His work suffered.

Terrified, he only knew something was frighteningly wrong with him.

His Head Clerk, a man named Taylor, ordered a visit to the Fort Surgeon. And to ensure he went, Taylor went with him.

Though in the present day, there would be privacy laws to protect Laurence, at that time, there was no such protection. Standing naked in front of the two men,

Laurence found the non-stop descriptions humiliating. Looking back, he realized his fortune was still with him. If they had known what he had become, they would have shot him.

"Observation of your blood reveals nothing far out of the ordinary. Speech is full and normal. The movements of your chest are full. No swelling of his liver or legs. No skin discoloration or abnormalities around his glands. No lice or ticks or other parasites. Your heart beats slower than average but is steady," Doc said.

Laurence asked his true fear: "It's not cholera?"

"What makes you think that?

"My sister died of cholera."

"You were there?"

"No, I was informed by letter."

"Then no."

The doctor decided Laurence's problem was suffered from anemia, brought on by a sailor's diet and exacerbated by the travel overland. As there was plenty of meat, he suggested letting Mr. Roch should eat his fill so he might continue his duties. And suggested his vegetables are mashed as one would give an infant to aid in digestion which should also help him sleep."

Then Doc really got going: "Mr. Roch, during your period of indenture—how shall I say this? Were you in the care of a woman, or more to the point, did a woman care for you?"

Insertion: The doctor was referring to the many European, and Asian women who indentured themselves to escape brutal husbands only to be assigned a man during their indentureship because society deemed it unacceptable for a woman to live alone. Worse, each baby lengthened their contract.

"Captain and his missus didn't approve of such things. She was the cook but really was First Mate."

"And you weren't allowed to marry?" The doctor insisted.

"I was not allowed to leave the ship."

The doctor met eyes with Head Clerk Taylor, then turned his gaze to Laurence. "Perhaps you'd do well to find a wife."

Now, as far as Laurence was concerned, his accounts were not nearly big enough yet to have a wife. "But how would I keep her?" He did not say in luxury; the images in his mind were of horsehair sofas, carpets, and painted walls just like the boss's house.

Taylor suggested: "Create a budget, hire men to build you a cabin..."

When Laurence hesitated, Taylor said, "Mr. Roch, while your work has been satisfactory, you ought to do a better job of being genial if you mean to continue to enjoy the luxuries of our community. The doctor is right. A wife is what you need."

"Alright, then, I will find one," Laurence assured them. Even when the political upheaval shattered his human family's security, he didn't remember being so frightened. There was nothing but wilderness around the fort. "How will I find a wife that my father would consider suitable?"

The doctor said, "What's suitable?"

"She'd need to be Catholic," Laurence said.

Then Head Clerk Taylor said, "I know a girl. She doesn't have much to recommend her though, but then neither do you." However, you ought to know my wife is fond of her."

The threat was clear enough. If he took this girl as his wife, he better treat her well.

"Who?" Laurence asked.

"Suzan Davis."

The doctor said, "If you wait, another fellow will scoop her up. Just you watch."

Head Clerk Taylor said, "She already said no to two men, but they only offered her a country marriage. She's a respectable girl, no matter who her parents are. Won't touch a drop of alcohol except in communion."

Suzan Davis had gone hungry too many times to count by the time she made her way to Fort Vancouver to have the youthful bloom of most seventeen-year-old girls. She stood tall, the way an older, more mature woman would, neither flinching nor flirting in Laurence's gaze. He was mesmerized by her.

Suzan thought Laurence was too skinny.

Her father, a French trapper and Catholic had her baptized Catholic. She spoke simply but well. She did not read but was good with a gun. She came to the fort to sell trinkets and found a job as a seamstress for the wives and daughters of the fort's leadership.

Mrs. Taylor said, "If you marry him, you will be

a gentleman's wife and receive quality rations, but if you wait for the trappers to come in, you'll be one of the lonely widows waiting for her man or traipsing around the countryside like your mother."

Suzan did not flinch physically, but Laurence saw her soul flinch as if Mrs. Taylor had struck her.

"If I'm to be your wife, it must be official under your God. I won't be a country wife only to discover that you've another." Suzan had said, her hands on her hips.

"Were you promised to another?" Mrs. Taylor asked Laurence:

"No, Madam. I wasn't," Laurence said.

"Good. It's settled. I'll call on the priest and make the arrangements."

A week later, Laurence and Suzan were married.

Laurence was shocked at how quickly advancement prospects reopened for a family man. Suzan was everything a wife should be: thrifty, hardworking, and diligent in her care for him.

With the household budget, she kept their small wooden cabin clean and bright and created wholesome, warm food. With her personal allowance, she kept chickens and rabbits in hutches attached to their home. He adored how she sang and stroked them when she fed them.

And Laurence wrote to his father and brothers to flaunt his good fortune with a sketch of his new bride to boast of her beauty. Then he doubled the amount of money going into his nieces' trusts. His sister-in-law wrote to him in thanks, and he introduced Suzan to her and the rest of the DaRoccos through letters.

Suzan did not fear his nightly wandering or his near-constant need for meat. She never complained, but about two months into their marriage, the doctor still claimed he was anemic.

She slaughtered one of her rabbits and collected its blood to make blood sausages which he ate with ravenous hunger. Then she made him mittens with the skin. He loved her so much, but she had many fears. One night she asked him not to drink his ration.

"Why?"

In stilted whispers, she repeated what he already knew: her father was a trapper who sold furs to Fort Astoria before it closed. Her mother was once a prominent native woman. "My parents died from too much rum and debt which came from it. Let me sell your ration to other men—who don't have families to care for. I don't know my mother's people. My father refused all that. Now he's gone, and I was lost. I fear what it means for our children."

Laurence didn't understand, but the sad fact was his knowledge of the indigenous was quite limited. Their stories were not told. Indigenous women lived near the forts and often married white or Hawaiian men. Sometimes in Catholic ceremonies, as Suzan had, sometimes not. Most spoke in a pidgin language that Suzan knew, but Laurence understood only the English and French words. All he knew was the depth of his wife's sorrow.

"You're Mrs. Roch. I'm American now, which makes you an American. Our children will be American." Seeing her concerns unabated, he added, "I will not drink a single drop. If you tell me to forsake the blood of Christ, I will do it."

She kissed him again. "We must take communion. Others watch. They whisper about you. Don't give them a reason to hate us."

She was obviously afraid, but Laurence was still too sure of his own destiny to hear between her words. "I will do whatever I can to please you. I will."

His purpose changed. He no longer cared what his father thought. All that mattered was Suzan. Someday he would build her a house with carpets, soft furniture, and painted walls. He would hire servants. He would become so rich that she would never fear her old life. Without a complete understanding of his illness, Laurence assumed he would leave her a widow financially and socially able to care for herself or remarry as she wished.

For two years, Laurence planned for his next promotion or possibly his death and in awe of his capable wife.

During an unusually hot summer, several children perished of an illness. Laurence could not know what. The whispers grew louder until the night Laurence thought he heard movement outside. The chickens were clucking. Someone at the rabbit pens untwisting the wires. The footsteps of men echoed in his ears.

He smelled pitch. Sparks fell through the ceiling.

Laurence pulled Suzan from the bed as the roof collapsed. She screamed and coughed as Laurence dragged her through piles of falling wood. A soldier barred their escape through the door.

"Let us out!" Laurence screamed, trying to remain out of reach of the bayonet stabbing through the door.

Suzan fell to her knees. Then the floor.

With strength he did not expect, he gathered Suzan into his arms and jumped from a shuttered window. They landed on the dry grass, embers sparking. She wasn't breathing. He tried to revive her.

"Hey, they're there!" A man shouted.

A bayonet sliced into his back. He screamed and jerked away from the agonizing pain. Somehow, he made it to his feet.

With men brandishing their muskets and bayonets on his heels, he stumbled into the forest. Branches reached for him and scratched his face. He raced towards the salmon-filled streams where the women often fished. Eventually, he found himself in complete darkness with a singular fear of the dawn.

Still bleeding, he crawled into a narrow fissure between boulders where he knew the sun would not touch him and prayed Suzan had lived. That the doctor, or perhaps the Taylors, brought her in their home.

Lonely terror took hold. Pain flared with an intensity unlike ever before. Every part of his being ached for an answer to this misery.

Dreaming of being reunited with Suzan in heaven, he followed the stream to the river and eventually to the Pacific, where he tried to drown himself. He vomited up the seawater and knew a thirst more powerful than he ever had known.

He tried to rinse his mouth in the freshwater river, but there wasn't enough water to quench his thirst.

Through beaches, headlands, primeval forests, he wandered, unsure he would ever be free of the horrible longing.

Perhaps I am in Hell. If so, this isn't like I expected.

He hid from the sun during the day and hunted at night.

When he was lucky, he ate the flesh of raw fish. When he wasn't as fortunate, he ate anything decaying. When hapless, he ate nothing.

One night, meat on a trapper's fire smelled delicious, but the pounding of the trapper's robust pulse called. As if the devil took over his soul, Laurence ripped into the man's neck from behind. Gore poured into his mouth. The rhythm of the trapper's pulse and sweet blood became a balm. Laurence took his heart as a snack for later.

More out of intuition than belief, he returned to Vancouver. Laurence never he was damned because he damned God. He believed he was a strogi, the male version of a strega so he ate the trapper's heart and dreamed of the rich, strong blood of the fort's soldiers. Terrified, he ran through the cabins and huts to the settlement's graveyard. He found two small slanted headstones beside each other. One read: *Suzan Davis Roch, 1808-1827 Devoted wife and friend.*

The other was blank but smeared with chicken droppings.

He knelt in front of Suzan's stone. "Damn you, God. You were supposed to take me and leave her a wealthy widow! Suzan never did anything wrong. She was an innocent."

He silently moved towards the walls. When he arrived, a strange compulsion overwhelmed any thought of vengeance.

He stole a bucket and scooped handfuls of dirt from the foundation of his burnt hut. He grabbed clothes off a line and any other odd pieces of trash that might be valuable. An infant's wail and a single bell cut through the darkness. He heard men speaking. He crawled to the fissure, where he took shelter.

Clutching at his bucket of Earth, he dreamed of the moonlight on Suzan's hair and the loving way she kissed him. He was truly happy until he awoke on the cold, damp stones of his cave shelter with a thirst for blood.

For decades, he roamed holding the bucket of earth, it turned from loamy dirt into clay, but the memories of his first wife still remained. Now in a suitable home, the dirt from the bucket has now been moved to a glass jar which holds those memories and other memories of other loves, of people he found the homes with William and Pascaline and his friends of the coven, Derrik and Norma.

And it is this earth that reminds him who he is, just as it reminds all of us who we are. And who we were to him and each other.

A WORD FROM OUR SPONSOR

Norma's Cleaning Service

Have you ever gotten intoxicated off alcohol in a victim' blood and wondered what to do? Well, Here is a wonderful testimonial from Laurence Roch.

"I was drunk off my ass after drinking blood from a stranger so I don't remember much, but I found myself tucked safely in my own bed, curtains drawn, fully dressed, except my shoes which I found next to the door and no mud tracked into my apartment. As I had a few texts confirming my whereabouts, my landlady was concerned about my hangover, but not overly concerned that I was a risky tenant on a bender. Norma and Carlos are the best!"

Remember Norma's Cleaning Service tidies all kinds of messes in the greater Seattle area. Depending on the circumstances: Guaranteed to solve your problem or ensure you never have a problem again! Licensed and bonded private investigator and house cleaner.

Call or download the App!

INITIATE QUESTIONS

INITIATE BRIAN ASKS: LADY LORETTA, THIS QUESTION IS MORE ABOUT LAURENCE THAN THE EARTH, BUT WAS LAURENCE A LIVING VAMPIRE?

Yes, he contracted the vampire virus on the train but did not die until two years later. This is why the sun bothered him, but he could deal with it to a certain degree. Bread was distasteful but he still ate it. He might have died of smoke inhalation, the bayonet, or might have drowned himself in the Pacific. Unfortunately, he really didn't remember dying, only being dead and very thirsty. He was a full-fledged vampire.

You can contract the virus without dying. But if you do not die, you will continue to age, and your body will shut down eventually. It seems to us it is better to die quickly and become stronger rather than weaken and become a vampire, but we may be wrong.

Initiate Linda asks: Lady Loretta, if you can see dinosaurs and such in the Earth, why didn't vampires discover dinosaurs?

Human Scientists did.

Imagine if someone came to you with no evidence except dragon myths about creatures that only they could see in a pile of dirt. They don't even have fossils, just the dirt. Would you believe them if they talked about unicorns or dinosaurs? No. And no one would believe us either.

Without evidence and the scientific method, you don't just discover things. Or if you do, people think you are crazy or burn you at the stake.

I would hope that no vampire is stupid enough to look at their Earth, which is a pile of dirt, and claim they can see all these things and understand them. Because you can't.

You have no idea how a dinosaur or unicorn experienced the world. You can only sense that they did.

Have a good day and sleep the sleep of the dead.

(Special Note: An unabridged version of the History of Laurence Roch was originally told in Immortal House, 2018.)

INTRODUCTION

Beloved Initiates and Other Listeners:

I apologize for the delay in lessons. As some of you know, the Paper Flower Consortium flooded, and the sounds of reconstruction slowed my recording schedule.

Tonight, I shall tell you the story of another type of vampire hunter that my youngest, Haley Avedo, ran into at a party. Moreover, Norma has seen more of this type as of late. The world has seemingly gotten angrier and colder.

This type of hunter looks soft and innocent, but they are not. Rather than coming on strong and violent, they get close. Moreover, they do not kill for money. Rather, they use their personal pain as an excuse to destroy vampires.

They don't even hate vampires or hold a grudge against us, but when we die, we leave simple ash. That is the only reason they kill us. I will also say these hunters tend to hunt the rogue vampire, but if they come upon a coven vampire and find a victim of opportunity, they will still strike.

This is just a warning for caution. All vampires should do what they would like to do. While Haley's description of a house party does not appeal to me, it is an amusement for this age, and dancing is a wonderful activity.

Haley was twenty-five when she was transformed in 2019. She entered the initiation program directly out of college. Haley loved the vampire existence – or at least most of it. She had a lover who wanted to be her enthralled human throughout her initiation. And that person who dumped her once she was transformed. This person left the coven and went over to Strawberry Fields, where they could bind themselves to an older, more exotic vampire.

I knew my daughter was hurt, the ending of a love affair is often painful, but I wish Haley would have confided in one of her coven siblings or me. She didn't.

I realized the danger she was in when the sun rose, and I began to burn with her. Now to be clear, Haley did nothing wrong. One ought to be able to go dancing and meet someone at a party. This is just a warning that our people must remain vigilant.

A HOUSE PARTY

October 26, 2019

Haley has always loved to dance, yet she felt breathless as she moved into the roiling crowd. There were some people in costumes, but most dressed in club clothes with a bit of Halloween flair or the Seattle uniform of jeans and tees. Haley fit in.

At twenty-five, Haley was the average age of the party goer, and as a young vampire, she did not have any out-of-time habits, which made her stand out. She had to focus on her bloodlust, but she ate before the party and had a pocket full of dried blood capsules that she bought from Norma.

The party was in one of the older U-district craftsman houses, which had not seen a renovation; instead, it was rented out to five grad students. By the simple décor and threadbare furnishings, most likely men. Not that she cared about the décor, but the smell of the musty, beer-soaked couch almost chased her back outside.

It had been three years since she had been to a human-mostly party, and she felt her movements were not paced with the tempo. She wondered if she should go to the bar in the kitchen just to have a drink in her hand. Her eyes glanced down to the floor. Her rhythm became even more offbeat as she swayed to the music.

In the privacy of a noisy crowd, she admitted to herself, that maybe it was wrong to begin the initiation program right after college. Maybe she should have experienced a little more life first. The other vampires had warned that enthralled humans liked vampires older-- a lot older --but she hadn't expected how hard it would hurt when an enthralled human told her she wasn't vampiric enough. That she was too normal to be a turn-on. Scott and Bruce (her brothers under Charles and changed in the '1983 and '90 respectively) tried to warn her it was hard to find an enthralled human. It took over two decades for Sophie to come into Scott's existence. And Bruce was still single. But as Haley was a beautiful twenty-five-year-old woman, she ignored the warning.

Dancing blocked the soul-crushing loneliness. The harsh feeling was held at bay by the movement. She feared if she stopped to think that in the dark room of pulsating bodies, a feeling so forlorn would take root in her heart and spread. She was all alone in an uncaring alien world.

Below her pounding feet, the floorboards squeaked and sagged. A cheer rose from some guys as the song changed. Four men bounced around with maniacal glee. She supposed that too was a type of dancing, but she found herself hoping the floor gave way, and they crashed into the basement. She shifted to the outskirts of the small room where she could move with the music on her own.

Haley knew no one at the party, but a twenty-something woman's short flouncing gossamer skirt tickled against Haley's thighs as the woman moved past with perfect rhythm to the thumping beat at the house party. This close, Haley caught a musky scent sticking to the woman's skin.

A shiver went up her spine. She had romantic intentions for the woman and hoped the woman would want her back.

The woman smiled at Haley and turned to dance with her. There was something hidden, laughter, passionate and mysterious in perfect amber eyes.

She called out, "You here with someone?"

Haley shook her head no.

"I'm here with friends, but they are somewhere in the crowd. I'm Layla, by the way."

"Haley." She immediately regretted telling the stranger her name. Feeling her body coated in glistening sweat, she loosened the lacing on her velvet vest, exposing the thin sheer black top and bra below. She was glad she wore black so no one would see she sweated blood.

Layla explained how she had been dumped by her girlfriend—who was weirdly claiming they broke up by mutual decision—two weeks before. She didn't understand because she and Kate had been through everything since college. Friends turned lovers just like in a romcom. A year after graduation, Layla had assumed they were working towards a future together. Marriage, dogs, maybe even kids. Two weeks ago, Kate moved out of their shared apartment, claiming she needed space to find herself, that they were too young to settle down.

Haley nodded and felt sympathy for the other woman's pain.

Layla took a hit on her vape pen, apologized for rambling about her ex, and offered her a hit of her vape pen.

Haley took a hit, but it didn't do anything. She didn't expect it to, but she felt it was something else she lost—which was weird because she didn't vape in the first place.

People raised their hands in the air to the song. Imitating the other dancers, Haley did as well. She saw how long and sharp Layla's nails were. They seemed too thick, more claw-like than fingernails should, but Haley shook it off as a Halloween fashion choice.

Suddenly, Layla pirouetted away from Haley and danced towards the foyer.

Haley was enraged, and as if she was in a waking nightmare, she saw blood on everyone. An earsplitting screech stopped the movement. Haley turned back, but it was just someone forcing one of the old windows open.

By accident or purpose, Layla hopped back in front of her, then rocked her body against Haley's.

Haley felt her fangs expand. She popped a capsule. The dried blood mixing with saliva tasted chalky in her mouth.

Layla suddenly pressed her lips against Haley's. Haley was worried, she'd freak out about the fangs or maybe the blood, but Layla whispered: "I want your claws to scratch down my back. I want to forget being dumped. Bite me."

Haley curled and stretched her toes as best as she could against the patent leather, releasing some of the pressure. Trying to slow things down, Haley ensured her voice was melodious and sweet. "Let's go somewhere we can talk?"

Layla followed Haley out of the living room away from the dancing. Though Haley was in the lead, she felt like she floated, unable to stop following the strange blonde woman with mysterious amber eyes.

In the foyer, she glanced at the mirror. She gasped in fright. She knew her reflection held only clothes and cosmetics. But the cosmetics had run down her face from the bloody sweat. Her fangs had expanded. Thank goodness it was so close to Halloween.

The women moved into the kitchen past the counters filled high with alcohol, sodas, and other mixers.

Trying to gain a semblance of control, Haley cried, "Hold up, I need a drink." She poured herself a cup of water from the sink and chugged it, and popped another blood capsule.

"Can I make you anything?" Layla asked.

Haley shook her head. Still wondering what she looked like, she poured herself another cup of water.

Layla took her time, carefully pouring out her fruity concoction of vodka, strawberries, and lime soda. She added a slice of lime for good measure. Seconds went by, longer than they should. This was eternity. Haley knew she would follow Layla as soon as Layla finished her drink. She had to focus on something else besides those uncanny eyes, but nothing else mattered.

Haley felt as if she didn't know herself anymore. Was this her broken heart or the vampirism?

Thankfully, another woman hurried into the kitchen before she finished. "Oh, there you are, Layla!"

Layla smiled, but it wasn't a true smile. It did not reach her mysterious eyes.

"Haley, this is my friend, Jo. You know how I mentioned I was with friends. Want something to drink, Jo?"

The women spoke to each other as old friends. Haley felt her limbs tremble with jealousy. She felt abandoned. She didn't understand what was happening. Maybe Layla was sensing the danger of leaving with a vampire. What if she read the whole situation wrong. Haley didn't want to leave and face an empty apartment. Or the sad, sympathetic looks of her coven siblings.

"Still coming?" Layla asked Haley.

Haley didn't move, unsure how to read the situation anymore. Layla shrugged. Holding their fresh drinks, Jo and Layla left the kitchen and parked on the stairs to watch some men play a silly drinking game.

Haley returned to dancing. It felt good to be one with music. Across the living room, Haley observed Layla talking with a different girl. This one wobbled a bit on her feet. She was drunk, too drunk to make a good decision. Haley's belly knotted, enraged.

We only spoke a few sentences with each other. It's not like she's my girlfriend. What's wrong with me?

She didn't want to be passed over for another woman.

Layla gently bit into the nape of the drunk girl's neck. No fangs expanded. It was just a love bite followed by a kiss.

Haley's heart thumped in terror, rising in her stomach and into her dry throat. She wanted to be loved. She knew people thought vampires obsessed over victims, but just once, she wanted to be the one who was more loved. She wanted to not feel the aching loneliness in her heart Dancing no longer held back the flood of emotion. She feared she might start crying in the middle of the party. Never a good look.

Across the room, the living amber eyes seemed awash in confusion. She left the other girl where she drunkenly stood and pulled Haley close, and breathed into her ear. "I thought you weren't interested."

"I am interested..." Haley smiled, exposing her long

fangs dripping with blood and saliva. "I just wanted to talk first."

"It's about time you made a decision. We can walk up to the gazebo at the park. It'll be private," Layla said. The hidden laughter in her amber eyes became full and bright.

Haley felt the uncontrolled, floating feeling return. Was Layla a witch or something? Or was she just one of those humans who didn't know she was a witch. Or a werewolf or something.

"I don't like it when you try to take control. That's what you're doing, right? I don't like it." Haley said firmly. "My creator showed me how to do it, but I don't like it."

The floating feeling disappeared.

"Oh, then I won't, sorry," Layla said. "But most people find it more pleasant when I do, so I do."

"You're my rebound girl, and I am yours—I want to feel it all."

Layla looked as if she might argue but said, "As you wish."

Now Haley was a young vampire, but strong and in good health, but she is not a telepath. Besides, even if someone told her Layla was a vampire hunter, Haley might not have believed it. She had seen plenty of vampire hunters in television and movies. They didn't act like Layla—well, maybe Buffy acted a little like Layla. In her mind, Layla was just another woman at the party.

The bright orange sun crested the hills of the Arboretum. Her back began to itch, then burn, but Layla's kisses were growing more passionate.

(At home, my own back began to itch and burn. My beloved, Charles, found Haley's location in the depths of the veil. Norma and Carlos immediately headed north.)

Haley escaped Layla's embrace as her shoulders started to smolder and her hair crackled. She jerked away, but Layla held onto her arms tightly. Her kisses became more passionate and fervent. The pain disappeared; Haley felt as if she were perched on the edge of pleasure. As if she was floating. She could not—no, did not want to-- move for a moment. She no longer cared if she burned.

However, as the topmost layers of flesh turned to ash, she screamed.

She bit down on Layla and yanked herself away. She fell from the park bench to the dirt.

"What's wrong?" Layla said, but her eyes were smiling with horrible glee.

Haley almost made an excuse. Thinking better of it, she scrambled to her feet and ran as fast as she could, and hid in a shaded grove of trees. Morning birds were singing. How could I be so stupid?

Panting in the deep cold autumn air, Haley realized she didn't have her phone. She didn't remember dropping it or handing it to Layla, but she certainly wasn't going to go back to get it. Whatever Layla was, she knew mesmerism. And she could mesmerize Haley.

She raced away from the park bench and hid in the shade of the trees until someone with a cell phone ran past.

She was glad to be female, young, and not someone who looked like a threat.

"Excuse me," she called. "I lost my phone. Mind if I make a call home?"

There is no way to know if Haley lost her phone or if Layla had grabbed it and threw it away. However, a jogger heard the insistent jingle of a cellphone ringing again and again. It grew louder as he ran south towards the gazebo. The phone in a glittering aquamarine case lay abandoned on the trail.

No one liked to lose their phone. Nice man that he was, though annoyed, he slowed his heart rate, he plucked it from the gravel.

The screen read Loretta. Before he could answer, I hung up.

There were obviously a lot of messages and texts from several female names.

The phone rang again. Norma.

He answered: "I found this phone."

"Are you in the Arboretum?" Norma asked.

"Uh yeah."

"Cool, my friend, Carlos, will be right there to pick it up. He's about six foot and has black hair, great shape in jeans, and a Halloween hoodie. He's coming up the hill. Can we give you a reward?"

"Reward? No."

Carlos still offered what Norma called a "C-Note" to the man who did decide to take it so he might get some brunch treats for the family.

On the ride back to the coven, Haley described what happened and gave Layla's description. Layla is still at large, though Norma has heard of other attacks by a perpetrator with Layla's description.

As for Haley, she still is looking for the enthralled human of her dreams. Fear not. The older vampires always ensure the younger ones are fed.

A WORD FROM TONIGHT'S SPONSOR

Photos Evermore

Are you an initiate concerned that a creature of darkness is unable to be caught on film and digital photography?

Photos Evermore records your photograph for posterity, future documentation, and identification. We even can future-proof your Instagram or Facebook Page with a hundred glamorous selfie-style photographs, which we can Photoshop into your future vacation, dog park, or dining pics! Affordable packages based on your needs.

Jingle: Before you disappear forever, think Photos Evermore!

Visit us on our website to schedule an appointment tonight!

INITIATE QUESTIONS:

DEAR LADY LORETTA, SO IS VAMPIRE DATING HARD?

I think all dating is confusing, but as I've said before, I never dated in the modern sense of it. I met Charles in the gardens of Versailles. We were infatuated with each other. Charles spoke to Jakub and Gaius to explain our intentions. Then he courted me. We had what you might call a long engagement since we couldn't marry until I was a vampire. Condoms were not widely available.

I repeat, Haley did nothing wrong, but there are bad people in the world, and one must be aware of that possibility. Haley went on several other dates with people where nothing happened. Forgive me; I should say that only pleasant things happened, such as good conversation and lovemaking.

In this unrestrictive age, my younger offspring tell me most of them meet dates on apps, they take adult entrenchment classes, such as pottery or painting, interest-based meetups, or volunteer work. Of course, everyone's dating existence ended with the pandemic. And many of them are lonely.

Have a good day and sleep the sleep of the dead.

The Guest in Room 014

INTRODUCTION

Beloved Initiates,

Tonight, we shall be talking about a most crucial topic: Manners. One reason vampires are sexualized in human society is that they often must fit into human society. Thus we work hard to be cultured, whatever that culture is.

Because we exist so long, we always act in such a way that creates a pleasant existence. We believe good manners show the best you have to offer and encourage others to be at their best.

Though our library has books on etiquette and courtly behavior of several centuries, and tonight's story mentions the procedures of dueling, I am not talking about perfect etiquette. I am talking about the basics of treating everyone with respect no matter who they are.

Now there are different expectations for several different species, but overall we have found they want to be left alone or they understand the basics of vampire behavior if they wish to interact with us.

Because if one doesn't, it is quite easy to find oneself in trouble around supernatural beings.

Now some may say manners are overrated as they repress straightforwardness or truthfulness. I disagree. No debate is ever won by bad manners. Even when someone believes that they have won, they have literally turned people away. And our Forty-fifth president exposed what bad manners can do to a democracy.

But let us not talk politics. In your own life, have you ever had a change of heart because someone trolled you online? I never have. I am guessing you have not either. And vampires must be careful not only their mannerisms but their enthralled humans' manners as well. We have seen firsthand how an ill-mannered enthralled human can hurt a vampire in reputation and personal injury.

I hate to use the now-common derogatory moniker of Karen, as I have a beloved family member and friends with that name, but the story I will tell tonight deals with that type of rude, entitled individual.

If you have ever worked in a retail setting and had a customer forget their manners, well, you understand tonight's story.

My darling Charles and four of his offspring work in the hospitality side of the hospitality industry.

Housing visiting vampires has always been important to the Paper Flower Consortium. As Seattle is a port city, we quickly learned that other species also need housing.

Now I've said the building, which is now the Night Owl Extended Stay Hotel is an older building finished in the late 1890s. We were housed there until the 1940s but converted into a hotel after our current building was finished after World War II.

However, we do not claim that we are something we are not.

The Night Owl is a three-star hotel. This means we strive to meet all the three-star standards in regards to the terms of lodging, though in some ways, we still are under older codes as we are a vintage building. We are in Full-time operation, seven days a week. As Seattle does not have a tourist season, we remain open all year.

As we have four floors, plus one underground, we did retrofit in the 1950s with a single lift-style elevator. All our Bedrooms, Bathroom, Public areas, and kitchen are fully cleaned daily.

Thankfully, Covid is not even the first pandemic we have existed through, so our cleaning standards were already higher than Covid-19 guidelines.

All floor surfaces are clean and in good shape. Our rooms get aired daily. A clean change of coffin, bed, and bath linen occurs nightly & between check-in. Clean and good quality linen are provided to the guest, and all rooms have attached four-piece bathrooms with toilet, bidet, sink, and shower/tub combination. As most Americans still prefer toilet paper rather than the bidet, we offer that too.

We provide full sunproof double caskets in every vampire room plus rollaway queen beds with pillowtop mattresses for their enthralled humans. And we do not charge extra for enthralled human accommodation in the same room as the vampire.

Only the giant room is set up differently with six queen beds lashed together because it is for giants. We also have 24-hour room service and breakfast and dinner service, but we do not claim to have the amenities of modern hotels. Indeed, most of our visitors enjoy what they now call a bed and breakfast experience.

I say all this, so you understand the fullness of this situation.

Now I beg your pardon, for I found myself chuckling as this was a comedy of errors in many ways, and if Charles and I had not stepped in when we did, it might have become violent. The Adams gave permission to tell this story – as did Courtney, and indeed they laughed with me when going over some of the points. The vampire guest remains unnamed other than the English version of the title they used. Messrs Smith and Lee would be well over ninety by now, but just in case they still live, I changed their names.

THE GUEST IN ROOM 014

Courtney had only been a vampire for a few years at this point, but they are rather shy, retiring, and sweet-natured. Courtney bends over backward to help our customers, which is why they are so wonderful with most people, but this tendency also means they tie themselves in knots when something goes wrong. None of that matters to the story except Courtney can be browbeaten by irate customers. That is exactly what happened.

Two very good-looking human men entered the Night Owl, carrying a latched travel coffin between them, though the sun had not yet risen. And wouldn't for a few hours.

"Good evening," Courtney said.

"This hotel is not downtown Seattle," the first man said, looking around the lobby.

"Yes, Sir. We are in Georgetown."

"Who goes to Georgetown?" the other muttered.

"Uh, we are convenient to the new highway and the airport," Courtney replied. "And we do have a car service if you need...."

Charles took over for Courtney as he could see these customers would be overbearing.

"I have no problem calling another hotel for you if you wish to stay in a location closer to the city center."

The first beautiful man did not answer. Instead, he said, "We have a reservation under Smith and Lee. "

Mr. Smith signed the register and passed over the credit card.

Charles escorted them to their room. He rolled the bags, but the men carried the coffin. Though they did not need to do so, we have a special trolley for coffins.

When Charles opened the door, Mr. Smith grumbled, "I would rather sleep on the street than stay here."

"You are welcome to do that," Charles said with a small smile.

As he expected: Mr. Smith snapped, "I want to speak to your manager."

"I am the owner. As I mentioned, if our establishment cannot serve your needs, I have no problem calling another hotel for you."

Then the basis of the men's dissatisfaction was made clear. They wanted to stay in the city center, but their vampire did not.

"We are here because our vampire wants to stay among his people," Mr. Smith said.

"Then how may I help you, Mr. Smith?"

"Those curtains are dusty—and much too thin."

Now all our windows are covered with three layers of window coverings. Full blackout curtains, sheers, and during that decade, full vertical blinds, which though dated now, looked very modern in 1969. Sunlight would not have gotten in.

Charles moved the trio three times. On the ground floor in room 014, Mr. Smith and Mr. Lee finally found the room they liked. They undid the latch on the travel coffin. And the vampire rose, whom they referred to as the Baron rose from his coffin wrapped in velvet with great spectacle.

Charles had the sense that he was a younger vampire than he claimed, not much older than the 19th century. Moreover, the Baron never told us what location he was the Baron of or any other information like his full name. Humans can be easily fooled as they only know the age they live, but it is harder to fool a vampire.

The Baron poked around the room, running his finger along the furniture and checking the taps.

Charles asked if he could get them more towels.

Finally, Charles was dismissed, but as he exited, he heard the vampire say: "What type of hotel lets a scarred man work the front desk? I thought the Paper Flower Consortium was run by nobles."

Charles ignored them. He has no shame about his scars. And if that shame ever does creep into our existence, I would remind my husband that he is the most handsome man in the world in my eyes.

Charles hoped that though they were demanding and specific about their needs, they would be quiet for the rest of their stay. Sometimes guests are like that. Unfortunately, that was not to be.

During that day, Mr. Smith was heading to the ice machine when he ran across two ghosts, a Mr. and Mrs. Adams, floating down the hall to the dining room.

While ghosts don't have huge appetites, they do like to smell, and they often enjoy seeing others enjoying themselves. And we offer small tasting plates at reasonable prices, which ghosts love since one or two bites of anything will fill them for months.

The ghost tipped his hat to Mr. Smith as he moved towards the elevator.

We are not sure if a bit of icy ether drifted past him or touched him, but we do know that Mr. Smith said, "You are crowding me!"

Mr. Adams tipped his hat again. "Forgive me, Sir. My wife and I were going to the dining room."

Mr. Smith nodded. He began muttering under his breath when he assumed they were out of earshot. "Your lady is a fat, pampered dog,"

And that was it.

Mr. Adams turned and said, "You offended my wife. That requires an apology, Sir."

Instead of apologizing, Mr. Smith said, "I am sorry

you have a fat wife."

Unfortunately for Mr. Smith, this particular ghost couple hailed from the eighteenth century. Unlike vampires who must remain in time because of our physical needs, ghosts really don't.

The ghost challenged Mr. Smith to a duel in the parking lot.

Mr. Smith called the ghost crazy and tried to shove them. Which, of course, he couldn't. It didn't matter that his hand just swiped through the ether; this was the worse thing he might have done because not only had he insulted the ghost a third time, a blow is never tolerated between gentlemen of the eighteenth century.

Mr. Adams told him he had the first shot, which according to duel rules, he did.

Mr. Smith ran back down the hall without an answer.

The ghost's voice echoed. "So you are a coward as well."

You see, Mr. Smith may or may not be a coward. He ran back to the room because he had expected his vampire, the Baron, to know what to do.

Of course, his vampire had no idea what to do about a ghost who wanted to duel.

He did know a ghost might pull the soul out of a vampire. He shouted at the ghost to leave them alone.

Mr. Lee ran and escaped to the front desk. There was a phone in the room. We think Mr. Lee wanted to get away from the chaos.

Charles had left for the morning, and Courtney was back at the front desk when Mr. Lee started screaming, "I want to talk to your manager! There's a ghost in the hotel!"

Poor Courtney stammered, "Of course, there is. They are guests. How can I help you, Sir?"

"My vampire does not approve."

"They are paying guests, Sir," Courtney replied.

"What are you going to do about this? Do you know who my vampire is?"

Courtney had no idea who the vampire was as they explained, "The reservation was under Messrs Smith and Lee. The vampire isn't listed."

"The Baron will rip the throat out of the next person who disrespects us!" Mr. Lee cried.

"I am sorry, but who is disrespecting you?" Courtney asked.

Mr. Lee slapped the counter and said something about dueling.

Courtney went to the room. Mr Lee followed but stood in the hall near Mrs. Adams.

Mr. Adams shouted at the Baron, "If your man is a coward, then I shall meet you in the parking lot."

And the Baron bellowed in return: "Leave my room!"

Courtney tried to calm both men, but Mr. Adams kept mentioning his satisfaction.

The Baron screamed every time the ghost came near. "Do something about this abdominal situation!"

He squealed and threw a table lamp across the room.

"He's no gentleman," Mr. Adams shouted back.

"If everyone would just please, calm down," Courtney began.

"Don't tell me to calm down, my lady has been

insulted," Mr. Adams shouted.

The Baron added, "Who are you, a hotel clerk, to tell me to calm down. I am going to call the manager."

And at this point, Courtney figured it was best to call the manager. And they ran to the courtesy phone and called us at home. Well I should say he called Charles, but I answered the phone. Before voice mail, I loved answering the phone— it was always a surprise to hear who was on the other end. What a marvelous invention; I'm sort of sad that everyone texts now. Sigh. Back to the story.

Of course, Courtney apologized for bothering me. They are a kind, gentle soul.

"Charles, my love, it's Courtney." I called to my husband, who was already in our coffin.

"The shabbaron in room 014?" Charles grumbled.

"It sounds like it. Apparently, they are upset there are ghosts in the hotel."

"I'm getting upset I allowed those prats to stay here," Charles said.

Through the phone, poor Courtney was growing more panicked. "Lady Loretta, I must speak to Charles. Those men... they are dueling with ghosts now!"

It was obvious a lady's touch would be needed, and by that, I do not mean my gender, I mean my previous position as a lady of the French Court.

I dressed quickly. Charles and I walked through the tunnel and into the ground floor of the hotel.

Courtney's eyes alighted upon Charles and me, but they didn't make eye contact with either of us.

"I tried to stop them. I messed it up, worse."

Courtney tried to hold in their emotions, but they were stressed and upset. They feared the threats that Mr. Lee was making and that Charles might blame them for letting this quarrel between guests get out of hand as it did.

We went to room 014, where the Baron and Mr. Smith were screaming at the ghost slipping in and out of the door. I could see Mr. Adams was taunting them, getting carried away by the excitement.

Mrs. Adams was still in the hall, covering the empty black orbs with wispy branches of ether. If I am honest, I think she was embarrassed.

"Excuse me," I said over the noise.

"He insulted my lady, and he placed his hands upon me," the ghost said. "I was not planning to hurt them, but I must have my satisfaction."

"This is a place of sanctuary for all," I said. "May I offer you something for your trouble? An upgraded suite? We have a lovely top-floor suite with a view of the forest. My husband shall show you the way.

"And I shall ensure they do not trouble you again."

Once Charles got Mr. and Mrs. Adams upstairs, I turned on the vampire. "It is well known this hotel caters to all species. If you do not wish to be housed in this establishment, I shall call a car for you."

Mister Smith took one look at me and made another mistake which exposed that undoubtedly his "Baron" was a pretender and not a gentleman.

He took a step towards me and knew I would not touch an enthralled human, so he used that rule against me to grab my wrist. I think they thought to cow me. I am what they used to call a "New Woman," so my honor is my own. Still, it was good Charles and Mr. Adams went upstairs as their presence would have undoubtedly worsened the situation.

"I would remove your hand, Mr. Smith, or you will lose it."

"Baron?"

The vampire sniffed. "A beauty such as yourself should not have to see scars for eternity."

"Insulting my husband does not endear you to me. Charles bears the scars he earned in battle. And he is nobler in character than you by far."

"How dare you insult me!"

"Because I am Loretta Fabron, Second Reborn of Lady Agata. Because I was born of the Viscount and Viscountess of Fabron, adopted by Lady Agata and Sir Jakub..."

You see, I only told him my noblebirth because I knew he would be impressed by such things. After all, he was a pretender, or if he was a baron, he recently bought the title.

Otherwise, he would have known the rules of dueling.

He quieted immediately.

After I had gained assurances that there would be no more trouble coming from this room, I found Mr. Lee and told him this scandal had been averted. And he might return to his room.

I climbed the steps to the suite where Mr. and Mrs. Lee were getting settled. Once again, I introduced myself with my full birth name and title and begged their pardon for what happened under my and Charles's roof.

The ghost accepted my apology and told me it was not my offense, especially after I offered my hand to Mrs. Adams and asked if they might enjoy dining with Charles and I.

Now if one is confused, this means they became our personal guests. If one is still confused, it means their meals were us. Indeed, for the insult, we comped the room.

Of course, poor Courtney was quite confused by the rules of duels and exactly what was happening, but they understood enough to get our private dining room ready.

And that was the end of the ugliness.

The Baron did play cards one night with a few other vampire guests of the hotel. His Mr. Smith and Mr. Lee remained in the room and ordered room service. They were much more polite to the waitstaff.

The Baron came for fellowship with other vampires, he tried to sidle close to the noble-born among us while ignoring our offspring. In Pascaline's case, he had the gall to ignore her husband. He didn't even thank Jeffery for the service or take his hand in greeting. Though we were not discourteous to Baron, he found he did not like the vampires of Seattle. He told us this city was spoiled by democracy.

He returned to the hotel for the rest of his stay and remained there until the car took him away.

This was fine because in 1969, we had several

fledglings of different nationalities and socio-economic statuses. The last thing fledglings need is a classist or racist or jerky vampire and their rude enthralled humans.

This is why it is always best to treat everyone with respect, no matter what their species. And of course, now it is even more important.

If we acted in such a manner to a hotel or store clerk or our enthralled humans did, it would be trending in ten minutes. We must always exist for the good of the coven, and manners are good for the coven.

A WORD FROM OUR SPONSOR:

MYT Clothier

Vampires, Do you dislike ripped denim, thin fabrics, and how well-made modern clothing is covered in labels? MYT Clothier creates handmade custom clothing in accessible styles for all body types from all eras—including this one! We use the best quality handwoven silk embroidery from China, Damask from France and Italian Embroidery and Leathers, and other fine fabrics. And if you wish to look like you stepped out of time or even reality with fantastical designs, we can make that happen too.

And werewolf friends, we have a wide variety of double woven stretchy materials for those quick transformations. If the cloth tears when you transform, we'll fix or replace the garment for free!

At MYT Clothier, quality is our style.

INITIATE QUESTIONS

LADY LORETTA, MANNERS CHANGE EVEN IN A HUMAN LIFETIME. HOW CAN WE BE CERTAIN THAT WE DON'T OFFEND PEOPLE OF DIFFERENT SPECIES?

Some people claim people are easily offended nowadays, but as you can see, people have always dealt with transgressions of manners.

People of all species want to be treated with kindness and respect, especially when people are traveling. Everyone expects minor inconveniences and, even at times, accidental offenses. If Mr. Smith had stepped out of the way and kept his mouth shut, there would have been no ugliness.

Even after the insult, if he had just apologized and begged pardon, there would be no talk of duels. Even if Baron had done so, as the head of his household, he might have relaxed the tension. They did not need me to step in.

LADY LORETTA, HOW CAN ONE ENSURE THEIR ENTHRALLED HUMANS ARE WELL-MANNERED?

My beloveds, though we need enthralled humans, one should never rush into an arrangement with a human just because they offer their blood. Spend time with them before a contract is signed and watch how they treat people—especially folks like the janitorial or wait staff.

Put simply, don't choose jerks for enthralled

humans. And don't insist that they press upon others to lift you up as the Baron did in my story.

INTRODUCTION

Welcome back, beloved initiates.

Tonight, we shall discuss pets and the strict laws against turning animals into vampires. This is the story of two ancient horse vampires. So be warned, innocent horses die and are reborn in the telling. I will also touch our beloved, Dash, who met death though Derrik was tempted to transform her. So I understand if you fear listening. This is a terrible subject, I know. However, I hope you listen carefully because this is incredibly important.

There are several misconceptions and old wives' tales about why most vampires don't keep pets—especially short-lived pets. Some believe the animal will sense our predatory nature and run away, but that isn't true. After all, in many cultures, humans also eat meat. Some eat blood. Humans are also predators also hunters.

The reason most vampires don't keep pets is the pain of loss.

Before the 1921 Initiation Laws forbade such things, history shows us that several vampires tried to transform their animals so their sweet unconditional love and acceptance might also be eternal. While some were successful, most animal transformations tried and failed.

I remind initiates since vampirism is a virus transmitted by blood and other bodily fluids, Now, the vampire virus does not seem to infect reptiles, or if they can be, they die quickly. Perhaps it is because they need the warmth of the sun to function. I have said before this is unclear to us.

History shows us small animals, mammals, insects, birds, and bats do not survive the transformation. Though many think bats can be turned, these are tiny little animals. They die quickly.

House cats and small dogs can be vampires, but their transformations have a high 83% failure rate. Generally, this is because the vampire takes too much blood from the small little animal, and the animal exsanguinates.

The animals with the best survival rate are primarily horses and large dogs. That is dogs over 100 pounds.

I personally have only seen one transformed animal: a beautiful warhorse, once part of the Roman cavalry, the magnificent Nix.

FATE OF THE MAGNIFICENT NIX

He was born as an animal who ate grass and grain, but death brought him back as a monster.

His eerie neighs and snorts reverberate into one's soul. To see Nix in person is to be dumbstruck by his great beauty and terrible countenance. As a former warhorse, he was built for carrying armed men into battle. His muscles ripple under his black coat. Unlike human-esques vampires, Nix cannot or chooses not to retract his fangs.

Yet, Gaius jokes Nix is a hidden unicorn. Indeed, he can be quite docile.

In 2019, before the pandemic shut everything down, Norma went to Europe on a job. And she said the only sad thing about coming home was leaving Nix. She said his coat felt like the softest velvet.

And Norma isn't the only teenage girl Nix loves. Even after Gaius stopped loving his former concubine, Julia, Nix never did.

For over a century, Nix allowed her to groom him and braid his mane. Indeed, when he saw her, he would happily trot up to her and nuzzle her.

Sometimes I regret that when I was a girl of seventeen and had the opportunity to pet the beast, I did not. I was still a human and frightened of those stomping hooves and snapping fangs. After all, Nix eats only meat and drinks only blood, and I was filled with both.

Imagine a giant dog who nips when he is happy, and you will understand my fear. Gaius was there, so he would have ensured I was transformed, but the Paper Flower Consortium's relationship with our progenitor has always been complicated. I simply did not know Gaius well enough to trust him with my safety.

And it is not just teenage girls Nix adores. Even though centuries ago, Jakub stabbed Gaius in the chest, Nix has always let Jakub touch him.

It is possible with so many battles and violence

in his existence, Nix does not or cannot associate these two events with violence. Or perhaps it is because Gaius forgave his progeny due to the circumstances of that event; Nix also considers Jakub forgiven. Obviously, Nix cannot tell us what he thinks, but he prances right up to Jakub. Jakub has always had a way with horses.

Let us begin the story of Nix, who begins with the story of Gaius.

Gaius still claims he has had two great loves in his existence. One is his former concubine, Phillipa; a former witch turned vampire who eventually usurped him due to his cruelty to other concubines. And the other is Nix, his eternal companion.

Now Gaius doesn't quite remember the year he was born, but it was the 4th century BC. Gaius's father was a senator and well known for breeding chariot horses. Gaius claims he had a happy childhood. He was well-loved by his parents and siblings. At thirteen, he left to join the service, and with his patrician name and history with horses, he was sent to the newly formed cavalry.

Gaius had already done one tour of duty when he returned home to his father's estate and met the yearling, Nix.

The black horse was originally planned for the chariots, but he did not take to the training. And any good horseman knows you don't force a horse to do anything.

Gaius asked his father to let him take the horse for the calvary, which needed several types of horses. Even if the foal couldn't be trained for war, there were other jobs for him. Gaius's father agreed, and Nix flourished in the calvary. The two, Gaius and Nix, were inseparable brothers-in-arms.

Gaius was an excellent general and won many battles or, at least, he won more than he lost. After several more accomplishments, Gaius was ultimately given control over the Carpathians, which had been under Roman rule for centuries.

As for the year they were reborn, Gaius claims Nix was close to ten years old, which would have made him approximately thirty.

Gaius became a vampire because he slept with the wrong woman. Phillipa had warned him to be careful, but he ignored her good advice. As a vampire, Gaius turned Nix along with the rest of his legion and Phillipa. He told his soldiers to transform their horses.

Many did die. However, during the years of the Roman empire, Nix had several horse companions too.

In 1509, when Agata met them, only Nix and Fidelles had survived the lean years. The rest were dead, sacrificed to feed the other vampires. The soldiers and their mounts were immortalized for their service to Gaius, but there were also hundreds of the concubines who were just bled and thrown into the sun.

Due to the multitudes of vampire death: soldiers, horses, concubines, Gaius made the treaties with the counts stationing himself as a protector even after the Roman Empire fell. He became the Legatus of the Mountains, and though many more things happened during those centuries, this is the story of Nix's fate.

Let us go to the twentieth century and World War

II. Because, of course, now people don't ride horses into battle. Nix was left remain behind when Gaius fought with the French Resistance. This situation was hard on the man but even harder on the horse. Nix once had an existence, a purpose, and it was gone.

No one was ready for the destruction which World War II caused though Gaius and his legion saw it coming and tried to warn us and other covens. When the bombs fell, the elderly, women, and children were killed by the thousands. Some of the impacts were so great that people were lifted up into the air. Thousands more were injured. Millions were made homeless.

But let us not get sidetracked. One night the town—which I will not name—was bombed. The structure which housed Nix collapsed. Nix brayed and kicked his way out of the falling stone and timbers.

In the night, the poor brute was terrified by sounds of other bombs hitting other buildings. People screaming. He raced across town with other horses and rampaging livestock only to be met by machine guns.

German soldiers mowed down fleeing civilians and their animals. If the bombs didn't kill, the guns would, and any who escaped would face starvation.

We know from Gaius, Nix was hit with at least three rounds. However, unlike other animals, Nix was already dead and could not be killed again. He reared up, and his hooves came down upon his assailants. The machine gun was found crushed, as was one of the operators. The other was not found with the gun.

Nix had dragged the other gunman into a nearby

cave and ate him in order to heal his pains.

Back in town, Gaius dug into the old barn with his hands and could not find his beloved Nix. Eventually, Gaius left his body and found Nix eating the soldier. By the man's defensive wounds on his hands, it was obvious the man had been alive when Nix dug into his flesh.

Gaius paced the day away. He heard the Germans whisper about a demon horse that he had seen the night before. One that had been shot but would not fall. They planned on capturing it for Hitler. With very little fanfare, Gaius spirited Nix deeper into the countryside, which was still bombed, but to a lesser extent.

Of course, though he is a legacy vampire, the law states if Nix bites anyone, he will be destroyed. If he changes anyone, he will be destroyed. Now Nix was eating someone.

Gaius moved, again and again, to keep Nix safe and away from the bombing. After the war, Gaius returned to Hamburg to ensure they were on the West Germany side of the border.

I was allowed to tell this story because Nix was tried by the council after WWII but has been found innocent of the wrongdoing. He was simply defending himself.

For Nix might not have human intelligence, but he does seem to have horse sense and always knows an enemy. Gaius has wondered several times over the last century if he should destroy the animal and allow Nix to experience the freedom of death.

Nix exists in a comfortable treed pasture and attached barn outside an unnamed European city. Gaius's legion does not understand why Gaius keeps the lovely creature, but Nix loves Gaius. And Gaius loves Nix.

Over the centuries, he has been stabled at times, so the stable doesn't bother him, but he is alone, except when Gaius is home and comes for their nightly ride. Just as a side note, Romans rode their horses without stirrups, which would come later from Asia, so Nix does not like stirrups which is one of the reasons he will not let most ride him.

Perhaps that's why the old stallion likes young women and girls. His horse sense has taught him that they want to pet him, braid his mane, and give him bits of meat. They don't tend to threaten him with machine guns and bombs. But it is a sad existence for a horse, I should think.

FATE OF THE WILD FIDELLES

Now I shall tell even a sadder story. In 1509, when Phillipa usurped Gaius, the two vampire horses were split apart. Nix is an expensive pet for eternity, but what happened to Fidelles was much worse.

And in this, I speak of Agata's vengeance against the vampire who infected her with the virus and destroyed her beloved life.

Nicheloa was a cruel lech of a man, and this ultimately got him killed, as Agata saw the only way to regain her honor was through vengeance. Agata would have her retribution against Nicheloa, but there were costs. And part of that cost was paid by an innocent beast.

For his cruelty and lechery, Nicheloa was cut into

small pieces, doused in oil, and burned. Then his ashes were burnt six more times in hot flames.

Agata felt the severing of the bloodline, and she suffered, but at least she understood what was happening. Poor Fidelles did not.

While this was happening, though in pain, Gaius escaped with Nix and rode away before any of his vampiric concubines or human servants tried to kill him. Fidelles, who was panicked as he experienced the dying of his creator, Nicheola, was left behind.

Fidelles recovered the severing of the bloodline. Though he did seem to wander from time to time looking for Nicheloa, Gaius, or Nix, he seemed happy enough racing through the mountains with Sylvia. As the vampires had for centuries, Sylvia kept the pacts with the surrounding counties who gave them sacrificial animals for protection.

However, as the Ottoman Empire moved west, eventually, the old pacts between the Counts and vampires dissolved. The vampire coven no longer had soldiers, as Gaius had eaten them in the lean times. And though Sylvia was a strong horsewoman, none of the women were fighters. They only had one manservant and some children at the time, so they did not even have a human who might negotiate with the Ottomans.

The old pacts fell, and food grew scarce. Sylvia took to hunting humans for food which Fidelles loved. However, eventually, they closed their doors to the outside world, locking in a few humans with them.

Fidelles's territory was now just the courtyard of the mountain fort. Sometime in the early seventeenth century, he rebelled from his existence. He could not stay trapped in the fort's gardens.

The poor horse kicked out of his stable several times until he got out during the day and tried to immolate himself.

I will repeat what some may have forgotten the first thing I told initiates: vampires cannot have an easy death. Vampires can be injured beyond any human measure, or in this case, horse measure. Vampires may be roasted by the sun, but unless it burns everything, we regenerate, reanimate.

And what does this mean? Apparently, night came before the giant warhorse found final death. His once beautiful gray coat was burnt and smoldering, exposed patches of scorched, blistered flesh underneath. Foamy saliva dripped from his mouth. His hooves were cracked and torn.

This went on for days and nights.

Sylvia and Julia tried to make him comfortable, tried to make him understand that he must stay within the garden. As Fidelles is only a horse, he could not understand. In the night, he began to heal; in the day, he would burn again.

Perhaps on the hottest and longest summer day, he might have been able to succeed, but not that year.

His eyes grew filled with rage and pain. Adrenaline coursing through his veins, he reverted to wildness. And as all vampires do when they get hungry, lust overtook him. He jumped over the stone wall.

He topped down to the other side. The sound of his

cracking bones was horrifying. But as he was a vampire, he shook himself off and limped away into the darkest forests.

Sylvia killed a man and tried to tempt Fidelles home with the corpse. She almost snapped a bridle on him. Fidelles reared up. He turned and bit off her hand—which thankfully though mangled, was complete and reattached later.

Fidelles bolted.

Sylvia, along with Julia, hunted him. They know his location. And Gaius has looked down the bloodline and found him as well.

Fidelles is now a beast of legend: a land-based kelpi if you will. He sleeps in a series of caves, but if anyone or any animal comes near, he tempts those he sees and drags them back to his lair.

Thankfully the land he lives on has fallen into a nationalized trust of Romania. Let us hope it stays that way because it means human prey is rare. Whatever the species, if they are lucky, they die quickly. We have heard Fidelles loves to rip the soft skin of the cheek first and delights in squishing eyes between his teeth.

Of course, with this social media generation, some have tried to find him. Such easy prey even stands still while they try to capture photos or video. By the time they realize the danger, it doesn't matter because a horse can outrun a human, and a vampire horse can outrun a human on uneven ground even when they have a motorized mount. Fidelles cannot be fooled by any human trickery. An ancient vampire can hear a heartbeat over a motor. A vampire horse knows no mercy. If you are wise, you will never try to find him. If you are not, you will die.

FATE OF DASH

Finally, I will make a personal observation. I thank God though Derrik was tempted to transform our sweet old sheepdog, Dash—which was still legal at the time—he did not.

Dash originally belonged to Jakub's enthralled human, Luc. She came with us from Europe to America. After Luc's death, Derrik, who loved the sweet creature, took her on. Though she was friendly to all of us, she loved Derrik best. She aged alongside him as he grew into a man. She slept with him in his coffin, and after he and Pascaline married, Dash slept between them each day.

If you remember our sixth lesson, it was Dash who comforted Derrik when he transformed into a vampire, and his telepathy battered his brain.

When Dash turned eleven, she was still quite spry. Derrik began to see the signs of aging and knew she would not have many more years in this world.

Jakub understood as he went through the same process with his warhorse Castor. He ultimately gave Castor the gift of death and suggested Derrik do the same with Dash.

Dash lived two more years. As her coat grew more white and her running pounce became a walk, Derrik grew more tempted. One evening, when Dash was thirteen, she could not rise out of the coffin. Derrik had to lift her out. Agata rubbed her legs, and Dash was able to temporarily walk again, but by sunrise, she was immobile again. The next night, the same.

Derrik asked to be left alone as he brought Dash into the pasture where our dog had enjoyed running. He bit into the dog's artery. She halfheartedly snapped at him in animal instinct.

Every second, Derrik was tempted to cut open his wrist and give his blood to the dying creature. Then Dash's heart stopped, and she breathed her last.

Derrik wrapped the dog's body in a quilt. He dug the hole and prayed over her. It was the last hole, indeed the last manual labor, he ever did. His last link to his human life had been snuffed out, but he said he was glad he had not acted in selfish depravity. Yet he mourned her for a long time after. Indeed, though he has never shown any unkindness towards an animal, indeed, he is very gentle with them. He refuses any pets in his home. When Norma was a girl, she wasn't allowed an animal companion. Even now his enthralled humans aren't allowed to keep pets other than fish.

Some call this heartless, but for Derrik, the temptation of transformation is too great.

The decision to keep pets or working animals is a personal one. All vampires must decide for themselves if they can overcome that temptation along with the understanding, that the coven will not be merciful to those who break this law.

A WORD FROM OUR SPONSOR

Norma's Cleaning Service

Messy Hunt? Unexpected worshipers? Are you just an elderly housebound monster caught in a pandemic? Norma and her crew of undead are licensed and bonded Private Detectives and house cleaners. They fix and clean up all types of situations, from getting groceries into your pantry to stopping a coven-wide blood feud. Problem will either be cleaned up to your satisfaction or you will never have a problem again.

ONE ANSWER

There will not be a question or answer period tonight because any question you ask on this topic has one answer.

Since 1921, a vampire cannot make a vampire out of anything other than a consenting adult human over twenty-five years, following coven and international guidelines.

Even if it is "accidental," we will destroy any coven vampire who converts anyone outside of the guidelines. It is ultimate cruelty to turn anyone without permission. Though animals love us with a full heart, they cannot consent.

Fidelles would not have wanted to be parted from Nicheola in death, yet they have been parted. And now the world has turned away from working animals and to machines. I fear—as should you all--what Nix might become if anything ever should happen to the Gaius.

I will also add, children and adolescent humans cannot consent. Norma, herself, admits she got lucky Derrik and Pascaline raised her with kindness and the coven paid for her education. Otherwise, she might have faced the fate that other vampires turned too young, faced.

A different girl from a different time or culture might not have survived. I have a number of histories of girls and boys who have cast themselves into the flames after they were transformed into a vampire. Even if you are one of my children, I will not show you mercy.

Good day, Beloved Initiates, and Sleep the Sleep of the Dead.

Loss of Reflection

INTRODUCTION

Welcome back, beloved initiates,

Tonight we will speak of reflections or, specifically the loss of reflections. Vampires do not reflect light and therefore cast no reflection. This means we are also terrible subjects for photographs. People in this modern age used to selfies are often shocked that we don't take pictures of everything, and we must complete our grooming without a mirror.

We ask and encourage initiates to stop using mirrors as early as possible during the first year of the program. It can be a true shock to lose your reflection, especially for those who are used to wearing cosmetics.

In fact, in my own long existence, I was glad I had six years to practice without a reflection, whereas Pascaline relied on Agata or me during her first years as a vampire.

Back in Versailles, I remember carefully applying cosmetics to every inch of exposed skin on Agata, Jakub, and Pascaline to ensure their entirety was covered, so no one was shocked by an errant lack of reflection in the Great Hall of Mirrors.

But let me tell you the story of my vampire daughter, Tabitha, who took the loss of a reflection quite hard. For those of you who don't know, she is the T in Paper Flower Consortium's MYT Clothier.

Before I start, I will give you a different warning. Never go unprepared into the mountains unless you have the experience and the gear to make the trip safely. A vampire can survive the cold; a human will die from hypothermia.

The mountains of the Cascades and Olympics are known to kill. I cannot stress this enough.

HISTORY OF TABITHA FORDE

Tabitha Forde was born an American but had lived in London when she was a teenager as her father had moved the family for work. She is a classic beauty by European standards and has always had an interest in fashion.

More to meet people than any other reason, she worked as a model as an adolescent. Her mother remained watchful, but Tabitha had quite a bit of freedom as long as she appeared respectful.

In Europe, she also devoured the Dracula flicks created by Hammer Films.

Her parents moved back to America when she was twenty. Though, at first, she did not plan to return permanently with them, while visiting, she happened to learn that vampires are real from one of her model friends who worked as an enthralled human in Bellevue.

As Bellevue was not seeking initiates at that time, they suggested she visit Seattle.

After Tabitha came to us, she claimed she found the men of the coven brooding, though I had no idea why.

Honestly, my Fifthborn daughter, Marion, is the most brooding of the vampires. Especially back then since, she was still a police officer.

As for the men, I suppose in the late 1960s, Derrik was a bit sad. After Norma moved out, he suffered from an empty nest though he was very proud of Norma's accomplishments. Jeffery began seeing women again, but he still grieved for his wife and child. Xiao was in torpor when Tabitha came. Courtney, though not a man, but presents as male, is reserved, but they are hardly brooding. Charles and his progeny tend to joke constantly, and they have a dry gallows humor common in former soldiers.

But hindsight being what it is, I understand Tabitha came to the coven because of her strong sexual attraction to the late actor, Christopher Lee. He stared in many Dracula films which she had seen as an adolescent girl.

Unfortunately for her, no vampire, in reality, can be nearly that fantastic. When she came here, she saw what she wanted to see. But I do not blame her because we all do that.

Her parents tried to talk her out of such a commitment to the coven. Though they called us a vampire cult, they were happy the initiation program kept her close by in Seattle. And before I go on, I will say, a diligent daughter, Tabitha visited her parents weekly and considered their well-being and comfort until her father's death, after which she moved her mother into the coven and cared for her most attentively until her mother, too left the Earthly plane. I can see why they wanted their daughter around.

But let's get back to Tabitha's initiation. Her time frame was four years, a bit longer than common, due to her age. Still, she was focused and studious during the program.

Tabitha and Mei Yeong became friends quickly. Their shared love of fashion and dressmaking became a successful early business, and they hoped to expand into menswear after Tabitha's transformation.

Tabitha could complete her cosmetic and grooming routines without a reflection. Yet she wasn't ready to be without a reflection. Some call this vanity or conceit, but that is untrue. She simply was pleased with what she saw in the mirror.

Tabitha was transformed in Winter of 1971. As a non-practicing Christian, she was comfortable accepting our prayers though she felt no need to lead one. I said a prayer for her. She held my hand and accepted my embrace and the embrace of her future brothers, siblings, and sisters.

The transformation itself went well.

After her transformation, Tabitha seemed a bit withdrawn, but she appeared at work and ate well at the party.

Then Mei Yeong told us Tabitha seemed distracted.

At first, we thought it was bloodlust, but she barely ate. That worried us. But Tabitha said nothing was wrong. We did not know she was studying photos of herself when alone. And we did not know the idea of no more photos frightened her.

One night, she pulled a new dress off the rack and tried it on, then stared at her empty gown reflected in the mirror.

Mei Yeong asked what she was doing.

"Am I empty?"

"Of course not!" Mei Yeong replied. "Changing into a vampire is huge, yet it never holds to one's expectations." Mei Young said, trying to encourage her sibling.

Tabitha nodded and apparently went to work, but she did not break for lunch. At the end of the night, she told Mei Yeong she needed a bit of time off. Remembering poor Walter again, I grew a little worried. I feared calling Tabitha's mother if Tabitha failed to thrive.

That morning, Tabitha returned to her apartment and changed into a pretty red dinner gown, and brushed her long hair in front of the mirror though she could not see herself or her hair.

I checked on her. For three days, I watched her grow slack with her thirst as she stood in front of her mirror, staring at the gown she was wearing. She cut open her wrists to see if she could see her own blood falling from her body. Of course, she couldn't.

When I discovered this and told Agata, who brought Tabitha a cup of her blood.

Tabitha's bloodshot eyes followed the reflection of

Agata's skirts and a cup of blood that was reflected in the mirror.

As Agata grew close, Tabitha leapt on her.

A vampire as young as Tabitha was no match for a vampire of five centuries. Agata batted her to the floor.

Agata explained she could give Tabitha final death if she wished it, or she could accept her bloodline progenitor's blood and exist forever.

As Tabitha was not suicidal or failing to thrive, she accepted the cup of blood without complaint or quarrel.

She explained something was wrong. No. Everything was wrong. There were too many people around the coven. So many heartbeats echoed around her. It took all her will not to reach out to someone and maybe hurt them. Moreover, though Tabitha could no longer see herself, she felt everyone was watching her. Maybe, everyone was laughing at her. That she was a fool to think she could be as fantastical as her version of Dracula, or rather I should say Christopher Lee's version of Dracula.

We explained no one was laughing at her. Everyone's transformation was difficult.

She explained how she didn't know who she was anymore.

"You are a talented fashion designer and fabric artist," Agata said. "These feelings are natural. We all went through this."

Tabitha cried and explained her bloodlust. "None of the stories about William stops the yearning to reach out and grab a human and expand my fangs into their throat. I don't know how I am going to be safe around an enthralled human."

"It is natural in the beginning to feel the bloodlust—especially when you are not consuming enough." And Agata gave her another pint of blood.

An Ill-Advised Trip to the Mountain

Tabitha left the coven the next night. I will repeat: never do this. Tabitha only survived because she is a vampire. She was not an experienced outdoorswoman but had many friends who climbed mountains. She had heard stories that mountain climbing gave purpose and clarity. So she drove south to Mount Rainer.

Not wanting to check in with the ranger station, she parked her car along the state highway and wandered through the forest. She pushed away boughs of evergreen trees and ferns until she found a trail. She could sometimes see the peak of the mountain but mostly hoped she was going in the right direction.

She had a slight shadow by the light of the moon. That at least gave her comfort that she existed.

She passed a creek and tried to see her reflection in the water, but all she could see was the rocky creek bed.

Tabitha climbed higher in the darkness. Her fur jacket protected her arms, but it was not made for mountain climbing.

The first patches of icy snow crunched underneath her feet. Patches became fields of snow. The snow obscured any landmarks, but at each clearing, she looked to the stars to find directions. Unfortunately, she could not read the stars.

The snow grew deeper. After the first time she sunk knee-deep, she picked up a large stick and pushed it into the snow to ensure she did not fall through. The night air sparkled with icy molecules which were blown off glaciers and yearly snow. The cold stung her skin.

Her eyelashes froze. The lengths of her blonde curls froze. Her once pretty dress became bloody tatters. Her fingertips turned blue, then burned from frostbite. Her toes turned black after her shoes cracked open and were eventually discarded.

She crossed a slope and found the lowest glacier. She would tell us later how from Seattle, Mount Ranier looked pristine, but the lower glaciers looked dirty up close. It is covered in rocks and dirt. It is still beautiful but quite different than what she expected.

Though she hoped to find some clarity, she felt nothing as she stepped upon the giant piece of ice which moaned under every footfall.

Even a vampire, even one as young as Tabitha, is quite a bit faster than a human. Tabitha knew that she had hiked for a long time but had no idea how far she had gone.

She still hungered for clarity.

The snow hid that the glacier was pockmarked with fissures and cracks, some small enough to catch an ankle, others large enough she might fall into. She had a passing thought she might become an abdominal snow woman.

Under the pre-dawn darkness, she watched the

world come alive. Marmots chirped. Deer walked with their young. Higher on the mountain, a bear wandered among the snow, seeking food. The idea of food made her stomach growl. She thought she might find a deer. Maybe just a mouse. Maybe nothing.

She wasn't hungry for food, but she hungered for clarity so she kept hiking until the sun began to rise.

She found a rock shelter and waited for night to come again. Under the shade of the deep rock, she asked the mountain to tell her, Who am I?

She did not find clarity. She only shivered from cold though out the day. She left her shelter early as there was thick cloud cover. She tried to remain close to trees, but they disappeared, and she found an icy-covered lake.

Near the lake was a small building. Curiosity driving her, she approached. Even before she arrived, she could smell it was an outhouse.

She peeked inside and found a hole with a wooden seat. How was she going to find meaning in such a place?

Why a mountain had more meaning than Seattle, itself.

She walked to the lake and looked through the ice.

That's when she heard human voices.

A small group of snowshoers hurried across the lake down the side of the mountain. She heard their fast, nervous heartbeats. She knew if she pounced on the last one, she might kill him. Yet, though she was famished, she did not feel like killing. She had no need to kill. She could get vampire or human blood back at the coven. And if she completely lost her way, she could always find carrion.

Though she had not gained clarity, she thought she might find understanding in the humans' love of the mountain. She decided to stalk the hikers' footsteps so they would lead her somewhere. She followed.

To be clear, they were not afraid of her. They did not even know she was there, or at least that's how they acted. They were afraid of something, however.

They feared the large dark cloud sliding across the peak. That cloud brought more snow.

Other than stopping for sips of water and checking their compass, the snowshoers moved fast.

Though her feet were in stinging agony, she easily kept up.

They led down to a visitor's center. Now we think she may have been at Paradise, but it is possible she may have wandered all the way to Sunrise. Honestly, we just don't know, and neither does she.

Tabitha was careful not to be seen as her presence and lack of hiking clothing would not make sense and would most likely cause a scene. Perhaps, someone might even call the authorities.

So she remained close to trees and watched the people. Mostly men milled about, but there were a few women and children in the Lodge. Someone set down a mug of bullion on a picnic table.

She lopped over to it and went back to hiding. She gulped it fast as she could and felt her cracked lips burn. She didn't know exactly where her car was compared to where she was, but she followed the road back to the highway until she found her car. That took her at least two nights. When she found her car, she slept for an hour.

Driving back was torture on her broken feet and hands, but she made it before another sunrise.

She looked horrible when she reentered the coven. Two enthralled humans, Aldo, who was an old man at that point nearing seventy, and Bernie, who was a young man at that point, saw her pulled up.

Tabitha was barely able to walk, but she declined their assistance. She asked them not to call Agata or me.

Bernie simply agreed with Tabitha and bowed at her, but Aldo was too old to listen to a young vampire, especially since he had served four different vampires.

Though he agreed not to call me, he called Derrik and Norma on the excuse that Tabitha might need legal assistance, and there might be a mess somewhere.

Aldo and Bernie washed and detailed the car.

Derrik, who, of course, was in the coven, easily caught up to Tabitha since she was moving so slowly. At first, she declined his assistance. As her feet were quite a mess, he offered to carry her up the stairs.

Tabitha admitted she did not want to face her apartment, so Derrik invited her to his home. Some people gossiped that they had a short love affair.

While Tabitha confessed she was attracted by his gentlemanly and brooding behavior, Derrik is not the type of person to seduce anyone who obviously needs medical attention.

Obviously, I don't know exactly what they spoke about behind closed doors, but Tabitha said, inside his apartment, he offered his blood, but there were no romantic intentions.

In fact, he tried to assure her by telling her how he gave his blood to Norma when she was an injured girl. Even less romantically, he talked about how much he missed his progeny since she moved out of the coven.

Trying to change the subject, Tabitha made the mistake of telling him his matchstick models were beautiful. His sadness disappeared as he excitedly told her how he painstakingly built them primarily in a 20-foot to 1-inch scale, though for the newer skyscrapers, he might go even smaller. He showed her his favorite types of glue and tools.

Then Norma arrived with a First Aid Kit and everything to make hot chocolate and marshmallows. So I believe Tabitha when she said nothing romantic happened.

Some say this trouble was caused by her vanity, but it was not.

It was the feeling of a door closing. Tabitha suffered from a mix of a false dilemma fallacy and impostor syndrome.

Tabitha was beautiful forever, but suddenly, she realized she could no longer work as a model. This was how she had met people, how she had an income until she became a vampire. Now she now not only was she a vampire, but she had a business to run with Mei Yeong. She suddenly worried that she wasn't a good enough fashion designer. Moreover, she worried about her partnership. She feared she might let Mei Yeong down, or maybe they would have a falling out. This is why Tabitha sought clarity.

Humans, Vampires, and Werewolves, all experience this during our existence. To claim it was just vanity does not get at the heart of the issue.

A week later, Tabitha was back at work. She was drinking the blood of Agata plus Aldo's blood of an enthralled human under supervision since she wasn't sure about that yet.

I thanked Derrik. He just shrugged. "I told her well-made clothing makes people happy."

And, of course, he's right about that.

A WORD FROM OUR SPONSOR
Photos Evermore

Are you an initiate concerned that a creature of darkness is unable to reflect light and therefore unable to be caught on film and digital photography?

Photos Evermore records your photograph for posterity, future documentation, and identification. We even can future-proof your social media with a hundred glamorous selfie-style photographs, which we can Photoshop into your future vacation, dog park, or dining pics! Affordable packages based on your needs.

Jingle: *Before you stop reflecting light forever, think Photos Evermore!*

Visit us on our website to schedule an appointment tonight!

INITIATE QUESTIONS

INITIATE FERN: LADY LORETTA, WHY HAVE YOU TOLD US SEVERAL CREATION STORIES WHERE THE VAMPIRES SUDDENLY REALIZE WHAT THEY'VE DONE. ARE YOU TRYING TO SCARE US AWAY FROM TRANSFORMATION?

No. Transformation is a personal choice.

My goal is only to show how some experiences trip up young vampires. You must be ready to experience everything: the bloodlust, loss of reflection, the need for ambitions and purpose. The need for change and changing technology.

Especially now that Seattle's population has exploded. Tabitha was able to accomplish getting on and off the mountain and remain unseen because the population was what it was. Then quickly through the rural areas of Tacoma, SeaTac, Federal Way, and Tukwila and back home due to the lack of traffic in the area in 1971.

That is why I warn you.

Now, if you need to do something like go to Mount Rainier, you must be aware that people will be around.

If Tabitha had gone to the mountain nowadays, she might have been seen. Or even gotten a parking ticket, or her car may have been towed by leaving it on the highway.

Though there are parts of King and Pierce Counties that are still rural, we are not rural counties but a major metropolitan area. That is why I warn you.

Now I'm going to keep this next question anonymous because I don't want Tabitha to feel anyone is judging her.

LADY LORETTA, THERE SEEM TO BE MANY SIDE EFFECTS TO BECOMING A VAMPIRE, BUT THE LOSS OF A REFLECTION SEEMS TO BE A SMALL ONE. HOW CAN THIS UPSET ANYONE?

My answer is this: There are many aspects to becoming a vampire, which are just different than when we are human. Though all initiates are taught to do their grooming without a mirror, that doesn't prevent the shock of seeing oneself walk past a shop window without a reflection. That does not prepare you for taking your first selfie and discovering you are not in it.

Any of these side effects which I have talked about can shock a vampire. Whether it is big or small, it doesn't matter. It matters to the person who is shocked. Be honest now, how often do you take a selfie? How often do you glance at your reflection? Different side effects will affect different people differently. It is not for us to judge. The goal is to let you know these things happen. If you are lucky, your transformation will be an easy one, but there is no guarantee of which side effects will affect you and which won't. I can only tell you these things happen.

Good day, Beloved Initiates, and Sleep the Sleep of the Dead.

Interspecies Kin

INTRODUCTION

Beloved Initiates,

Forgive me the reprieve from recording, but the Paper Flower Consortium is mostly fixed from the flood damage! Our home is complete, baseboards and all, though a few apartments must still be finished. It is such a relief.

Tonight I am going to speak on Interspecies Relationships. Due to the huge amount of what is now called "shifter fiction," this question has begun to pop up more and more. *Can Werewolves and Vampires have love affairs, and more importantly, can they live happily ever after?*

My beloveds, vampires do not live. We are dead. But yes, our existence can be happy. Interspecies relationships can be complicated, but they too can be happy. However, a warning: no relationship with a living being, and some of the undead, lasts forever.

However, before I go on, I would first ask you, dear initiates, If you are still a human and want to be with a werewolf, why are you seeking an existence in a vampire coven?

Why don't you join a werewolf congregation?

Our friends at the Howling Moon have openings in their HOA too. They have a Winter Fellowship and Summer BBQ, which are open to the public and offer an orientation to their initiation program. Like ours, it is three years and discusses in depth the pros and cons of transformation.

There are fictional accounts about how vampires and werewolves were sworn enemies and engaged in open or hidden hostilities. Maybe some groups in some parts of Europe may have competed for land or resources, but that hardly means all vampires and werewolves are enemies.

All the werewolves I have met have just lovely people.

Obviously, as a librarian, my experience with groups outside the coven is limited, but my husband has an inn, and my brother-in-law has had werewolf clients. My sister has acted as an official witness in her capacity as coven liaison. My daughters' company MYT Clothier has a whole line of clothing made specifically for shifting species and extra-large monster sizes. And Norma has always had friends and clients of all species.

The other more insidious fictional stereotypes about Dominant/submissive fantasies are not real life. Werewolf females have complete freedom of their person and wealth. Men do not call women the B-word unless they are jerks. In heterosexual relationships, but most women don't want a "bad boy" we want men who respect us and help raise children if that blessing is in our future. The words Alpha, beta, and omega don't exist in their lives, though they might have fun with such things from time to time behind closed doors. However, the very idea of it is based on faulty science, which has been debunked multiple times.

Here are some generalizations that I have found to be true. Werewolves are wonderful parents and have close family relations. They raise their children with gentleness and kindness and do not glorify violence. Indeed, this is why Derrik contacted them for assistance when Norma was a struggling teenager. For those I know to speak to, I've found most to be quite houseproud. Their homes and gardens are simply lovely, and their community property is well kept. Their motorcycle club also seems to be quite motorcycleproud. Their quilting club seems to be quite quiltproud. My darling Charles purchased the most amazing quilt for our coffin when they had a convention at the Night Owl. I am sure you understand. They are simply people, just like vampires, with a virus that at times is inconvenient but also provides a certain set of gifts.

But let us say you are a vampire, and you meet a werewolf and fall in love. Well, my beloveds, that very thing has happened to one of our allies. Unfortunately for those involved, it happened in a time and place before condoms were readily available. We will return to France in the fourteenth century.

Now France during this time period had some attitudes that we do not share now, especially that a woman's worth had to do with her ability to bear children. Some listeners may find this offensive, and so you should.

You may remember our friend Marcus had

transformed the sweet sister of mercy, Sophie, into a vampire, and Sophie turned her charges suffering from the plague into vampires. For much of their early existence, Sophie and her offspring survived as a wandering horde, feeding off unfortunate humans or dying animals. It was the Good Sister Sophie who told Agata this story of her ill-fated Fifthborn, Amice.

Before I continue, I will remind you, my beloveds, that Sophie transformed all her charges from the hospital. Back in the 14th century, there were guidelines in the official vampire communities, but there were no laws or even a council, so though child vampires were frowned on, they were not illegal. Some failed to thrive. Others joined her in death. And dear ones, know that young vampires meet their end in this telling.

WAITING FOR TRUE LOVE

Amice was a girl of sixteen who was sent to the hospital to die by her parents when they found the tale-tell black tumors. Sophie believes Amice was most likely from a merchant family. She could read and came with funds both for a bed at the hospital and to pay a priest to bless her into heaven. However, Amice never spoke about her human family. She rarely spoke about anything. She was very shy. She was gentle with the younger children. Sophie's Firstborn, David, and Amise were friends

People of this age do not understand the unending cold and darkness of the night and the harshness of day. The horde did not have coffins. They found grottos or dug holes and slept in the earth of France. To keep themselves comfortable, some vampires coupled up in love or lust and held each other in the cold ground. Amise did not -- though she, at times, tried to protect the younger children from the coldest winter days. In those early years, several child vampires stopped existing. They would wake frozen and hungry, unable or unwilling to move during the night. The horde was too hungry and weak to care for them. Dawn would come. Sophie burned with her offspring. No amount of prayer could save her from it. But David and Amise did their best to comfort her.

Sophie told us each morning before Amise covered herself with the earth of France, she prayed for true love to find her. After a time, David asked her to be his, but she refused. His form was but thirteen. The others pestered her and told her it was wrong to deny David, but she still refused. She was waiting for true love.

Sophie told her horde to let the girl be, so they did.

And so it was, one night, the horde came across three men at arms who protected a group of pilgrims. The horde thought to pick off the elderly, but Amise kept her eyes on the youngest gendarme. Sophie believes he was seventeen or eighteen. I am told he was quite dashing with a thick mane of brown hair.

Of course, the men at arms heard the horde in the darkness. They fed their fires and encircled their charges. They put their swords outward looking for danger.

With only fingernails, teeth, and sticks for weaponry, the horde sought easier prey. Amise was smitten by the lad. She said goodbye to Sophie and David to await the dawn.

The men at arms moved their charges during the day. Amise tracked them at night. For weeks, Amise buried herself at the previous camp and practiced what she might say to the lad if they chanced to speak. She feared approaching too close.

One night she heard his name was Timeo. She learned he had a father, mother, brother, and sister at home. The leader of the men at arms was his uncle, Theo. The other was a family friend.

Yet this information did not help her in the wooing of Timeo.

On the day before the first full moon, the men at arms did not move the camp. Instead, they hobbled the horses and undressed to prepare to change into their wolf form. They raced through the night and began their transformation. At first, Amise feared their claws and snapping teeth. The elder vampires and humans before them had sometimes told stories of wild beastmen, but Amise felt she was beastwoman. So she waited in the shadows for Timeo to return to human form.

But as a wolf, he had a wonderful sense of smell and found her.

At first, he growled as she was close to their camp.

"Timeo," She said and stepped toward him shyly. "I am a woman alone. A French Woman."

Timeo growled something and hid behind a tree as he was naked.

"You're alone?"

"I left my kin," she said. "Where are you going on your pilgrimage?"

"To Jerusalem."

"Will you take me there?"

"You're a vampire. Set apart from God," he said.

"My people claim we are closer to God," Amise said. "And say your kind is set apart from God."

"I am a son of the crown and a man of God," he said. "You won't seduce me, Vampire."

"You wouldn't have stirred my heart if you were not," she said.

Timeo was not sure what to do, so he stood behind the tree, grumbling for a time. Eventually, he said, "Well, I suppose if you really have no protector, you should go to the fire, but give me a few minutes, I'll tell them you are coming." And lopped away and covered himself with a tunic and cloak.

His uncle, Theo, was not pleased, but Amise was an educated woman alone. She asked out their pilgrimage and did not act in any way unbecoming.

Theo had her look at his crucifix. She did not burn. She held it. She knew the Lord's Prayer. She was gentle with the elderly and children in the group. So Theo agreed, she might stay.

For a month, they remained apart. The werewolves moved in the day, every night Amise followed and came to their fire. She quoted the Bible and Anne of France's Instruction for my Daughter with ease.

One night, she told Theo she loved Timeo. Fate brought them together and she wanted to marry him.

"Werewolves and vampires cannot be together," Theo warned them. "Amise cannot bare children. Her womb is dead."

This of course is true, but as you already must have realized, the young lovers succumbed to their youthful lust and growing love.

Theo was angry with them both, but to keep Timeo on the right side of the law, he gave his blessing for them to marry. Timeo and Amise traveled as husband and wife. He protected her from the sun, and she protected the party in the darkness, always taking her turn at guard. Obviously, Amise could not bare Timeo children to their grief, but they grew closer to each other in their sorrow.

After the pilgrimage, they returned to France. Timeo's family refused a vampire wife. He took work as a night magistrate. A decade passed. The young gendarme became a man in his prime. They existed happily even as the hair about his temple turned gray.

However, their neighbors took notice that the beautiful Amise had not changed. And washerwomen sometimes saw black puss staining her clothing. Of course, she never allowed the sun to hit her flesh. Whispers of witchcraft followed them. Before the whispers became hysteria or violence, they returned to Timeo's parents.

Though unhappy with the situation, his father and mother welcomed the couple. Their anger had softened in the time Timeo was away. Because a mortal's time is short and Timeo's mother was dying, she especially wanted Timeo and Amise to exist in felicity.

Later his father died, but Theo was still part of the village so the two remained. And death came for Theo. Though they mourned him, Amise and Timeo still lived with the werewolves quite happily.

However, in a short blink of existence, our brave and dashing Timeo became an old man. Sweet Amise still loved him and cared for him in his dotage, yet as his powers decreased, they became more erratic. He no longer could run in the light of the full moon. He needed to run every night. He could no longer control his turning. In the end, he grew forgetful and at times, forgot her name. She stopped loving him as a man and began to love him as one might love an old faithful pet, yet she still cared for him until the day he died.

That's when the screaming started. You see, beloveds, Timeo awoke during the day, and he awoke hungry.

The screaming brought the other werewolves to their cottage. And with fire, the werewolves drove Amise and Timeo out of their village and into the forest. Several times that day, he shifted halfway, his bones cracked and popped. Hair spouted on his face, and his skin twisted and tore only to heal again.

Their flesh burning, Amise carried him until they found themselves deep in the wood. Amise set Timeo down on the mossy ground and dug a large hole. She buried them in it.

In the night, Amise sought food, but only came across mice. Still she forced them down her husband's throat. Then she buried them both before the dawn came.

However, during the day, he clawed his way to the surface of the earth, breathing deep and burning his flesh. He would turn to an animal, to a demented man. He would forget her all over again.

And the cruelty of a vampire's existence is we burn with our offspring. All Amise could do was drag him back under the earth to ease their pain. This means Sister Sophie felt the rebirth of Timeo and the flames and agony of her two progeny. She sent her most powerful clairvoyant to find his sister, but the man did not easily find them through the bloodline's torment.

Later, in the deepness of night, Timeo returned and begged his wife: "Stop this pain, Amise, Kill me. Let it end. Why did you do this to me?"

"I don't know how this happened, but I will fix it."

She buried him a final time.

In the dead of night, she wandered until she found a church surrounding a village. She stole what she needed: a silver crucifix, copper ring, a clay pot to act as a crucible, and a firepot primarily for speed.

She built a fire in the firepot and stoked the embers until they were flames. She set the clay pot over the flame. And within, she set the silver crucifix and copper ring inside. The metals melted and bubbled.

She uncovered Timeo from his grave.

As dawn crested the horizon, she poured half of the molten metal into Timeo's open mouth. His lips blistered from the heat, and he screamed until he could scream no longer.

Amise screamed with him.

Through the agony, she drank her own draught of melted silver and copper. Neither could not breathe and both felt the pain of suffocation. Their lips burnt and throats scorched and filled with metal, they lay in a grassy field as the sun rose.

When the horde finally found them, Amise was still broken and blistered flesh, her beloved Timeo was nothing more than ash. David called to her from the shadows, she refused to budge to save herself.

David was close enough to dash into the sun and pull her back into darkness, though it was an ill attempt and just delayed the inevitable.

Sophie peeled the metal from Amise's face. She chipped it off her tongue and pulled out the slag which was caught in her throat. Amise began to heal in the cold earth of France.

When able to speak, Amise explained everything to Sophie and claimed she would be rejoined with Timeo in heaven or hell. It didn't matter to her. Sophie tried to bind her and David set a guard.

David asked her if it had all been worth it, just to suffer now.

Amise said it was.

On the first day in the earth without bond, Amise climbed to the surface and set herself ablaze.

Sophie burned for the next day and vomited blood in the night due to the pain. Amise's ashes were collected and burnt seven more times that night. At the next dawn scattered into the wind.

The moral of this tragedy is not werewolves and vampires cannot co-mingle. Vampires and werewolves can have a close kinship. They can even be lovers if they are consistent about condom use and caps their fangs with a mouth guard or other methods to control saliva and blood transfer.

If you chose to have a relationship with a werewolf, you must always be a careful and considerate lover not to spread the virus to each other because death will come for the werewolf, human, or any living species you chose to love.

And if you love your partner, you will care for them and let them die.

Obviously, we don't know all such things they did in the decades they were married. Amise and Timeo's exchanges were most likely that of bodily fluids in the acts of love.

Remember, the vampire virus does not kill you. It brings you back. You can live on for many years. Our friend Laurence died years after he contracted the virus. Our Lady Agata was strangled by a priest. Timeo died an old man, unable to control his transformation. He came back as an old man, unable to control his transformation.

If you have questions about safe sex between species, please discuss it with Agata in the clinic.

A word from our sponsor:

Sirens of Salish Sea

Ladies, Honored Individuals, and Gentlemen Vampires, You may be forever the age you were at your turning, but that is no reason to neglect your skincare routine.

To help you look and smell your best in eternity, Sirens of Salish Sea produce perfumed skin-nourishing soaps and lotions using all-natural sea salt, non-invasive species of kelp, cedar, berries, and grasses held together in delightful amalgamations of discarded sea serpent scales and the blood of careless sailors which are collected, manufactured, and bottled from our own local sea and shorelines.

Our main store is still open every day, and satellite store in the Paper Flower Consortium, Suite East B, is run by vampire staff and open every night from 9 pm to 6 am. Come on by!

INITIATE QUESTIONS

INITIATE FERN: SO TIMEO TRANSFORMED WHEN HE WAS A OLD MAN, BUT WHAT HAPPENS IF A YOUNG WEREWOLF WANTS TO TRANSFORM INTO A VAMPIRE?

We do not know what would happen and currently, it is illegal to knowingly transform a werewolf into a vampire and vis versa.

Though there are fictionalized accounts of werewolf/ vampire hybrids, we have never met one.

It may be that we are undead that their virus cannot be transformed into us, or perhaps it can be. I am assuming their lives would go on just as our lives go on. Basically, I'm saying they'd be nothing special. They'd still have to do their dishes and pay their taxes.

INITIATE LYNN: LADY LORETTA SO ARE YOU AGAINST SHIFTER FICTION?

Not at all. People enjoy these books for fantasy fulfillment. Not reality. So as long as you comprehend it is just a fantasy, I don't see the problem with it. Plenty of people enjoy such things.

But becoming a vampire is a serious matter. And the idea you would become a vampire or a werewolf or anything due to some expected romantic entanglement is not a good idea.

INITIATE TROY: THIS IS A TERRIBLE STORY. WHY DID AMISE KILL HERSELF FOR LOVE?

Initiates, I warned you this would be a tragedy. Amise might have killed herself for love, but I would also say she killed herself because she could not see beyond the time that her existence would be one where her nights and days were dark and alone. She did not want to be part of the wandering horde again, always hungry, always cold.

She had Timeo's love, yes, but she also had the protection of love. A warm, comfortable home with someone who truly loved her in return.

It is a great privilege that you were born to a century with cheap heat and light. Unless you have suffered homelessness, you cannot understand Amise.

Good Day Beloved Initiates and Sleep the Sleep of the Dead.

INTRODUCTION

Welcome back, Beloved Initiates,

You are here because you wish to be a vampire. Most of you wish to be a vampire because of eternal existence, at an adult age in which you are fairly healthy and strong. Some of you are not healthy and strong and wish to know a vampire's strength. That is understandable.

We will discuss an incredibly hard topic: the importance of forgiveness between vampires.

This is a difficult topic because not all vampires have acted in moral ways. And certainly, we have acted in ways that we know now are hurtful.

The current generation has a term for this. It's called being "woke," and its meaning is something a vampire experiences after their first human life. We awaken to the possibility that our actions have hurt people. This is one of the reasons it is important for a vampire to be humble.

Generations change. A word that once meant

the best of humanity becomes the worst or at least old-fashioned.

If one wants to experience eternal existence: forgiveness of one's self, one's former culture, and even one's enemies becomes important. Humans and young vampires might not understand this because they hadn't seen centuries.

You are not perfect. You will not be perfect. You will not always choose the correct side. There will be personal grievances and offenses between you and your coven siblings. Our coven and others.

Some will be simple misunderstandings. I pray that is the case for all of you. However, you may claim your current goodness to Heaven or where ever you believe your God dwells, but before this time of peace, vampires knew all types of human cruelties. Many of us, especially the ancients, indulged in them at one point or another.

And a warning, my beloveds, you will painfully learn about the holes in your knowledge. One day that knowledge will be before you. You can accept it and change or stew in your prejudices for eternity. Buried in your wickedness, no other vampire offers you friendship. And you will be alone.

If you believe you are one of the chosen wise, ask yourself this question: who decided the age of adulthood and marriage/sexual relationships? In western cultures alone, this has changed throughout the centuries it has been dependent upon socioeconomic and gender.

In vampire society, the age of consent to vampirism is twenty-five. Though initiates and enthralled humans may come to the coven younger, they find most vampires after their first century won't have sexual relations with a person younger than twenty-five – even though that is not the law.

Now overwhelmingly, in American Culture, we claim the age of eighteen is the age of adulthood? But why? We know the average age of first teenage sexual activities happens younger.

I believe because I lived through this change before, society chose 18, primarily it is because it is when the end of mandatory schooling. It is the age when people are allowed into the military. It is the age when people are allowed to vote. I believe this because I existed in a time when boys went to war at age thirteen, and though they were not often married until much later, they might be.

To be clear: the elder vampires and I are happy we no longer send boys to war as children. We no longer marry children off to protect a family's land and titles. We are happy we existed to see slavery abolished. We are happy to see women have rights that they did not have when we were human girls.

We hope the world will continue to move forward to destroy the horrors that humanity, vampires, and all other sentient beings have wrought or been party to.

If you cannot imagine how disconcerting this is, consider how strange it is for someone to have lived when the age of marriage was younger. Agata and Jakub married when Agata was 15 and Jakub was 20. Agata and Jakub married their elder human daughter to a spice merchant when the girl was also 15 and the boy was 18. Their son married at 17 to a girl who was 16. This was common and considered good for society.

Now Agata and Jakub are not ashamed of their marriage or that they were married to secure a silver contract for their fathers. The fact is, the relationship which defined marriage five hundred years ago is not the relationship that defines marriage now. It was closer to a business relationship rather than a romance. Agata thought her soldier husband was dashing, but it didn't matter if he wasn't. Jakub thought his bride was thrifty and had good sense. These attributes were much more important than love when they were married in the late 15th century. Love, respect, and trust grew between them. Agata helped her father negotiate the terms, which included their own house and a small herd of cows to ensure that their children had an inheritance as Jakub was the younger son.

To make things even clearer how things change: Jakub thought he was being true to Agata as he only had sex with the officers' laundress or other men while at war.

The officer's laundress would be a questionable relationship today, but he believes he was offering her an opportunity for greater comforts and protection than she had with anyone else. She also had relations with several other officers. When she became pregnant, the old term "Son of a Gun" was applicable though this was before the widespread use of guns. I suppose a better term would be "Son of a Sword."

Regardless, Jakub paid for the midwife and child's apprenticeship—though there was no guarantee he fathered the child. It was irrelevant. He was the commanding officer and a nobleman. His duty was to ensure the laundress's care. At the time, there was nothing untoward about it.

Do you judge something that happened 500 years ago? Initiates might. But then you exist for a century or two, and some of the things which you have done will be, at best, obsolete.

Now, what about the atrocities?

So here we are and we must ask a question that people do not want to be asked. How long did it take Agata to forgive the man who threatened to rape her, who attempted to bring her to final death?

In the same vein, how long does it take Gaius to forgive the woman who killed his closest companion and helped his concubines usurp his lands and title?

It took Gaius and Agata approximately two centuries to forgive each other for the crimes which they committed against each other. I cannot speak for Gaius, but he claims he has always had respect for Agata since she bested him twice.

But I can speak for Agata because I have her words.

Agata hated him. And she hated that Jakub didn't. That Jakub's honor was assuaged and had forgiven him after he put a sword through his chest as an atrocities of war. As another soldier, Jakub had to forgive him.

For two centuries, it didn't matter. Gaius was in Prussia. Agata and Jakub were in France.

In the seventeenth century, we had an idiom about how adversity makes strange bedfellows? I am not sure if you still say that, but hopefully, you understand the truth of Gaius and Agata's relationship. Agata never wanted to forgive Gaius. Agata did not forgive in the way people sometimes mean it.

She does not forget, but she saw the wisdom in our current association with him. And that is why she has been our leader for so many centuries. She rarely deals directly with Gaius, but she has pushed her pain and loathing deep into herself, so Jakub may deal directly with Gaius.

VERSAILLES, 1687

For those who are unaware, Charles was captured in the Franco-Dutch war. His gentle birth and training meant he was taken as a prisoner of war rather than killed on sight. He was taken to a POW camp run by Gaius and his current Firstborn, Gunter Bach.

Charles hated them. But they did bring him back to France because Gaius had something he needed to negotiate with Louis the XIV. Moreover, Gaius sought out Agata and Jakub.

Even though it smelled to high heaven and was noisy, Versailles was so beautiful. In the beauty, it was easy to forgive the dirty poverty of Paris. One might think I would be safe surrounded by the soldiers of Versailles, but in truth, there were many temptations to a maiden. The days which held the most dangers was when the King when hunting.

I was sitting among the fountain of Apollo when a man I did not know approached me. This fountain was one of my favorite places to read. The statue is of a golden god burst forth from the water in anticipation of his daily flight above the earth. And looking at the statue, it might make you feel like you might fly.

I was charmed by his smooth tongue as he told me that I looked as beautiful as sunlight. However, then he dared touch me though we had never been formally introduced. I knew he was an impostor. Or he was a man who may have been of gentle birth but thought I was for him. Many men did assume that in those days.

I backed away from the man and excused myself with a curtsy and the excuse, I must meet with my father for dinner. He loomed over me. His gentle words of love became whispers of a different type. Though I was still a maiden, I wasn't shocked. I did not know what the end result this man thought he would get from me, but it wasn't of the pleasant sort.

I hurried towards the north wing of the castle, where my family slept. Fear quickened my steps. The gravel path seemed longer than before. I looked for another woman, for a group of people who might offer some protection, but there was no one who was an ally. I think I remember people laughing at my distress. I didn't dare scream or cry out because that simply was not done.

I was closer to the castle's main wing, but I only knew a few people there and no one who I felt I could ask for help. While it felt like I was chased for hours, I am sure it was simply minutes that passed. Times slows when one is frightened.

I had met Charles, and certainly, I liked him, but this was before Charles had asked Jakub if he might court me. The idea I would throw myself at him was simply not something a lady of the Court would do. And Agata hated

Gaius. I did not trust him.

I felt I had to keep moving. If I stopped this man would be upon me. Somehow I got lost in the garden, and before was a dark and horrid grove. The King, for all his foibles, was gallant towards women, and if I fell upon his hunting party, I would be under his protection.

Branches and underbrush grew thicker, reaching out and pulling on my heavy skirts. I could barely see a few feet ahead. I sensed the darkness closing in. Sweat and facepaint stung my eyes. It was impossible to know what could be waiting.

I realized this man might be driving me toward something. I sensed something undead. I smelled tobacco and hoping I had found one of the King's men, I hurried that way.

For a moment, I thought what I saw might not be real. Indeed for a moment, I believed I saw Apollo in the flesh smoking a cigar and with him a black horse with glowing eyes and fangs.

Knees trembling, I clung to a tree.

Gunter looked as if he wanted to consume me. He was a vampire of that century and never trained to control his bloodlust, yet he made no move against me. He smiled at me, his fangs exposed. "Charles wasn't lying."

I had no idea what that meant. "My father will be looking for me..."

Gunter patted the giant's horse, bowed at me and Nix dropped his head. Then slowly approached my pursuer.

"And my father told me to watch over you. Come, Lady Loretta. You should not see this. On my word as a vampire and my hope that Charles will join our people, I will allow no harm to come to you."

The lech screamed as Nix ripped into his throat. He screamed for a long time, because Nix likes his food warm and alive.

I was frightened, but Gunter just brought me to Gaius.

The apartment was on a grand scale unlike our tiny one in the Northwing. Gaius's Roman attitudes were hidden under the most gentile of Prussian attitudes, but I sensed something older in him. His French was not good, but Charles translated. At any rate, he fed me a fine dinner, as Charles also needed to eat human food. Gaius tried to push sweets upon me because, as he claimed, I was still so young. Then he said I might pet Nix if I wished.

Deep in my heart, part of me wondered if this was staged for Agata and Jakub's benefit, and certainly, they considered the same as they entered the fine apartment with Pascaline.

We cannot know. Gaius always does what he thinks is right. In any case, Charles was innocent of such knowledge. Gunter told me only that Gaius tells him what he needs to know and little else.

What we do know is Gaius needed Jakub as another general to lead undead troops into battle several times over the next century. He needed Pascaline's beauty and viciousness. He used them both. Right or wrong, France and her allies depended on Gaius. And we depended upon France. This association also gave us the information we would get to Gaius ensured we were ready to leave France before the guillotine did its dreadful work.

No company of the Paper Flower Consortium wanted to sponsor this episode, so Gaius did

A Word from our Sponsor

Gaius's Legion

Are you a person of questionable morals? Have you seen a lifetime of battles and want more? Do you want to become a vampire without all the moral posturing of the official covens, such as the Paper Flower Consortium? Contact Gaius's legion! It's like Norma's Cleaning Service, just on an international scale.

Immediate opening! Excellent opportunity for a too young or otherwise ill-fated vampire with an innate gentleness towards animals. Nix is quite lonely and needs someone to ride him when I am out of town. You will be responsible for his care and grooming. Nix loves young innocents; he may be a unicorn in disguise. You will be under my full protection. The council ignores me as it is wise to do so. If someone hurts you or touches you without your permission, Nix will eat them for you. And I will always have your back because I love Nix.

My word is my bond, and Norma can attest to my trustworthiness in such matters.

Initiate Questions

Initate Fern: Lady Loretta, if I do something

WRONG AND DISCOVER IT LATER, HOW DO I DEAL WITH THE GUILT?

The same way people deal with anything. They make amends, including at times by leaving the hurt party alone. They confess to their spiritual advisor and their God if they have one. Perhaps they give money to charities that work to combat whatever wrong they did. You must find your own path to forgiveness.

INITIATE LYNN: LADY LORETTA, WHAT IF WE SEE BAD CHANGE TODAY? HOW DO WE STOP THE WORLD FROM FALLING BACKWARD?

Beloved, unfortunately, there is no way to stop the world from falling backward that doesn't require direct action and killing on our part. We exist apart from humanity, except for the humans who decide to join us. We exist in an open secret with our governments because we do not get directly involved anymore.

We may still write letters and sign petitions. As registered voters of our districts, we vote and support candidates who we believe will protect our world. We may even choose to protest, but understand if you are caught overnight in jail, you may be immolated in the morning.

Good Day Beloved Initiates and Sleep the Sleep of the Dead.

Summon Demons at your Own Risk

INTRODUCTION

Good evening, beloved initiates I shall begin tonight with some unfortunate news. Initiate Ellen has failed the Initiation program. You all know the initiation program takes a minimum of three years, but as we have said, depending on your age and experience, the process might take longer. Ellen lost her patience and decided to try to become an immortal another way.

I warn you: you cannot hurry the process. You must endure the wait.

However, my beloveds, the wait serves a purpose. Vampires learn to exist with forbearance as eternity is a very long time. There is no way we can know exactly when something is going to happen. We cannot know what the future holds or when danger will find us, but existing with patience permits us to analyze different situations and keeps us calm and in control.

Now I have heard the grumbles we ought to have done more to save Ellen. However, that type of talk only spreads ill will. Hopefully, the entire story set in an official manner should stop it. If you find you cannot abide by what you hear, you are free to leave the initiation program.

While I wish I could have stopped Ellen from destroying herself, there is little to nothing a person can do when another adult decides to follow the path of folly. I hide nothing from the initiates. The coven must be able to trust you for eternity as a vampire. Unfortunately for her, my stories piqued Ellen's interest.

Our library holds many books: most of them are safe. There are fables and myths from all over the world. Some hold blood-chilling terror in the fictional section if that is what you desire. Some are non-fiction. Some are journals of our past. We have several complete sets of encyclopedias and scientific studies.

These books come to us by way of estate sales when there is a death of a witch, wizard, warlock, enchanted humans, werewolves, or members of other short-lived species. I keep this knowledge as safe as I can, but it is knowledge and meant to be shared. People in this modern age are often shocked about our collection of dangerous knowledge and even more shocked we keep them out for anyone to peruse. My only comment to that is what good is the book if I do not allow our residents to peruse them.

If I, and the coven, cannot trust you to act with respect to the world's dangerous forms of knowledge now, than how is the coven supposed to trust you once you are a vampire?

SUMMON A DEMON AT YOUR OWN RISK

If you choose to explore summoning a demon, you do so at your own risk.

I am not your mother, I am the librarian.

Over the summer, Ellen began spending more and more time in the library. I knew she had pressed deeper into the stacks. She has always loved history, and as the summer weather was so miserable this year, she was also coming for the air-conditioning.

I thank my God Above, Norma has moved back home where she belongs.

I also thank my God Norma happened to be in the library.

She and her friend, Carlos, were assisting Ryan Jones with a research questionnaire about pollutants. You see, he is trying to ensure his surveys are written with respectful language to the sea peoples who he researches.

For those who don't know him, Carlos is Norma's shade friend whom you might see on occasion at our Fellowships. The word Zombie is now out of favor with this community as it gives most of the populace ideas of flesh-hungry, brainless monsters and the shades are none of those things.

Norma and Carlos were in the library because their own work had dried up during the pandemic. It was Norma and Ryan who felt Ellen's intentions change, from learning to be a vampire to finding out knowledge that would give her power. Perhaps that was always her intention.

While Derrik ensured his surviving offspring were educated enough that they don't often read people's minds without permission when their focus is elsewhere, it is easy to fail in that effort. At that moment, Ryan's focus was on Norma's experience with Sea Serpents and the Children of Poseidon. And Norma and Carlos were both focused on Ryan's questions.

However, I saw Norma's eyes look up. She turned her head as Ellen crossed the library with a large ancient leather-bound book in her hands.

"You don't want to do that," she called over her shoulder.

Ryan saw that Ellen had caught Norma's intention. His eyes opened wider, and he rose from the table. "Ellen, don't do it!"

Carlos grunted. (As some of you know, his larynx was crushed when he perished.)

Ellen threw a dirty look at them but said nothing.

"It's your funeral," Norma warned. I could see by the intensity on her face that she knew there would be a problem. She looked over at me and mouthed: "The box."

My heart sank.

Carlos patted her hand. Norma always has had too big of a heart. I am glad she has a friend who knows her so well. She whispered something to him. He rose and left the library.

You may remember in Lesson 5, Norma and Marion had captured the demon who went by the name Harold or Harry Taylor. They had put him away for a few decades or even a century. Some say that it was in punishment; some say it was more of a vacation, and some vampires look at it as a torpor. I don't say anything of the sort.

Only Mr. Taylor knows the truth about why he is in a bottle.

Just as all of you do, Initiate Ellen knew of the box where Mr. Taylor the demon was held in his bottle.

The day before, when all the vampires were sleeping, she took down the box out of the infirmary closet and brought it into the library. She shoved it in the back of a long row where she knew I wasn't likely to find it.

A little before midnight, she came to the library.

She plucked the book of ancient spells to summon and bind demons to her will from the shelf.

She untaped the box and unpacked the glass bottle from the layer of sand, and opened an ancient text. Then she began to read. "Dear God, Hear my prayer! I ask for your blessing to bind these creatures of darkness who have forsaken your warmth and light."

Norma jumped to her feet and raced to the back of the library.

"Who mock you by mimicking the steps of your blessed Mass."

Ryan and I followed her.

Ellen kept reading. "I compel thee, Creatures of Darkness, Bind thee to my will. I have the glorious God's blessing to bind you all to my will. I compel you... Creature of darkness....I have the Glorious God's blessing."

The library was suddenly filled with ghastly sounds of ancient tongues spoken with an American accent. Then there was something worse: A horrid sound of silence followed by the cruel sound of wood breaking against soft flesh.

The box was open, and the wine bottle lay on the floor and so was Ellen.

You see, Ellen hadn't finished her summoning when Mr. Taylor's spirit collided into her so fast; he knocked her to the wall then the floor and the breath from her body. She took in a mouth full of smoke or mist or what ether followed him.

"Damn it," Norma said. Quickly, grabbed a handful of salt which had spilled from the open box and made a circle around Ellen, the box, the bottle, and hopefully Mr. Taylor's spirit. Now before you complain that our Norma didn't even try to help Ellen...well that is false.

As I said, Norma had warned her. Ryan warned her.

Moreover, she saved your still human existences.

Norma, Carlos, Ryan and I would not have died. We are vampires and Carlos is a shade. But if Mr. Taylor had escaped into the coven, it might have been a blood bath among our humans who aren't so foolish as to summon a demon.

Thankfully, Carlos pushed past Ryan and me and threw a box of salt toward Norma. She caught it. He gestured Ryan and me back as poor bloodied Ellen grabbed a nearby chair for support and as if gravity suddenly didn't work, it toppled on top of her. Then an unseen force flung the wooden chair scratching our lovely pine floor, and tossed Ellen into the wall, damaging the plaster. Of course, we, vampires, could hear Ellen's heartbeat, her muscles in pain and screaming for the blood that was soaked into the plaster. We knew she was still alive.

"Damn it, Damn it, Damn it," Norma muttered to herself.

"Don't swear," Ryan muttered for some reason.

"Damn it, now I have to fix the wall," Norma said this time louder.

Carlos grunted. His dead stare held a warning.

Always keeping herself between us and the demon, the coven and the demon, Norma created another barrier.

I'm not sure if Norma heard the apology over the noise, but Ryan did mutter, "Sorry."

From the outside, we watched as the chair leg was broken off and Ellen was stabbed in through the chest. It screeched through her torso and into the floor below. She screamed in agony.

"Mind the floor, Taylor!" Norma shouted.

There was a loud bang as an unseen force hit the circle of salt, but it held.

Inside, blood spilled from Ellen's eyes, nose, and ears. Her fingernails began to bleed. Beside me, I felt Ryan's bloodlust pique. However, Norma remained calm.

The force darkened into a form of a middle-aged man in a burgundy velveteen leisure suit and matching plaid shirt straight out of 1969. Harold Taylor blinked as his eyes adjusted to the light.

"Hello, Miss Rollins."

"Hi, Mr. Taylor."

"Has it been a century?" He stretched his arms and back.

"Not yet. It is 2021. Why? You ready to come out now?"

"Tell me what's going on in 2021?"

"Well, there's a pandemic, and the economy's not so good right now. Want a paper? Oh, and most people don't read the paper on papers anymore, but Madame Onfoy still gets it for the library."

"No need. Economies are never good after a pandemic. You need to live a few more lifetimes." He licked his lips in a salacious manner. "How's Miss Marion?"

"Great. She's the head of security now. Got tired of the force," Norma said brightly.

Mr. Taylor nodded. "Good for her. Glad to hear it." He looked beyond Norma and stared at me then as if just noticing the vampires and shade behind Norma.

"And you remember her vampire mother, Madame Onfoy," Norma said.

"Yes, you are as beautiful as ever, Madame."

Demons are often polite and when they are not hungry make lovely guests. It is one of their more dangerous attributes.

Still, I thanked him for his compliment.

"And this is my coworker, Mr. Perez, and my bloodline uncle, Dr. Jones."

Careful not to touch the salt barrier, he bowed at them. "My compliments, Sirs."

Then he smiled too widely, exposing his stained, too sharp teeth.

"So the summoner is.... soon to be was...a human. And I am a bit peckish." He smiled at me again. "Dr. Jones,

Madame Onfoy, you might want to turn around."

"Indeed," Norma said.

Ryan and I should have listened.

Mr. Taylor's mouth open wider and exposed his rows of teeth. Mr. Taylor bit into her cheek. I do not deny we knew she was still alive when he took the first bite. We knew she was alive when he took his fifth bite. We did not turn so at first, but Ryan's pallor didn't look good when Ellen squealed of agony.

Carlos, gently, took Ryan's arm to ensure he did not faint as Ellen beat her arms against his body.

By the licking, slurping, sucking, and smacking of Mr. Taylor's lips, Ellen apparently was scrumptious. Though of course, we all wish demons eat with more cleanliness. They tend to spill their saliva a bit, and they just leave bloody bones and torn clothing on the area rug.

Once satiated, Taylor asked if he might check out a few new mysteries, for his time in his bottle was slow. He slipped into the bottle and brought out some older library books.

As pleasant as Mr. Taylor was, he was quite disappointed to hear Agatha Christie's passing in 1976.

I admit I was worried he might throw a tantrum and break something else. You see, he was one of the Londoners who rioted when Sir Arthur Conan Doyle killed off Sherlock Holmes. Fortunately, he kept to his polite, genteel behavior that night. Of course, Norma had him trapped in concentric salt rings. As requested, I found him some new traditional mysteries to read before he returned to his bottle.

So for those of you who knew and cared for Initiate Ellen, I am sorry for your loss.

A WORD FROM OUR SPONSOR

The Law Office of Derrik Miller.

Derrik Miller has assisted the paranormal community of the greater Seattle area with their legal needs for over one hundred and seventy years! He can assist you in the formation and purchase of a new business, the closing of an old business, and preventing disputes by fair and ethical contracts. He is also experienced in supernatural immigration, including assisting in asylum hearings and paperwork. Call for an appointment tonight

INITIATE QUESTIONS

INITIATE JASON: LADY LORETTA: IT SEEMS TO ME THIS HAROLD TAYLOR IS TOO DANGEROUS TO EXIST-ESPECIALLY WITHIN THE WALLS OF THE COVEN. WHY DOESN'T NORMA KILL HIM, AND WHY DID YOU LET HIM CHECK OUT LIBRARY BOOKS?

My kindhearted Initiate Jason,

Harold Taylor is a true immortal. We, and by we, I mean Norma and Marion, can trap him in a bottle, and of course, he can travel to Hell or other dimensions, but we have no idea how to kill him. Or even if he can be killed.

One issue we've seen with many horror films and books concerning demons is that the humans win. Humans never win when dealing with demons. At best, there is a short time of delicious power or wealth before the human is consumed either quickly or mind-numbingly slow.

Moreover, Mr. Taylor is a resident of the Paper Flower Consortium and therefore has lending privileges at the library.

In many ways, Ellen was lucky that Mr. Taylor was hungry. Perhaps some night, I will tell a story of when a demon ate a vampire. For now, just know, that it is best to stay polite and act in kindness which is good advice when dealing with all types of people.

To give you time, my beloveds to decide if you are still interested in vampirism, we will be taking a break in the lessons.

Have a good day and sleep the sleep of the dead.

ABOUT THE AUTHOR

Elizabeth Guizzetti is an illustrator and author best known for her demon-poodle based comedy, Out for Souls & Cookies and For Blood Bones & Biscuits: The Legend of Walnut Razor Fang. She also loves vampire stories which is why she created the Paper Flower Consortium Universe.

Guizzetti lives in Seattle with her husband and dog. When not writing or illustrating, she loves hiking and birdwatching. To follow her work:

Twitter: @E_Guizzetti
Instagram:@Elizabeth_Guizzetti
Facebook: Elizabeth.Guizzetti.Author
Web: www.elizabethguizzetti.com

Novels & Novellas

Norma's Cleaning Services Mysteries

Death Pulls a Stake Out, 2018
Death Hears a Siren, 2019
Death Sticks a Pixie, 2019

Immortal House, 2018 (Laurence's Story)
Honor Among Vampires, 2019 (Agata)
Chivalry Among Vampires, 2020 (Jakub)

(And More Stories to come!)

Vampires of the Paper Flower Consortium Podcast

is found on most podcatchers!

OTHER NOVELS

Other Systems
The Light Side of the Moon
The Grove

COMICS

For Blood, Bones, & Biscuits:
The Legend of Walnut Razor Fang
Faminelands
Lure
Out for Souls and Cookies
The Prince of Artemis V (Illustrator)
A is for Apex (Illustrator)

Paper Flower Consortium
Visit for a Night;
Stay for Eternity!
Seattle's largest
Vampire Community

www.ingramcontent.com/pod-product-compliance
Lightning Source LLC
Chambersburg PA
CBHW061048190726
48286CB00006B/1661